SURFING WITH SHARKS

The following story is entirely true, except for the parts that aren't. The names of people and places, as well as the sequence of events, have been changed to protect the innocent from ravenous woke cancel-culture mobs.

SURFING WITH SHARKS

Madness and the Tumultuous Summer of 2020

SEVE VERDAD

To all those who lost family, loved ones, and/or their livelihoods due to the summer riots of 2020.

PALMETTO
PUBLISHING

Charleston, SC
www.PalmettoPublishing.com

Surfing with Sharks
Copyright © 2022 by Seve Verdad

Disclaimer: The following story is entirely true, except for the parts that aren't. The names of people and places, as well as the sequence of events, have been changed to protect the innocent from ravenous woke cancel-culture mobs.

First Edition

Hardcover ISBN: 978-1-68515-871-2
Paperback ISBN: 978-1-68515-872-9
eBook ISBN: 978-1-68515-873-6

TABLE OF CONTENTS

CHAPTER 1

PRINCESS

Antonia phoned at six in the morning to let me know that my business in Van Nuys had been vandalized.

"What year is it?" I said.

Antonia snapped, "Still 2020. The nightmare. And my—"

I interrupted, "Still 2020…shit… Only vandalism?"

Antonia sounded on the verge of tears. "Come and see my store. It's a *puta madre* disaster."

Antonia and her husband owned Nuestro American Hardware, next door to my bait and tackle shop.

"I should see that. I'll be there in an hour or so."

As news of the riots unfolded last night, I secretly hoped my business would be looted and burned to the ground. I was facing bankruptcy anyway. If my bait and tackle shop were torched an insurance settlement should result, though I wasn't sure if I was covered against general anarchy.

I laughed out loud. Not to keep from crying but out of exasperation, and for the hell of it, and to remind myself I felt pretty good, physically. Sometimes I wondered about my mental state though. Every morning I woke up delusional, filled with false hopes, envisioning a new day, a new year, a new era. The past few months had been but a bad dream and today would be different. Yet the nightmare persisted. It was still 2020, the reality relentless, wearing me down, my mind rebelling, on constant lookout for an escape that did not exist, a cure to the madness.

Actually, there was an escape, a cure. I just couldn't see it. All would come clear in a matter of months however, as the COVID pandemic, quarantines and lockdowns, a looming prison sentence, bankruptcy, riots, aliens, and zombies all colluded and conspired to torture and kill me…and wound up making me a killer, a killer who finally found his escape, got his mind right and cured himself.

A goddamn plot, a conspiracy. That's what it was. A conspiracy.

Seems obvious now, but back in June the conspiracy against me and multitudes of others remained intangible, something I'd contemplated but was shrouded and obscured by my delusions and false hopes… I hadn't become a killer yet. There was no cure or escape for me. The next hour passed with all the anticipation of a dreaded sixth-grade school day, except I refused to feign illness to miss it; Antonia could use a helping hand, and, as it turned out, so could Princess.

Princess became my guardian. Not a guardian angel, parent or caregiver, but a confidant and benefactor. She was sitting on the side of the road when I discovered her, behind a gutted and scorched car parked opposite a smoldering pharmacy, about a half-mile away from Antonia's hardware store. I braked the moment I saw her, my Toyota 4Runner coming to a stop several yards from her splayed legs. A small child, that's what I envisioned—a golden-brown child dusted in ashes and dressed in a pink jumpsuit stained with blood. The moment I leaped out of my car I could see I was mistaken and released a strangled breath. It wasn't a child but a stuffed animal of some sort… A bear…a stuffed bear seated forward as if poised to begin a stretching exercise. I was about to abandon her but something in her eye—a sparkle of early morning sun—detained me. I squatted next to her. Rather tall for a teddy bear, over knee-high if I stood her up. She was beat up pretty bad, her snout twisted and bloodied, but retained all her appendages, except for an ear and button eye. Her blood-spattered pink bonnet had been torn from her head and dangled helplessly down the nape of her neck, and darkened blood covered her head in the shape of an inverted crown. I imagined it was blood from her previous owner, perhaps a little girl gravely injured during last night's upheaval. Had the bear been a passenger in the gutted vehicle behind her? Possibly. Or maybe the blood belonged to a looter. I examined the bear's jumpsuit. The stains could have been paint, spaghetti sauce, or ketchup, but why jump to that conclusion? Why diminish our encounter with unsubstantiated assumptions that did not conform to the evidence? This was a warzone and the poor thing had been abused and discarded like trash and resembled a war casualty. She'd suffered greatly for that blood and deserved the recognition and empathy that came with being splattered with blood. I refocused on her face, searching for grimacing signs of torture. Her button eye was white with a black iris, and the stitched mouth below her snout formed a W elongated into a smile.

Smiling in the face of death, I thought and smiled back.

"Alligators are always smiling," I said. "But you're a bear."

No response.

I broadened my smile. "Smiling like me."

Her head listed.

"Enjoy yourself last night?"

I placed a finger under her white tuft of a chin and straightened her posture.

"National and social media make it sound like all you folks across the country have been having just a grand ol' time, all a social-justice peaceful protest party."

I removed my finger from her chin. She fell to her back, spread-eagled on the pavement.

"That's quite a hangover you got there," I chided. "Or do you have COVID? Both?"

"COVID" was a reference to the Chinese pandemic infecting the world, "hangover" a self-projection. I resolved to rescue her. She reminded me of myself, either what I had become or strived to be—a survivor; a tattered and bloodied, unbowed, hungover survivor. She'd make a perfect mascot and guardian.

Antonia squealed with revulsion when she saw me cradling Princess outside her hardware store. "Looks like roadkill," she sputtered, hand to her heart. "Just what we need around here, more death and destruction."

Her feral expression was hidden behind a nuisance mask, but I could see it mirrored in her eyes, my "roadkill" a macabre distraction from the destruction inside her hardware store.

Antonia's husband, Manny, put a positive spin on my roadkill in broken English: "Thee firs' death here. She fit in wit' el disastre…"

Manny had always been the cooler head between the two of them.

"Princess is a survivor," I said, "and will protect us." I stood Princess up against a lamppost, but she couldn't quite support herself and toppled facedown onto the sidewalk.

Manny said, "Parece que Princess haf a con…cussion." Princess' pink bonnet had shaken free, exposing her bloodied head.

The sidewalk was littered with debris from last night's activities. I retrieved a stray board, leaned it against the lamppost, and dusted off Princess as I propped her up to it, reposed but on her feet, her bonnet snugly in place.

"Beautiful."

Antonia huffed, "Stop clowning around, Colton. I thought you were here to lend a hand."

"Now we can work secure in the knowledge that Princess has our backs," I announced happily.

Manny released an involuntary laugh and massaged his temples.

According to this morning's local news reports, downtown Los Angeles, 25 miles south of here, was wracked by more destruction last night than Van Nuys—more fires, more looting, more general mayhem. What the hell happened? Nothing out of the ordinary for cities across America these first few weeks of summer. "Bad elements within peaceful social-justice protests" was how a legion of politicians and media talking heads described those behind the anarchy.

The word play was a frontal assault on me personally. Not a slap in the face but Tyson punches thrown with bad intentions. I was being railroaded by the state for incitement to riot and hadn't so much as struck a match during my peaceful protest, much less gathered mobs bent on destruction. Yet real rioters across the land were allowed to run wild. Why the double standard? The question had been gnawing at me for weeks, gnawed at me this morning, and was all consuming when I spoke to my public defender yesterday.

"*I'm* a bad element," I told him. "I can accept that. And these angry mobs are rioters, plain and simple. Draw a clear distinction between me and them and you can demonstrate I'm innocent of the charges against me."

"I'm not so sure the prosecution or judge will be swayed by that argument, Colton. And what is a *bad element* anyway?"

I'd given the matter quite a bit of thought last night and was still thinking about it. Unwanted party crashers are bad elements. Hecklers at a comedy act are bad elements. Had "bad elements" devastated Manny and Antonia's hardware store, torched that car and pharmacy and wounded Princess? Were armed bank robbers thugs and thieves or bad elements? Were angry mobs bent on destruction bad elements or rioters? Well, they sure as hell weren't peaceful protesters or rowdy teens cruising the boulevard looking for a good time like a scene out of *American Graffiti*.

Was rioting a "good time"? I supposed so, at least for the rioters and looters and arsonists. Were peaceful protests a "good time"? More or less. I'd witnessed a few in my younger days and had participated in one several weeks ago; the protesters did look animated, and I'd felt animated, spirited, as though engaged in a taxing team sport. Was there a difference between peaceful protest and rioting? How 'bout a riotous comedy act and burning down a house? A riotous party and ransacking department stores?... A riot of a movie like *American Graffiti* and a matinee drive-by shooting in gangland Chicago?

Riotous behavior, a riot of a comedy, a riot of a good time... Riotous mobs or "bad-element" mobs? "Bad elements" in the streets or riots in the streets? Why use the term "bad elements"? Even my attorney had trouble defining it. Had it become part of a politically correct lexicon?

I used to get upset and angry when people twisted the definitions of words to suit an agenda. Princess cured me of that, for the most part. Her sanguine bearing and supportive attitude were contagious and relieved me of negativity. And she was a great listener, still is, the only one who has never tired of hearing me talk...

Within a couple of months of discovering Princess, my public defender finally told me he was tired of listening to me. "I'm tired of listening to your same old argument," he said.

I beseeched him, "But the numbers are in, Mister Bartholomew. Dozens dead across the nation in five-hundred *real riots*, and billions of dollars in property damage since Memorial Day when Floyd was murdered—"

"No one has been convicted of murder or anything else yet. And I told you—"

"Mister Bart."

"*Bart* will do."

Mr. Bart was prematurely gray and had developed a nervous nose twitch since we personally met in mid-May. We'd been meeting on Zoom, online, since then. His features were sharp and pearly smooth and suggested youth, but for his prematurely graying hair and this newfound twitch which my persistence may have induced but I attributed to other cases of his that must have been more stressful than mine.

I persisted, "The prosecution, the state, must be aware of these numbers. And if they aren't, they must be *made* aware."

Mr. Bart twitched. "They don't care about those numbers. They care about your behavior. And frankly—"

"My behavior?" I interrupted, rocking back and forth in my seat. "Compared to what? Murder and arson? They're accusing me of incitement to riot for Christ's sake. I gave you a video of the so-called riot they're accusing me of inciting. Show me the mayhem, please, show me the anarchy."

Mr. Bart's blue eyes grew large beneath his graying eyebrows. "And you have injected yourself into other riots, Colton. You've given me the video evidence of that as well."

"I've injected myself into *real* riots to record the mayhem and draw a distinction between them and my peaceful protest. And who's calling those real riots *riots* except me, and now you?"

Mr. Bart flushed, and backtracked: "I meant *unrest.*"

"Upheavals, maybe. *Riots* are what they are; real riots, not like the imaginary riot I inspired."

"Of course. *Imaginary riot...* We're back to that. Not much of a defense, but there is someone you should speak to about your imaginary riots, Colton. She might help us get you off..."

Doctor Bolton. Her last name rhymed with my first and she had a pitchy nasal voice which, I'd eventually discover, was in harmony with her tortuous logic.

"When you say *imaginary riot*, does that mean *riot?*"

I shook my head. "No. That's why I call it *imaginary*."

"And do you have many imaginary riots?"

"Only when referring to the one the state has labeled a real riot and is accusing me of inciting."

"But if you know it's imaginary, why do you persist in calling it a riot?"

"I don't. I call it *an imaginary riot*."

"How can a riot be imaginary?"

"For one, when I'm innocent of inciting a riot when there wasn't a riot in the first place."

"What is a riot, Colton?"

Good question, one I grappled with throughout the summer and beyond. Whether or not police were accused of murdering a black man, like they were with George Floyd in Minneapolis, or whether or not they'd subdued or shot a black suspect somewhere or were involved or uninvolved in anything particular or unparticular anywhere, social-justice and defund-the-police demonstrations and protests ensued, demonstrations and protests that gained momentum and were regularly succeeded by unrelenting mayhem, anarchy and...riots.

Riots? The night before I rescued Princess, I'd seen television newscasters describing images of angry mobs and burning structures as "incendiary peaceful protest." In accordance with media and politically correct denials of reality, Antonia, Manny and I called our work "post-party cleanup." This was our first post-party cleanup, but we hadn't thrown the party. We were an unsuspecting family returning home from a June outing to find their house and neighborhood ransacked and torn to shreds, the perpetrators nothing short of hoodlums, thugs, rioters and thieves who had indeed enjoyed quite a blowout.

There was just enough light Inside Nuestro American Hardware to see that there'd been a jailbreak. The overhead florescent bulbs were dead, but morning sun filtered in through the shattered windows and the devastation was clear—it looked like there'd been a *puta madre* jailbreak. What wasn't stolen had been smashed, tossed and scattered. A thick odor of machine oil hung in the air along with...spiders...hundreds, thousands of tiny spiders suspended by diaphanous threads. I walked straight into their ambush, didn't notice them swirling and twisting in the semidarkness until they were upon me, tickling my neck, arms and face and threatening to penetrate my nuisance mask.

I bellowed, "What the fuck," and squirmed and ran my hands over my neck and body like an erotic dancer tweaked on crystal meth. "There are spiders in the air..."

Antonia stammered, "S-spiders? Where? It's only the dust, Colton, you friggin' clown."

I tripped over a stray piece of pipe, landed on my ass, and craned my neck, in search of the vermin. They seemed to have disappeared but… "There are spiders," I said. "Little tiny ones. I saw…and felt them."

Manny stepped over to me, broom in hand, and stopped short at the jarring thump of a falling object from the far end of the store. We stared at each other in silent alarm.

"That sounds like a big spider," I said.

Manny nodded, "Sí," and helped me to my feet. I retrieved the pipe for defense and Antonia joined us as we plodded towards the darkened office at the rear of the store. Antonia shed light on the scene with her iPhone, illuminating the grimy floor and a toppled shop-vac in the hallway. There was a shadow of movement beyond the shop-vac, a specter of limbs and a woolly head. I raised my pipe. Antonia shined her light upon the figure and gasped at the gaunt, ashen continence before us.

"Charlie," she breathed.

"*Pinche* Charlie," echoed Manny.

I recognized Charlie as well, though his face looked like he'd stuck his head through a hole in the drywall, his chocolate brown complexion muddy gray and framed by a whitened afro. He shaded his eyes from Antonia's light and said, "Deconstruction," through parched lips.

Antonia lowered the light from Charlie's face. "You been here all night, Charlie?" she wanted to know.

"Just came to see deconstruction at work," he answered, and wrung his hands together as if lathering soap. "Lots of deconstruction everywhere. Predictable…yes? Deductive…yes…"

I approached Charlie, placed a hand on his back and swept my gaze over his figure, searching for blood or signs of injury.

"You okay, Charlie?"

"Oh yes. Yes, yes, yes. Past the point of no return."

"Come along, Charlie," I said, pleased to find him uninjured. We'd formed an unlikely bond these past couple of months of COVID pandemic lockdowns. Unlikely because I was an entrepreneur and Charlie...well... At first glance and until you got to know him, Charlie looked like an ordinary vagrant...

Antonia waved us forward. "Let's get you outta here, Charlie."

Charlie shuffled along behind me and the four of us made our way out. Manny paused beneath a shattered florescent light and raised his broom to a fresh hole in the ceiling. He swept his broom over the hole and headed for the morning light at the entrance to the store. Outside, Antonia recoiled at the sight of Manny's broom—the brown threads of tiny spiders covering the brush.

"Looks like you have an infestation problem up there," I said.

Charlie took me by the arm, his opaque right eye flickering on Manny's broom, the other focused on a spot on my forehead. Charlie had an afflicted and lazy right eye, a likely result of examining every side to every question, like the strain of examining every side to every question had jarred the eye loose to accommodate the effort. According to Antonia's and my accountant, Ned, Charlie was a Stanford-grad genius, a cosmologist and Cal Tech tenured professor driven to madness by the death of his wife and child and an insatiable desire for explanations as he delved into Evolutionary Behavioral Sciences. Not only did all phenomena have an explanation, but explanations themselves were theories that had to adhere to strict criteria. For Charlie, a walk in the woods or along a beach did not inspire awe and appreciation for Mother Nature, God, Buddha, Brahma, yin and yang, Quetzalcoatl, Yoga, Yoda, The Force, or Shakespeare; for Charlie, a simple stroll down the block revealed a world and universe replete with questions and phenomena requiring explanations, explanations that were within his reach and the power of his mind. Within reach and forever out of reach, for Charlie's brain and communication skills were fractured by the feverish exercise, his lazy famished eye and lucid amber eye relics to wonders Charlie resolved to know from every angle but could rarely enjoy or fully explain.

Anxiety, overthinking psychosis, bipolar disorder, Ned had even described Charlie's condition as a mild form of schizophrenia. Ned could have been a doctor, was not a doctor but could have been, had mentioned as much to me on a few occasions. "I would have been a doctor," he told me on my second or third visit to his office on the second floor of the office building kitty-corner from my bait and tackle shop, "but the hours I keep as an accountant are far more agreeable." Ned's office smelled of the sweet fresh tobacco stuffed in his meerschaum pipe that he frequently drew on but never smoked from in his office so as not to possibly offend clients or perspective clients, and he had a mildly agreeable habit of running his hand over his balding pate while he gave careful consideration to an accounting difficulty and reassured himself that he hadn't lost all his hair yet.

Ned had an imperial Roman nose and a less agreeable habit of pointing it and the stem of his pipe at you to make a point. "I'm no doctor," Ned confided to me one February evening after

I'd seen him chatting with Charlie at a bus stop after work, "but that man Charlie is extremely high-functioning, for a nut case." Ned lit his pipe and pointed the stem at me. "Sometimes I think I should have been a doctor."

Maybe so, for I concurred with Ned the would-be doctor. In fact, before long I'd give Charlie more credit than Ned did. On the first day of spring, a few months before discovering Princess, I came to the conclusion that Charlie was far from your average run-of-the-mill vagrant when he predicted my bankruptcy due to the state's COVID pandemic lockdown. "Only a chosen few will outlast the lockdowns," he said, reading my mind. I gave Charlie a ride home that evening and eventually came to view him as a sort of loony savant…or eccentric clairvoyant and mentor….

In his youth, Charlie's face must have held an exuberance of concentration and fervor for life. Now it was a mask of impassioned serenity, a veneer of comedy and tragedy, a veil of humor and hurt and yin and yang as his mind and eyes struggled to focus. Antonia was gentler with Charlie than with other vagrants who lingered on the sidewalk before our storefronts, joining him in conversation while moving him along; Charlie did have valuable and interesting things to say, if you could decipher them.

Charlie loosened his grip on my arm when I offered him some water. "Shall I give you a ride home?" I volunteered, and extended a small bottled water from Manny's ice chest.

"Deconstruction," he said with a sip of water.

"You mean destruction," I clarified.

Charlie's broad nose increased in girth with a flare of his nostrils. "That's the result," he said. "Deconstruction, postmodern…yes…is the cause…"

I nodded convincingly, "No doubt…"

Charlie brightened, his teeth even and white through his ragged beard, his cockeyed gaze stuck somewhere in the middle distance behind me. "She knows," he said.

Princess. Charlie saw something intriguing in Princess and stooped to greet her, as to a small child. He paused, and cocked his head to her, listening. Then he stood abruptly, turned on his heels and pointed to the sky in triumph. "Yes, I did predict it."

Charlie hitched up his bedraggled trousers and ambled away, talking to himself and drinking his water.

"Charlie, el loco lúcido," Manny said.

"More lucid than crazy," I replied in English.

Antonia sighed, "Let's hope we all are…"

CHAPTER 2

HELL TO RAISE

Charlie was right. I had a feeling he might be on that first day of spring back in March. It pained and angered me to admit the truth but before long my dwindling business bank account and the anxiety pacing through my chest left little doubt: only a chosen few would survive the pandemic lockdowns, and my business was not one of those chosen few.

Like so many, I'd been deemed "nonessential" and forced to close shop, yet I could have weathered the storm if California's lockdown had only lasted the promised two or three weeks. But by May well over a month had passed with most everything shut down, from beaches and parks to restaurants, gyms, salons, and schools, and my business was all but sunk.

There was nowhere to go except to buy essentials, almost no one to talk to, and my fiancée was quarantined in El Salvador with family. Most all nations on earth had imposed some kind of pandemic lockdown policy, El Salvador one of the strictest. Other than to buy essentials, I did manage to escape my apartment a couple times a week to take and retake inventory at my drowning Fisherman's Shore Bait and Tackle, crunch numbers I'd share with my accountant, Ned, in an effort to hoard money and avoid inevitable bankruptcy, and chat with Antonia and Manny at their hardware store. Hardware stores were deemed "essential" and allowed to remain open, as were liquor stores and Walmart. You could buy an ice cream cone at Walmart but not at the nonessential ice cream parlor down the street from my bait and tackle shop. The 7-Eleven a block away was open and I'd walk there for coffee. There was little traffic, the sidewalks practically deserted, like strolling to the 7-Eleven might get me arrested.

I ran into Charlie at the 7-Eleven one afternoon in early May, about six weeks before I rescued Princess. At that juncture, experience and Ned's insights had led me to the conclusion that Charlie was far from an ordinary vagrant. He looked the part of a vagrant if you weren't paying attention. If you did pay attention, you'd notice that his clothes were aged and disheveled rather than tattered and dirty, that he may not be well groomed but had bathed not too long ago, and he did not beg for money. He might even be holding a 7-Eleven coffee he'd bought as he loitered and shuffled here and there.

Charlie greeted me with a "Good morning, good morning, good morning" in his reedy tenor voice when I exited the 7-Eleven with my coffee.

"Afternoon, Charlie."

Charlie scanned the sky. It was cloudy—threatening rain.

"Morning in Hong Kong," he said. "Morning in Hong Kong."

"And it's five o'clock somewhere."

Charlie worked his jaw, the lines in his forehead deepening, calculating where on earth it was five o'clock right now. I was referring to the Alan Jackson song, that it was cocktail hour somewhere, and was going to mention as much, but Charlie was way ahead of me.

"In the middle of the ocean, yes. The Atlantic…the Atlantic…

"I suppose so. And it's morning in Tokyo as well as Hong Kong."

Charlie dipped his chin and shrugged, and his lazy eye fluttered, his slight frame forming a question mark, his mind somewhere in the nether regions. I sipped coffee and beckoned him with a wave of my hand. We drifted across the parking lot.

"You been to Hong Kong or Tokyo, Charlie?"

"No more China," he said. "No more…"

I took that to mean that he'd been there, perhaps as a student or professor, and would not return. Charlie had gone from tenured professor and research scientist at a highly respected university to a life of semi-derangement in a section-8 housing project, supported by social security and a reduced pension due to early retirement. His astonishing downfall was a poignant reminder that no one is immune to misfortune, destitution and even madness, or at least I wasn't. I'd lost everything—all my assets—once before and managed to rebound, but after four weeks of this lockdown and with bankruptcy looming, I wondered if I would do it again or go crazy trying.

Charlie began babbling when we reached the sidewalk: "South China Sea, Taiwan, Japan, India, Hawaii, California. The New World, the Old World, the moons and Mars. All are part of the center-earth empire. It is written…" Charlie stopped in mid-stride and ran his hands through his graying afro. "I have the equation, a proof. Promising…yes…promising…" He bobbed his head up and down to a monologue that had become interior, fingers massaging his heavy lower lip.

"Come along, Charlie," I said. The light at the intersection was green and I placed a hand on his back to guide him forward. I'd yet to see Charlie in the middle of the road disrupting traffic like other mental cases, but I didn't put it past him. We crossed the street without incident and strolled towards Fisherman's Shore Bait and Tackle shoulder to shoulder.

"Did you know the lockdown would last this long, Charlie?" I asked. He'd told me that only a chosen few would survive the lockdowns and I remained fixated on what appeared to be an accurate prediction on his part.

"More to come," he said. "Always more to come. Yes, more to come…"

I paused and tugged on Charlie's shirtsleeve to keep him from advancing beyond me.

"You mean this one will last longer, or more are coming when this one ends?"

Charlie bounced his eyebrows at me, his chocolate brown complexion singed by a surge of emotion.

"Yes, yes, yes," he said. "I have it all worked out. It's in the math and data. The historical congruences are astounding." He lifted his gaze to the heavens. "My lord, *all the lords*, it is predictable."

Charlie brought a hand to his hairline and twirled his afro between his fingers, eyes lost in the clouds, his teeth clenched and exposed in a bleak smile.

"Deductive, deductive, deductive…general, general, general…causal, causal, causal…predictive, predictive, predictive…meaningful, meaningful, meaningful…"

He repeated himself again and again, in tempo, his thin tenor lending a lyrical quality to the words. He wasn't singing, more like chanting. The chants and prayers of a madman…

I snapped my fingers in front of his face a few times.

"Charlie. Charlie… Get a grip, will ya?"

He looked around, confused, as though shaken from a dream and unaware where he had woken up.

"Back to reality, Charlie?"

He squeezed his hands together.

"Oh yes. Yes, yes, yes… Past the point of no return."

I grunted a short sigh, continued walking, and stopped before my darkened storefront and its immaculate façade.

Looks like I'll have to take down that colorful banner up there…

I read from it, mouthing the words: NOW OPEN… Fisherman's Shore Bait and Tackle…

I'd begun dreaming of expanding the moment I opened for business. The idea was to include surfing gear in my inventory. Not surfboards so much as wetsuits and fins. I was an avid bodysurfer, had competed some in my younger days, and a good selection of wetsuits and fins would attract spearfishermen as well as body whompers…

Can I keep the dream alive?

"Downtown will suffer more."

Charlie. I smirked at him. "You think so?"

"Numbers don't lie. More hell to raise…more trouble…"

"Hell to raise? By whom?"

Charlie shook his head slack-jawed, his expression one of repentance, like he hadn't meant to insult me, though I didn't feel insulted, only puzzled.

"Not by you," he said, "but your antipodes."

"Antipodes?"

Charlie waved me forward, an invitation to accompany him.

"Come. I'll show you. I have it all worked out."

I pulled the keys to my bait and tackle shop from my pocket.

"I'll give you a ride later, Charlie. I'm going inside to call my accountant."

Charlie sang a tune as he padded down the street: "Trouble, trouble, trouble…right here in River City…right here…"

Come summer, I'd realize that Charlie had it right again…

CHAPTER 3

JUNE

After clearing debris and boarding up broken windows, we dedicated ourselves to scrubbing and painting over the graffiti scarring the walls and doors of our businesses. Manny's "primos" would help tackle the disaster inside Nuestro American Hardware in the days and weeks to come.

"Maybe my shop escaped looting because they knew I was closed," I said, "and thought I didn't have much to steal."

Manny nodded in cadence to his scrubbing motion. "Tal vez," he replied. Perhaps. Manny was from Guadalajara, Mexico, and we regularly spoke Spanish together, a language I was fairly fluent in thanks to my studies and Salvadorian fiancée. "Or maybe the rioters know nothing about fishing," he added, his Spanish acquiring a cynical tone that cleaved his nuisance mask.

Antonia snorted.

"Oh those *pendejos* know how to fish…with dynamite…"

I released a short laugh. Antonia had a sharp tongue that belied the soft contours of her oval features and prim figure. I'd dined with her and Manny several times. They were an entertaining couple, and Antonia was three months pregnant. Her charms attracted customers and acquaintances alike, yet vagrants attempting to loiter outside her hardware store didn't linger when confronted with her rapid-fire bilingual harangues and the broom she used daily to sweep the sidewalk. She was born in California, but her parents were Spanish, had immigrated to the U.S. from Spain. As opposed to her husband, Antonia spoke flawless English, and the three of us often communicated within a blend of English and Spanish. She was a fair, hazel-eyed woman and had her blond-streaked hair tied up in a bun, her jeans and two-tone work shirt dust filled from this morning's "post-party" cleanup exercises.

"Never thought of stocking dynamite," I said. "But maybe I should, for self-defense…"

Manny glanced at me sideways, his Spanish laconic, "You planning on reopening, Colt?"

"No." I might have expounded but Manny and Antonia knew my circumstances. My bait and tackle shop was barely three months old when lockdowns due to the COVID pandemic closed all "nonessential" businesses. Fisherman's Shore Bait and Tackle failed, my bankruptcy soon to be finalized. And while Manny and Antonia's "essential" hardware store was allowed to remain open, they'd now suffered another kind of shutdown at the hands of rioters.

I adjusted the mask covering my nose and mouth. Masks were requisite due to the pandemic, but they also served to fend off the dust during our cleanup, the dust and noxious odor of the paint thinner I was using to remove graffiti.

Antonia gestured with her paintbrush, across the street and down the road a piece, at the ice cream parlor.

"They were closed due to the mayor's and governor's lock-downs, and they got looted..."

Manny and I looked over our shoulders. A black couple was hard at work clearing debris littering the sidewalk in front of their ice cream business. "Unlucky," I said, with the accompanying thought: *And maybe I'm somehow lucky...*

Manny chuckled, "You're lucky, hombre. Be thankful that the looters were so hungry for ice cream they left your business alone in favor of the parlor down the street."

This was a theme I'd heard before, albeit not exactly in this context. "Stop your belly-aching and be grateful you have a roof over your head and food on the table," my parents would tell me as a youngster. Sometimes the reproach actually stopped me from sniveling about one thing or another. And within the next couple of months, Dr. Bolton would put it different way:

"Make a list of things to be grateful for, Colton, and you might not be so cynical."

"What's wrong with being cynical?"

"Cynicism can be a barrier to happiness."

I scratched an incoherent itch at the base of my skull.

"So I should be grateful..."

"Yes."

"Grateful that my business didn't burn to the ground, for example?"

"I should think so."

"Even though I'd be better off with at least some insurance money if it had?"

"Fires are quite destructive, Colton. Things turned out better this way."

"I don't believe you."

I didn't believe a lot of things. Right now our post-party clean-up was an unbelievable burden. My bankruptcy was unbelievable. The riots were unbelievable. These friggin' lockdowns were unbelievable. COVID was unbelievable. About the only thing that was believable were the delusions I held every morning that somehow today would be a new day, a day of escape from this recurring nightmare. That new day might never arrive but believing the delusion for a short time did provide brief respite and a semblance of happiness.

Manny grabbed a ladder and leaned it against the wall beside me. The graffiti we were removing was decipherable. I took my scrub brush to a red anarchist sign, an Antifa calling card—an A encompassed by a circle. The sign blustered and bloviated below the red letters BLM and a black word—**RACIST**—that had become so utilitarian it might apply to stores, shops, highways, hairstyles, monuments, national parks, apple pies, clothes, buildings, math, people, or the bloodied pig face in a police cap with its eyes X'd out that Manny was scrubbing.

"And they wanna throw me in jail for incitement to riot," I grumbled.

Manny chortled, "No *mames*." "Híjole…" He switched to Spanglish: "Pinches cabrones…dey don' do nada to you después de this, *real* puta madre montines aquí en L.A. Y ha habido muertes in Seattle y San Luis y otros places…" Fucking assholes…they won't do anything to you after this, *real* motherfucking riots here in L.A. And there have been deaths in Seattle and Saint Louis and other places.

About a month ago, I got arrested during a demonstration. The protest was against COVID pandemic lockdowns and had nothing to do with subsequent incendiary Black Lives Matter (BLM)-Antifa social-justice demonstrations and marches like the one in L.A. yesterday. I planned to defend myself against the charges, one of which was incitement to riot, though there hadn't been a riot, nothing resembling the wanton destruction consuming so many American cities now.

My neck and shoulders, stiffening from this morning's work, loosened up at the unfortunate irony of Manny's argument. Perhaps the destruction here and downtown, destruction resulting from bona fide riots, would work to my favor when I faced the judge. After all, not only was I not guilty of incitement to riot, there'd been no riot—no destruction, no violence. Some unhappy people had made their voices heard, but a riot? Compared to what? A walk in the park? A family picnic on the beach? A nap in the shade? Birds chirping at sunrise?

I'd been preparing my defense and returned to it now, imagining all those in the courtroom—spectators, the judge, my public defender, the bailiff—hanging on every word of my testimony as I compared videos and photos of scorched businesses and cars here and in downtown L.A. to the peaceful protest I'd managed to inspire in Malibu…

Had there been a death in L.A. as a result of rioting?

Not yet, I thought morbidly. And if there had been, would a judge and jury give a shit when comparing my "crimes" to murder?

The world had been turned on its head. If what happened last night here in L.A. was legitimate peaceful protest, then contemporary standards held no standard at all. Now something else struck me as believable: In this topsy-turvy universe, I could easily be found guilty of incitement to riot and sentenced to years in prison as if convicted of murder.

On the other hand, convicts of many stripes, including violent criminals, were being released from jail, partly due to fears of pandemic outbreaks in prisons, partly due to prison reform, and also as a result of demands from social-justice protest warriors. If convicted I'd surely be set free, wouldn't I?

Maybe not. Maybe they'll let me rot behind bars to set some kind of example...

Made sense, especially since I had a prior—a record. But nearly a decade had passed since then. And it was for marijuana—penny-ante shit compared to violent crime. They wouldn't hold that against me, would they? My release from prison seemed a lifetime ago. By comparison, it really was only yesterday when I got arrested again...

CHAPTER 4

MAY

I got arrested again. A decade had passed since the last time—a bullshit marijuana beef that landed me in prison for a spell. I was a state-licensed medical-marijuana producer in those days, but the feds didn't care about that—a state license for weed. Weed was, and remained, federally prohibited, state laws be damned. This time it was city cops who dragged me off to jail. Not for drugs, robbery, a DUI, or violent crime, but for holding up a sign and pacing back and forth along a short stretch of the Pacific Coast Highway (PCH), Malibu. Essentially, I was arrested for exercising my freedom of speech.

That's the way I see it. But perhaps it's not so simple.

I know from experience that cops don't have to tell you why you're arrested when they slap the cuffs on you. They'll read you your rights, but you may not know the charges until booked. In this case the charges read: Incitement to riot and violation of Executive Order N-33-20.

Executive Order N-33-20 was commonly referred to as the California Shelter in Place Ordinance. The ordinance locked down the entire state in response to a pandemic, a most contagious virus—COVID-19. Yet another in a long list of pandemics that had originated in mainland China (Hong Kong flu, Asian flu, and SARS a few of the others).

COVID pandemic lockdown regulations were imposed in most every state to stop the spread of the disease, and at first most every American adhered to them. But before long many began to challenge the distinctions made between "essential" and "nonessential" work or activity. It wasn't too difficult to understand why those working in law enforcement, emergency services, healthcare, food and agriculture, the financial sector, infrastructure and the like were deemed "essentials" and remained employed. But within a matter of weeks over 30 million were newly unemployed, the economy shattered, and the whole idea of what was "essential" and "nonessential" work began to be questioned. After all, poverty is the biggest killer in history, and that's where the nation appeared to be headed—self-inflicted poverty.

What was COVID's actual mortality rate? Conflicting statistics abounded, but it was nowhere near the killer poverty was. Dire estimates put COVID's mortality rate at about 1-2 percent, with the elderly and those with comorbidities the most gravely affected and about 40% of people infected asymptomatic. And for folks in my category—well under 60 and strong—the mortality rate was infinitesimal.

No doubt COVID was dangerous, but it was not a death sentence, even if you caught it while convalescing in a hospital or nursing home. Where could you catch it? Considering the hysteria, everywhere, though if that were the case Costco would have been crippled by it.

Why the hell could you buy fishing gear at multinational corporate stores like Costco but not at my Fisherman's Shore Bait and Tackle? Was Costco honestly able to enforce pandemic mask and social-distancing regulations better than my staff and I could? As a man in the "nonessential" bait and tackle business, the classification criteria for determining essential and nonessential work seemed arbitrary at best to me. Controlling behavior and choosing economic winners and losers looked to be the real goal, an eternal goal for those in positions of power. The true nonessentials were the politicians and bureaucrats making up these arbitrary rules and regulations. Maybe financial ruin as a result of my forced shutdown had made me more cynical than usual, but after a while it appeared to me that those in state leadership positions were getting paid off by enterprises they allowed to stay in business.

It's easy for those living on Easy Street to demand that the rest of us close shop and lockdown…

The assholes destroying my and thousands of other small businesses never missed a paycheck. Did they really believe their own bullshit? I doubted it, and my judgement was borne out over the coming months as politicians were regularly photographed and recorded breaking all the mask and social-distancing rules and regulations they imposed on others.

They should be shot. What's the mortality rate of a bullet to the brain?

Why could you buy fishing gear at Costco and not at my bait and tackle shop? Why were liquor stores open and churches closed? Why were schools and parks and restaurants and gyms closed but Petco allowed to remain open? Well, aside from what I saw as corruption, "science" was the rationale, the go-to justification for politicians and easy-street bureaucrats to dictate the lives of others. Science, science, science. At the outset of the COVID outbreak in China, scientists at the World Health Organization (WHO) parroted Chinese propaganda and insisted that the disease was not transmittable between humans and was contained, proclamations that turned out to be total bull. As COVID spread in the States, science and government-appointed scientific experts dictated that the general population didn't need to wear masks in public. Then, in an abrupt about-face, it was imperative that everyone wear a mask. Could those who were asymptomatic spread COVID? At first the answer was "rarely"…later a definitive "yes," like the experts weren't scientists but baseball umpires who had to make some kind of call and couldn't admit they didn't know. In the name of science, state and local governments declared lockdowns, lockdowns that were not equally applied yet promised to last only a few weeks. As weeks and weeks passed, government "experts" then warned that the lockdowns would last throughout the summer, maybe longer. But as Memorial Day approached, some of those same science-minded experts admitted that prolonged lockdowns could be worse for mental, physical, and economic health than the disease. Other expert epidemiologists, doctors and scientists who were not government appointed but managed to have their voices heard every now and then went further and declared all lockdowns an "unimaginative and destructive" solution that lacked focus on those who were most vulnerable to COVID. Yet the lockdowns persisted…and were justified by government-appointed scientific experts.

Was the "science" based on biases, opinions, evidence, or subject to political whims? Scientists would say their conclusions and edicts were based on the evidence, but what evidence? Which? Who controlled that evidence, China? U.S. government or private agencies? International agencies? All of the above? The outbreak began somewhere around Wuhan, China. Even the commie-fascist sonsabitches running China had great difficulty hiding that fact within their blatant lack of transparency. But was there a conspiracy to conceal and distort evidence to protect those, including Americans, who were guilty of mismanaging the spread of the virus and perhaps developing the virus in a Wuhan, China, lab for research or more nefarious purposes? Had science been politicized? Sure seemed like it to me.

A conspiracy. Definitely a conspiracy.

"Calling it the Wuhan Chinese virus is racist," was a common refrain amongst politicians and media talking heads, a refrain I called bullshit. Nowadays, whenever someone had something to hide or couldn't support a position with evidence, they labeled their opposition "racist!" If calling the COVID-19 virus "the Wuhan Chinese virus" was racist that really meant there was a conspiracy between China and their American corporate-political-media-scientist lackeys to obfuscate the true origins of the disease as within the Wuhan Institute of Virology lab.

Science, science, science. Did science demand that masks and social distancing (six feet of separation between people when in public) be the "new normal"? Or did science indicate that masks and social distancing could not be the new normal, would indeed lead to abnormalities as such impositions disrupted the healthy social development of children, as well as their education, and stymied communication integral to human interaction? Such were the questions in the year 2020. Ridiculous questions, if you asked me, with a rational self-evident answer: No way were we living a new normal, unless Elvis, Sinatra, and The Beatles woulda been better this way; Brando and Loren; Lady Gaga and Jay-Z; Marilyn with her face masked... Sure. New normal...if we were to become a race of mutants, a shadow of what was formerly the human race. But when it came to science and socio-economic issues and questions in the age of COVID, rational answers were as elusive and ineffable as much of the science itself.

I knew that scientists could be misguided or flat-out wrong sometimes, and that an accepted scientific truth today might be refuted tomorrow, but as every tomorrow blended into the next and one group of scientists and experts were overruled and silenced by politicians, news outlets and Big Tech media in favor of another who were supposedly more brilliant, more sophisticated, and more forward-looking, tomorrow never came; there was no relief in sight, the only saving grace for nonessentials an inspiration to drink (I did)...or do drugs (I was considering it)... abuse your spouse and children (I had no spouse or children but there was a scourge of power-hungry politicians and bureaucrats I'da loved to get my hands on)...or simply grow fat and diabetic and suicidal in front of the television and sicken yourself in compliance with government orders to save yourself and others and shelter in place (I would not continue to shelter in place, a decision I never did come to regret).

After serving my prison term for producing marijuana, it had taken me years to work up the ladder at a few bait and tackle shops before I could apply for the loans and licensing (the biggest hurdles for anyone with a criminal record) to start my own bait and tackle business. My business was just beginning to show some real promise when, BANG! in the blink of an eye bait and tackle shops were decreed nonessential and forced to close. My dreams were dashed, and I was on the verge of bankruptcy. This was the second time the government had robbed me and I was pissed as hell, ready to shoot up the town. When the feds busted me for marijuana, they shut down my Fisherman's Shore Bait and Tackle and stole all my assets, and this time the state of California was bankrupting me by arbitrarily enforcing a draconian ordinance. I was not alone, of course. If misery loves company, I had plenty. The internet and TV news were awash in stories of economic desolation due to pandemic state ordinances.

I'd also had plenty of company when the feds busted me for weed, yet I accepted responsibility for my crime almost immediately. Naturally I bitched and moaned to my lawyer about states' rights and how the feds were just out to rob assets and control consensual behavior, but after a while I had to admit that the man most responsible for my demise was the guy I viewed in the mirror. I was licensed and in compliance with state law and thought my license would protect me against federal DEA agents, and I had no idea the feds could seize all my assets before I pled guilty, but I did accept responsibility for my crime, the first step to making a comeback. Lesson learned. Now however, with this oppressive pandemic lockdown, I had to unlearn my lesson. How the hell was I to blame for this, a totalitarian takeover and ruination of my livelihood? I must have been right from the start: unconstitutional government strongarm tactics are the problem, not me. No fucking way!!!

My fiancée and I had recently moved into this apartment, but I was alone, Michelle quarantined in El Salvador with family. Bad timing—she'd arrived in El Salvador for a planned visit a week before her native country enacted one of the strictest pandemic lockdowns in the world. Our apartment had now become my own personal dungeon, the walls closing in on me for what seemed like an eternity. Days of dirty dishes and frozen-dinner trays were piling up, the monotony suffocating my initiative. I needed to escape, to get back to work, or a back to fishing, surfing, and sailing—something to break out of this toxic existence. Fishing would garner me some food, but I'd settle for surfing… or robbing a bank. Desperate times call for desperate measures, but bank robbery? I'd met a bank robber in prison. He'd gotten away with a half-dozen robberies before getting caught. I should be able to pull off a heist or two…

Perhaps turning to drugs was a better option, and the ultimate final escape. But I thought again…

Best to cleanse my mind, body and soul with a surfing session before considering such drastic steps…

The lockdown prohibited surfing, which inspired more inaction as I mulled over the non-option…and inaction breeds frustration.

Shadowboxing, a practice I perfected way back in my Golden Gloves days, relieved some of the frustration, but what I really needed was the beach, and Michelle.

The impetus behind my latest arrest, the tipping point, occurred after a conversation with Michelle. Had we gotten married before she left to visit family in El Salvador, she might be permitted to leave the country and enter the U.S.A. under strict pandemic supervision. As things stood now, we had no recourse but to wait until restrictions loosened up. The conversation left me deflated and I spent the next hour or so nursing beers and channel surfing the TV in vapid indolence. I was considering a big night out—taking out the trash on my way to pick up some fast food—when suddenly I saw black and strong hot anger boiled up inside me. A television commentator had inflamed my emotions and I side-armed my glass of beer at the TV with an "Unfuckingbelievable" in disgust at my impotence in the face of the lockdown. Beer splatter glazed the TV screen—CNN assailing peaceful protests in Michigan against COVID lockdowns as "COVID health hazards"—and the splintering sound of glass shattering against the wall jarred something loose in my brain. An epiphany, or what alcoholics refer to as a moment of clarity, washed over me. Relief could be at hand, deliverance from my tortuous inner turmoil within reach. All I had to do was show some initiative…and sharpen my weapons.

Protest signs were useful, but my tongue would be my sharpest weapon. Like carefully arranging well-crafted arrows in my quiver, I prepared a litany of refrains, maxims, and slogans sure to hit their marks. I'd probably windup facing police and that'll always get you in trouble—mouthing off to cops. But..."What the fuck..."

If we can't practice freedom of speech and protest in the face of authority, when can we practice it? You don't like it? Go to hell. Offensive speech is precisely what the Constitution protects. No need to protect speech shitheads all agree with...

There was a method to my madness, a method I didn't employ when I was arrested for marijuana a decade ago. I had nothing to gain by mouthing off to the feds back then; they got the drop on me and I took my arrest (but not the rap) passively. This time I'd been emboldened, pushed to my limits and forced to willfully violate the governor's and mayor's executive lockdown orders and would pull no punches. I was bound to attract like-minded supporters, and given the nature of my premeditated violation, as well as the clash of values between my protest and the government's unconstitutional iron-fisted tactics, why not push the edge of the envelope with smart-talk, get arrested and gain publicity for the cause? Didn't Martin Luther King Jr. do something similar in Birmingham, Alabama?

To say that the feds "got the drop on me" when I was arrested for weed is a vast understatement, like calling arsonists, looters, and vandals "bad elements." Cops literally tore my house apart in a six-a.m. no-knock raid, replete with an armored SWAT team, flashbang grenades, and automatic weapons, like I was Pablo Escobar or holed up with MS-13 gangsters. I was home alone and escaped serious injury, yet had they simply knocked and presented me with the warrant for my arrest I'd have complied without a struggle. The experience made me a huge supporter of police reform and inspired me to compile a list of those who were far less fortunate in similar no-knock raids:

Walter Parks, 47 years old. SWAT announced their no-knock drug raid with flashbang grenades. Walter's 14-year-old daughter cried out for help. Fearing a home invasion, Walter grabbed his rifle. He was shot to death in front of his wife and daughter. The raid was carried out at the wrong address.

Azuma Thomas, 9 years old. Azuma was shot and killed by law-enforcement officers as they exchanged gunfire with one of his relatives during a pre-dawn drug raid.

Juan Sanchez, 19 years old. Juan was standing at the front door to a house where he had come to repay a $25 debt. A drug raid on the house commenced and he was shot in the head by SWAT.

Silvia Reno, 86 years old. Silvia was bedridden with the flu when her house was raided. A narcotics officer kicked open her bedroom door and accidentally shot her.

Jeffery Bucks, 66 years old. Jeffery was watching TV when SWAT officers shot him to death during a drug raid. The house did not match the description on the warrant.

Alejandro Diaz, 10 years old. The fifth-grader followed police orders during the SWAT drug raid at his home. He was laying facedown on the floor when he was accidentally killed by a shotgun blast to the back of his head.

Colton Davies, 26 years old. An informant told police of a marijuana operation at Colton's home. A SWAT team executed a no-knock warrant. Colton was shot to death in his living room. There is no conclusive evidence that he was in possession of a gun, but he did have three budding marijuana plants in a bedroom closet.

Tamika Jefferson, 25 years old. Tamika was a single mother of five. SWAT executed a raid on her house to arrest her boyfriend on small-time drug dealing charges. An officer was upstairs with Tamika when he heard shots fired downstairs. He was startled, didn't know that his partners had shot the family's dogs. He accidentally shot and killed Tamika. She was unarmed, on her knees and cradling her 15-month-old son as she died. The son she cradled was shot as well but survived.

Michael Woods, 44 years old. Police conducted a no-knock raid on his home. When the front door to his house was kicked in, Michael emerged from an interior door with a baseball bat poised high overhead. He was shot three times and died on the spot. Police found a small quantity of marijuana and an empty vial alleged to have contained other drugs.

And on and on and on...

I was no stranger to the abuses of militarized police forces, and after my arrest for producing marijuana, I harbored a hatred for police and "the system" for quite some time. A deep-seated hatred. Yet upon my release from prison and following sobering bouts of reflection, I came to understand my hatred as destructive and illogical. A cop might be evil, but many of the laws cops were legally bound to enforce were more so, especially laws that criminalized non-violent consensual behavior and encouraged Napoleonic no-knock raids and the precipitous forfeiture of assets. And while too many sane cops refused to take a stand against the insanity, there were far more psycho criminals lurking about than there were psycho police. I'd met some in prison—flat-out crazy bastards—and other crooks, thugs, hoods, and swindlers as a matter of course in my life. Even in America's most dangerous, lawless ghettos where police might be particularly ridiculed and despised, police were the ones called in response to gang shootings and brutality, weren't they? Who else you gonna call, social workers to face down bullets? your mayor, governor, local congressman or state senator, have their private security forces and cops come out there and take care of business? Yeah, right. Good luck. You had to be a stupid moron or part of a broad criminal conspiracy not to see that humans were far from angels and that there were some mean, bloodthirsty thugs, gangsters and murderous psychopaths out there who woke up every morning aching to jack your car, steal your possessions, and literally kill you, your family and all your pets, and the vast majority of them were not police officers. Public law enforcement was essential, and "the system," while odious in many respects, did present countless routes to legally prosper in America, as long as I didn't allow myself to be blinded by hatred for The Man and his System. I tried to avoid police, and felt better when they weren't around or needed, but I refused to hate them and, as a result, did not fear them and figured that facing cops at a peaceful protest would be a completely different circumstance than facing them in a no-knock raid. So I prepared myself for the possibility of arrest without trepidation, left my wallet, IDs, smart phone, and cash in my lonely apartment, my car (with a hide-a-key stashed behind the wheel well) secured in the apartment complex garage. Wore swim trunks under my cargo shorts; running shoes, a Dodger cap, cheap sunglasses, a six-week beard (unemployment is an opportunity to grow out your hair), and a Catalina Island beach shirt. Nothing on me for the cops to confiscate except forty bucks and my backpack should my protest take a not entirely unexpected detour to the jailhouse…

CHAPTER 5

SCRUBBING AMERICAN GRAFFITI

Antonia lowered her mask, blew her nose into a handkerchief, took a couple of lung-clearing breaths and stared derisively at Nuestro American Hardware's defaced storefront.

"See many of these *puta madre* rioters and thieves wearing masks in the news?" she snarled. "If they are wearing masks it's not because of the pandemic but to disguise themselves as they destroy and loot. And social distancing? Ha! Prick bastards don't really give a damn about anyone, much less spreading a virus…"

Although the media and government experts touted the importance of social distancing, the absence of social distancing amongst rioters and social-justice activists was mentioned about as often as the term "riot." Apparently, rioters and BLM-Antifa social-justice warriors were blessed with a COVID immunity gene, a gene unrecognized back in May when peaceful protests against COVID lockdowns, like the one I was involved in, were regularly vilified as virus "superspreader events."

I lowered my mask to drink some water.

"They must be blessed with immunity to COVID, as well as immunity to prosecution."

Manny said, "Hijos de puta. Marching for la justicia? Veremos que justicia reciben." We'll see what justice they receive.

"They're too privileged to receive the justice they deserve," Antonia said. "They don't even get arrested." She waved her paint brush in a sweeping motion across her storefront. "No one's been arrested for this. No one. Pinches BLM-Antifa *social-justice warriors* should be—"

A vehicle pulled up at the curb, interrupting her little diatribe and drawing our attention. The woman behind the wheel of the midnight-bule Ford SUV said, "Why are you removing Black Lives Matter slogans?"

"Those are valuable messages," echoed her partner in the passenger seat.

Both women were caramel black, their voice inflections patronizing rather than accusatory. Neither wore a pandemic mask, and their expressions held the sort of forced composure that recalled grammar-school teachers exasperated by their students.

The driver smirked and shook her head. "Hell of a way to practice white privilege," she said.

Manny and I exchanged a puzzled look, eyebrows lifted as we deciphered her remark. Was she referring to me? My mask was lowered but even if it were covering my face you could tell I was white—brown hair, green eyes, tan arms. And Manny? His mask covered his mouth and nose but his straight black hair, almond-brown eyes and swarthy dark complexion… Were they referring to him as well, a Mexican? We stared at Antonia. Her mask was below her chin revealing a fair complexion flushed with seething rage.

"Puta madre pendejas," she spat. "You're the ones who are privileged!"

Antonia reached for a shovel leaning against the exterior wall of her shop. She thought again, grabbed the broom and swept clouds of dust and debris at the women in the Ford as she advanced, cursing them in a string of Spanish profanity worthy of a Chilango gangster in Mexico City. The women in the car yelped and shrank from the attack, their faces contorted in shock and confusion—shock at Antonia's precipitous eruption, and confusion at the streak of Spanish expletives fired from a white woman right between their eyes. Princess teetered within the commotion and toppled from her station against the lamppost, landing on her knees, face planted on the sidewalk, her bloodied ass directed at the SUV.

Manny bounced on his toes with the emotion of a spectator at a prize fight…and pointed a finger at Princess—a ringside casualty.

"La mataron."

Was Princess dead?!? My face screwed up in bitter anguish, tears flushing my eyes. I'd lost a loved one, my guardian and confidant!…our bodyguard. In a last desperate gesture of defiance, Princess had shoved her ass in the face of slings and arrows and assassins to protect us from exploding grenades! I sprang to her rescue, determined to breathe life back into her. Mouth-to-mouth showed no result, and I held her aloft, our fallen hero.

"You've killed her!" I declared, my head lifted to the heavens. I gnashed my teeth, dropped my gaze to the women in the Ford and extended Princess' bloodied visage. "Pray for her," I said, "for she has paid for our sins."

The women in the SUV screeched, screamed and screeched at the roadkill I held before them, as if confronted by troops of walking dead. The driver threw her car into gear and pealed out, throwing dust in the air, fishtailing and running a red light.

Manny applauded. Antonia glared at me, like I was to blame for the altercation. "Those BLM bitches are the ones who belong in jail," she hissed, "not you, Colton." She pulled her mask up over her nose and mouth and pointed her broomstick at the black couple repairing damage to their ice cream parlor down the street, one of them painting over graffiti. "Are they practicing white privilege too? White privilege my ass... *White privilege*— just another bullshit slogan and rationale for losers to justify their own failures."

Manny's eyes smiled at his wife. "Careful, cariño," he said. "No quieres que te llamen racista." You don't want to be called racist.

Who's gonna call her racist?

I surveyed the streets. There were few pedestrians, none of whom was paying enough attention to Antonia to curse her as "racist," or applaud, laugh or cry at our performance. As it turned out, someone did manage to record us on an iPhone. The video would wreak havoc on us in the coming months, but the havoc did help inspire me to cure myself.

Antonia rolled her eyes and laughed as to an inside joke. "Oooh nooo!" she chortled and cried and trembled. "Not *racista*. I better shut up and tow the party line or the woke media, politicians, and social-justice warriors will call me racist." She shook her head in exaggerated exasperation. "Those *hijos de la gran puta madre* call anyone who disagrees with them racist. I'll wear the label like a badge of honor, though the way the word is tossed around these days it's lost all meaning."

"That's quite a woman you got there," I said to Manny in Spanish, and pulled my mask back up over my mouth and nose.

"She knows how to work and play," he replied, "and picks her fights carefully—"

"When threatened," Antonia interjected, her Spanish sharp and deliberate. "I know how to pick my fights when threatened. And people like those two *putas* are trying to destroy our lives." She leaned her broom against the wall, retrieved her paint brush, and continued, "BLM scumbags pretend to better *black lives* but destroy everything they touch. If they really care about black lives, why aren't they in Chicago? Plenty of black gangsters are killing thousands of blacks there. *Thousands*, including children and babies… Goddamn social-justice warriors should move to China and receive the treatment they deserve. BLM's largest donors are funded by Chinese slave labor anyway."

Manny said, "Ándale, amorcito…"

I regarded Antonia, stirring the paint in her bucket with care, her eyebrows knitted in grim determination. I'd seen her heated before, manifested by sparks of affected anger to scare off a vagrant or two, or flares of histrionics as she reproached me for not stealing Michelle back to the United States against international quarantine regulations. Antonia was not hesitant to remind me—sometimes eloquently, other times in colorful language—that love conquers all; if I was truly in love neither famine, war, nor Black Death itself would prevent me from being with Michelle. As I considered Antonia now, I thought of Michelle, our plans to reunite and how pleased Antonia and Manny would be to see her again. And I reflected on Antonia herself. I'd come to appreciate her plainspoken honesty, as well as our occasional bantering. Yet this furious outburst of hers against those "putas" in the Ford, while not totally out of character, revealed a feral aspect to the woman I hadn't witnessed before, like a momma bear protecting her cubs.

She's pregnant.

I bent to my work and let my mind drift. Michelle was not nearly as confrontational as Antonia, but would her personality transform when she got pregnant? Probably, at least a little. I was fifteen years her senior, could I adapt my bachelor ways to marriage and a family? Yes, it was time. And what about my pending court date, the specter of fines levied against me, maybe a jail sentence, and my looming bankruptcy?...

Love conquers all. Michelle and I would be reunited soon, hopefully within a matter of weeks. We needed each other and were in constant contact—FaceTime, texts, email—and she knew all about my troubles, past and present. The fact that I was a convicted felon seemed to work to my favor when we met, not due to the attraction good girls may have for bad boys but for my determination to rebound and open my own business. How long had it taken me to open this latest incarnation of Fisherman's Shore Bait and Tackle? Years. And it took but moments to have it destroyed…

CHAPTER 6

SURFING WITH DOLPHINS

Summer appeared to have arrived early this year in southern California. May was shaping up to be one of the warmest on record. I hopped off the bus at the Malibu Pier well before noon with one other passenger and walked a piece, meandered within the closed parking lot and then along the highway, the beach off my left shoulder. A spectacular southern California day—crystalline sky, shimmering water, a three-foot swell. The breeze was still offshore, suspending waves at their peaks in sequence to a long glassy break. Not a surfer in the water, shocking under normal circumstances; and this was a Saturday. The Malibu lineup should have been a surfer's battleground paradise.

But these were not normal circumstances. California's beaches were all officially closed.

Sunshine, fresh air, exercise, the ocean; all strengthen the immune system, the heart, mind, body and soul...and kill viruses.

On a spring day like this, parked cars were usually bumper to bumper along this stretch of PCH, with tourists, locals, and valleys (like me) frolicking all along the beach. Not today. A-frame barricades, orange cones, and no-parking signs prevented street parking. Yet people were here, and they outnumbered the bicycles and skateboards. Some might have arrived by bus or Uber, but others must have come on foot, either from nearby homes or their cars parked on side streets. Handfuls of wishful beachgoers were milling around here and there, a daring few venturing onto Surfrider Beach, others, young men mostly, standing at the rim of the highway, stymied fingers running through windswept hair, hungry eyes staring out over the ocean. Everything about those hungry eyes suggested kindred souls: water rats—surfers, paddle boarders, parasailers. Unemployed or employed, they'd have already been in the water today. Now they were idle and restless, and likely unemployed due to the lockdown.

I was a young man once and know that, in general, young men are a volatile species, especially volatile when weakened, wounded. Like many animals, young men can be most dangerous when wounded. Unemployment is certainly wounding to anyone, but combine unemployment with pandemic shelter-in-place orders from the mayor and governor, forcing young men to be confined to quarters, their idle hands consumed with raw, boundless energy… These are the ingredients for a powder keg, the stuff violent revolutions are made of…

Was I here to start a revolution?

Maybe twenty years ago…

I'd witnessed a revolution of sorts in 1995, twenty-five years ago, in Chiapas, Mexico, where the Zapatistas struck a mighty blow for communism in San Cristóbal de las Casas, right after the

North American Free Trade Agreement was signed. The uprising made international headlines, and I wrote a couple of undergraduate essays on the subject. I tried to be evenhanded in the essays, neither pro nor contra Zapatista. I'd gone to Chiapas on a quixotic quest, as a non-credentialed erstwhile journalist in search of the truth. The adventure—diving headfirst into a regional conflict in a foreign land—carried some inherent risks that were thrilling rather than scary. I was young and more idealistic back then, a dreamer and truth seeker, like so many at that age. And I was faster too. Athletic. Probably overconfident in my ability to escape danger. Fearless. By 2020, my right knee tended to stiffen, as did my lower back. I was no longer fearless, but that didn't stop me from surfing, sailing, and fishing. Only beach closures, unheard of, unending pandemic beach closures, could do that.

In Chiapas, I was there to witness a revolution. Was I here now to do the same or start one? Somewhere in the recesses of my mind, I had a romantic notion of channeling George Washington and inciting revolution to recapture American ideals of E Pluribus Unum, federalism, and liberty, ideals that, given current nationwide lockdowns and my own personal experiences with the criminal-justice system, had been trashed. In reality though, I knew there was no chance of revolution.

I had no clue that violent revolutionary outbreaks and riots were at hand in the USA. I'd merely come to Malibu to help initiate what I believed was on the brink of happening: a non-violent protest against beach closures and the state lockdown in general. To my knowledge, no demonstration had been planned in Malibu, but they had begun to spring up across California, and police always made their presence known. Police in Sacramento were enforcing an outright ban on protests, but peaceful protests against COVID lockdowns in Newport Beach, about 80 miles south of Malibu, were going strong. Via social media and my own instincts, I sensed that Malibu must be ripe for an all-American demonstration of the First Amendment. Two young men were arrested here last week for surfing in violation of the shelter-in-place order.

I'd never initiated a protest before, hadn't even participated in one. I'd seen my share of them however, both here in the U.S.A. and abroad. Some protests were organized beforehand and required permits, others spontaneous. Timing had to be key to inspire a spontaneous protest, and now was the time; but even if I stood alone, my voice was the most important voice to be heard. E Pluribus Unum—one man's voice, a single individual's rights hold as much value as those of the multitudes. The mob cannot be allowed to rule, and I had something to say.

To my mind, "the mob" constituted a majority imposing its will on a minority. Within a month or so I'd experience the tyranny of a minority, the wrath of violent mobs who, had they been in the majority, would have literally burned the nation to the ground...

A whiff of marijuana slowed my pace. I paused about ten yards from a gaggle of young men and adolescents, none of whom were practicing pandemic social distancing. I didn't see smoke from a blunt, and none were wearing a pandemic mask like most of the others around, including me.

This is as good a spot as any.

A police cruiser coasted by. It seemed to slow as it passed me, sending a tingle up my spine, a scintilla of what remained of my young blood, a flicker of exuberance in the face of danger. Perhaps my real motive for coming here was to recapture my youth, my daring-do and idealism. I set my pack upon an embankment above the beach below, an inaudible crack in my knee a reminder that, while I might retain some youthful idealism, at 48 my body was old and slow, much older and slower than it was twenty years ago…

I unzipped my pack and fished out the bottled water from underneath my towel. The chicken salad sandwich could wait. A couple slugs of water fortified me. I scanned the horizon, and the waves, my mask beneath my chin. Dolphins were surfing, their dorsal fins tracing paths through wave pockets, impact zones in their wakes. Two or three leaped, confirming they were dolphins, though little confirmation was needed for frequent beach farers. The newly initiated might think "shark" at first sight, but sharks don't surf, certainly not with the agility of dolphins, and tend to avoid the swifter, highly intelligent mammals. Dolphins have been known to ram sharks and kill them in self-defense, self-preservation, and are superior hunters after similar piscine prey. Unlike sharks, dolphins never prey on humans. Indeed, they often surf with humans, a surfer's best friend, so to speak, for where there are dolphins there are, generally (but no guarantee), no sharks. Many of those standing along the bank above the beach gestured towards the dolphins, releasing whistles and howls in admiration and jealousy.

"Can't quarantine them," snarled a rawboned young man to one of his friends.

Quarantines are for the sick and vulnerable, not the healthy and active...

He and his friends stood about ten yards away from me, but I could hear their grumblings without straining, their slang and languid speech giving them away as surfers. I studied his blond, unmasked, indignant features, and judged him a probable ally, along with most everyone else in sight. They had to be. Despite the lockdown, in defiance of the lockdown, all had been drawn to this spot, called by Mother Nature and the healing, rejuvenating powers of the ocean and beach. We had a need, a right to swim and surf with the dolphins, and it was clear to us, like a unified moment of clarity, that the dolphins were teasing us, as well as challenging us to join them.

Another police cruiser cruised by, this one noticeably slowing along its way, as though the cops were judging, behind tinted glass, when to begin issuing citations and making arrests for violations of shelter-in-place orders. My gaze followed the cruiser south till it pulled into the pier parking lot. I wondered how many of his buddies were there to greet him, but the thought passed as quickly as the flip of a dolphin's tail. I was on a mission and reached into my backpack for one of my weapons. A free-speech weapon, a twinge in the pit of my stomach lending it the feel of a firearm as I pulled it out.

The size of my signs was limited by the dimensions of my backpack, about 34" X 18". I'd used colorful Sharpies for the lettering so the slogans would stand out against the white cardboard. I chose my preferred sign, kept it close to the vest as I neared the highway, and then held it high overhead and trumpeted its words in a booming voice: "Give us peace and open beaches!" I repeated the refrain a few times, my focus on passing cars, a technique I'd learned by observing Tea Party activists over a decade ago in Portland, Oregon. My voice was more likely to be heard by those around me than the drivers, but everything—my sign and chants—worked together to gain support from all quarters. Individual rights aside, there is power in numbers, and I did hope to capture the desires of as many people as I could. I switched to a slogan on one of the other signs secured in my backpack: "We are all essential!"

California surfer dialects answered me: "Wow, Bro, you're awesome!" and, "Rad! I need to get me a sign too…"

The surfers remained yards away, off to my left and aft, just beyond my line of vision. I was standing in place, focused on the cars passing in front of me, from my left heading south. The folks to my right, south of me, were the ones I noticed, and I was drawing their attention, fingers pointed my way. The surfers to my left were involved in animated conversation amongst themselves. One said, "We'll be right back," as I resumed my protest with words from the third sign in my backpack: "The beach is the cure, not the disease!"

Surfers approached me from behind: "You da *man!* Killin' it!" "Dig it. We been thinkin' on doing this." "Malibu cops don't have a lot of patience sometimes…"

This last comment trailed off as a police cruiser passed on the opposite side of the street, heading north.

I pivoted, pulled my mask over my mouth and nose in deference to pandemic regs, and focused my attention on the surfers, their exuberant, rebellious sun-tinged expressions. "Wanna help?" I asked and motioned to my backpack so I could distribute my signs.

Within fifteen minutes, a couple of the surfers had split and returned with surfboards in the bed of a pickup. The five of them worked in shifts, two holding my signs and chanting, the others protesting by surfing with dolphins. Time passed quickly and inside of an hour I noted a spring to my step and a stirring rush of energy I hadn't experienced in years. I wasn't running around trying to inspire people, more like skipping as my surfer allies and I gained support. Additional signs appeared out of nowhere, as did more people, along with a smattering of American flags. Newcomers didn't recognize me as the inspiration behind this spontaneous demonstration, but I was getting lots of fist-bumps and thumbs-up from those who did. The skip to my step must have revealed that I relished the role and truly believed in the right to protest as well as the cause, a cause that begged questions and observations too deep for a protest sign: There is no plague exception in the U.S. Constitution allowing for totalitarian rule. Which part of the Bill of Rights is incomprehensible because it's written in Chinese? As in today's China and North Korea, as well as the old Soviet Union and NAZI Germany, totalitarian rule is invariably justified as in the public's best interest.

Somewhere along the line I forgot that I'd prepared myself to get arrested, that I had expected police intervention. When law enforcement disembarked their cruiser at the edge of the highway to my left, about twenty yards north of me, I finally noticed that several cops were already hassling protesters well to the south. Across the highway, an officer spoke through a bullhorn: "Disperse or you will be cited or arrested! You are not immune to this virus!..."

He sounded like one of those drones I'd seen on the news lately, drones that flew around following people, harassing them, warning them to go home or face the consequences. And it struck me that these cops were much like drones or robots, similar to the cops who had arrested me a decade ago: mindless, following their programming, and obtuse—blind to their abuse of power.

Just like prison COs...

The thought, the memory, infuriated me. I reminded myself to focus my anger, to stay calm as I utilized the sharpest weapon in my arsenal: my tongue.

I drifted north, to my left, my face dutifully covered. Three cops in pandemic masks and latex gloves were maintaining social distance from four of my surfer allies, one of whom was recording everything on his iPhone.

Before the end of summer, I'd study that video in an effort to aid in my own defense against the state and make a key discovery I was certain would blow the prosecution's case apart.

"We have a right to be here," said a tawny teenager to the officers.

"And a right to protest," added the rawboned 'can't quarantine dolphins' young man.

" 'Fraid not," replied one of the cops. He was flanked by a partner on either side. They wore uniforms, not riot gear, but between their caps and masks it was impossible to get a read on their expressions. I could barely make out a furrowed brow on the cop doing most of the talking.

A diminutive surfer with sharp blue eyes chimed in: "But I get allergies in the valley. The pollen swells my eyes." The kid was probably sixteen but looked twelve. And I doubted he was a valley. It had taken him and a friend nary fifteen minutes to jam outta here on skateboards and return in a pickup loaded with surfboards. He crossed his eyes and puffed his cheeks. "And swells my face too. I need the beach."

His antics elicited laughter from his buddies. The cops shook their heads and exchanged surly glances. The officer in the middle spoke up again:

"Sorry son. I'll have to issue you and your friends citations if you don't disperse immediately. Orders, you know. Just following orders, like we all need to do."

"Sounds familiar. The Nuremberg defense. You remember that from school or does it come naturally?" The words escaped my mouth with minimal forethought, like a response to a slap in the face. Yet I'd prepared for this and had lowered my pandemic mask to make sure I came through loud and clear. The cops scowled at me, then cocked their heads at one another in a group effort to decipher my words. My previous experiences with law enforcement had taught me not to underestimate cops. Certainly some are ignorant brutes on a power trip, but more than a few are sagacious; I judged that two, maybe all three knew exactly what the Nuremberg defense was.

One of the uniforms pointed a crooked finger at me. "He's the instigator," he said. "I saw him earlier." My surfer friends released inflated "Ooooo"s and "Whoa"s.

"Sounds like an instigator," said the cop in the middle. He approached me, and paused the requisite six feet away, conscious of social distancing. "You looking for trouble?" His masked voice sounded like it emanated through a rotating fan—a Darth Vader voice.

"Has trouble been looking for *me?*" I asked, thumb to my chest. "Looks like it may have found me." One of the officers turned his back to speak into a handheld radio.

Vader said, "Let's see some ID," eyeing the sign I now held below my waist rather than overhead.

I patted down my cargo shorts. "Don't have any. You really citing people for peacefully protesting, exercising their First Amendment rights?"

" 'Fraid so." He pulled an electronic citation device from its holster. "I'll need your name."

"Doesn't failing to protect freedom of speech violate your oath to protect and defend the Constitution?"

"Emergencies call for emergency measures. Name..."

"Emergencies call for emergency measures," I recited. "Say that in the Constitution does it, as a rationale for totalitarian rule?"

He pierced me with a coal-hot stare. "Look, Asshole," he said. "These are serious times. Lives are at stake. You," Vader waved a hand over the crowd, "all of you are putting lives at risk."

"And I'm sure you have the numbers to back that up and strike fear into our hearts."

The creases in his furrowed brow deepened in calculation of those numbers.

I forged ahead: "There sure are a lot of conflicting numbers and experts. You know what Twain said about that…?"

Vader released a low growl. "What the f—"

"There are lies, damn lies, and statistics."

He narrowed his gaze, his voice dripping disdain: "Looks like trouble doesn't have to travel very far to find you. We don't need malcontents like you causing chaos at a time like this. Now give me your name or we'll run your ass in right now. In fact, we're gonna—"

"Ahhh…from Nuremberg to China. Like trouble, you get around as well."

He motioned to his partner. I didn't resist in the least, but they manhandled me anyway (social distancing be damned), grabbed me by the back of the neck, stuck my mask on my face, slapped cuffs on me, and searched me before I could expound: the Chinese justify totalitarian rule as the only sure way to avoid chaos, and it's for the benefit of the general population, naturally…

Catcalls and whistles from my supporters echoed in my ears as a police car pulled up. "Free my sister!" screamed a woman not far south of us, which caused a minor stir of confusion in my brain. She clarified: "Open her salon so she can feed her kids!"

I was occupied, but not unexpectedly or to distraction, and appreciated her illumination. This demonstration wasn't all about the beach but the general lockdown as well. An equal-opportunity demonstration. My own impending bankruptcy had driven me to this, and I instantly recalled a story out of Dallas of a single mother jailed for opening her "nonessential" business so she could put food on the table for her family. The judge called her selfish…

The cops tossed me in the back of the squad car, followed by my Dodger cap and sunglasses, Vader in the passenger seat. We headed south. I surveyed the crowd. Most wore pandemic masks, yet heated frustration registered throughout. Despite the emotion, there was no violence, and many appeared to be communicating calmly with police. And I remained calm, supremely at ease, proud of myself, like basking in the afterglow of a championship football victory. I chuckled, a sated smile spreading across my face and penetrating my pandemic mask.

Vader glared at me. "Name?" he said.

"Puddin Taine. Ask me again and I'll tell ya the same."

He snorted. "Smartass."

He didn't know that I'd been conditioned for this; I wasn't putting on airs. I had faced the feds and held no fear for these guys. And the USA hadn't become indistinguishable from China just yet; I wasn't heading for a gulag (best to act now before gulags became commonplace in America). Once they ran my prints, they'd know my name, and my record. But I'd considered that already. What the fuck. I'd been clean for years and wasn't gonna let that bullshit marijuana beef prevent me from taking a stand for the First Amendment, the Bill of Rights, and the right to surf with dolphins. I had no intention of living the rest of my life that way. Give me liberty or give me death, by virus or any other means. Don't matter if your life and liberty are threatened by redcoats, a virus, or both; the fight for liberty is arduous and, as history has proven, unending. Not that I compared my role in today's skirmish to Washington's valiance against the redcoats. Washington had risked his fortune and his life and, upon victory, refused to rule as king in favor of establishing a constitutional republic. Most unusual in the annals of history. On the other hand, my life was not at risk, I had no fortune, no military victories against overwhelming odds under my belt, and absolutely no chance of being king. And Washington had a smallpox epidemic to deal with during the revolution, a disease far more deadly than COVID. But that didn't deter him or his troops from wiping out tyranny. I hadn't wiped out tyranny but might have inspired small steps in that direction. That's the way I saw it anyway... In my ignorance, I did not consider how tyranny can take many forms, including the tyranny of a minority that I'd be experiencing soon enough. At the moment, all my thoughts and feelings were focused on what appeared to be a small yet significant victory for me. Everything I'd planned had gone down without a hitch. I was putting up a fight against lockdowns that had closed my business, and the people were demonstrating their support and exercising their freedom of speech. They knew no fear of man nor virus. My arrest was a small price to pay to provide them more inspiration, maybe some publicity, and to set an example: neither arrest nor jail nor risk of infection stays the fight for the Bill of Rights. There was indeed a method to my madness.

"Where do you live?"

"Homeless. Thanks for putting me up for a spell."

Once they ran my prints, they'd pull up my driver's license. But my license identified me with a previous address I hadn't gotten around to updating with the DMV. Inertia caused by the lockdown was part of the reason, but ultimately the epiphany that led to today's activities convinced me not to update my license at all, at least for a while. This little ride to the jailhouse was predictable; no way in hell I was gonna give these assholes my real address so they could raid my apartment.

Vader grumbled, "I don't believe a damn thing you say."

I used to have a spotless record. I went to college, started my own business, and played by the rules. Even when the feds busted me for weed I was adhering to state guidelines for marijuana production. Following my marijuana arrest, it would have been easy to dwell on the injustice of it all: federal intrusion on states' rights; destructive, cyclonic police raids on my home and business; how I was forced to forfeit all my assets before found guilty of any crime; and the lockdowns and shakedowns in prison, how those prick COs harassed us prisoners every chance they got. Nonetheless, upon release from prison I put all that behind me and endeavored to live on the straight and narrow. I could bounce back. This was America, the place dreams are made of. Nothing could stop me, except, as it turned out, totalitarian rule in response to a pandemic. Never would have occurred to me. After all, the country had survived pandemics before without taking such drastic actions. Once again the State, a government "for and by the people" was bankrupting me, and these cops in the car were reminders of those infernal prison COs...

Anger roiled within my chest, threatening to overwhelm the calm that had washed over me moments ago...

Relax. You still have arrows in your quiver...

"We'll identify you," Vader said. "And something tells me you have something to hide."

I fired a few shots: "When were the Bill of Rights suspended? Didn't know the Constitution contained a plague exception to justify a totalitarian takeover. Is suspending the Bill of Rights like occupancy laws or requiring shoes, shirt, and sanitary conditions in restaurants?"

Vader's dark eyes turned black. He reached for his mask to pull it down and give me an unobstructed piece of his mind, thought again, and showed me the back of his head.

Nothing like implementing and enforcing lockdowns to inspire abuse of power…

"Saw that video of cops brutalizing a Chicana for selling flowers in violation of your ordinance. Friends of yours?"

"Shut the fuck up."

Lincoln suspended habeas corpus; but he was dealing with a civil war, and it dawned on me that such extreme measures could *cause* a civil war here in the USA and most all western democracies… I reflected on George Washington again, channeled Martin Luther King Jr. on his way to jail, and then looked out the window, over the ocean. A couple of dolphins leaped high into the air. A miraculous sendoff. I'd been rejuvenated, reawakened, restored…and would be leaping as high as those dolphins the next time we surfed together.

CHAPTER 7

EDNA

Tiburones," Antonia said. "Todos son tiburones en un frenesí de alimentación." Sharks. They're all sharks in a feeding frenzy.

Antonia and Manny had invited me over for Sunday dinner after another hot, grimy day of post-party cleanup, the third time I'd visited their home in this quaint middle-class neighborhood a few blocks north of Ventura Boulevard, in Sherman Oaks. I'd gone home to wash up and arrived a couple hours before dusk, through the gate to the backyard. We were seated at a long picnic table out on the patio polishing off a meal of barbeque chicken, potato salad, and tossed green salad. Antonia's elderly mother, Edna, seated at the head of the table, tilted her head at her daughter's remarks.

"It's always been that way," she said in Spanish. "Individually people may be reasonable, but in packs they're wild animals."

Edna's English was passable, but she hadn't spoken it much since her retirement from the hardware store business she'd left to Antonia and Manny after the death of her husband last year. This was her house and she'd relinquished the master bedroom to her daughter and son-in-law, preferring the sanctity of the guest room with a view of the garden. Edna suffered a stroke shortly after her husband's death, and while her mind remained sharp English required an effort she'd rather expend on her early evening walks. In deference to Edna, we principally spoke Spanish this evening. I sat opposite her, at the far end of the table, practicing social distancing.

Antonia shook her head, her Spanish retaining a Peninsular Castilian accent not always evident in public or exchanges with her Mexican husband: "Most of the peaceful protesters might be reasonable, but I doubt any of the rioters are at all, especially their leadership."

"Which means we need sharks of our own to defend ourselves," Manny said. "But the police and the mayor, they don't do a damn thing, not here or in Chicago, New York, Portland, Seattle, Minneapolis…anywhere." He took a pull from his bottle of beer. Unlike his wife, Manny was slow to excite and not given to histrionics. But the damage done to his business at the hands of the mob had taken its toll on him, his open, pleasant face pinched in unaccustomed anger. "Our insurance might cover some of our loses," he added, "but our rates are sure to go up. We have to reopen or go broke." His hardened gaze softened and settled on me. "I'm sorry you went out of business so quickly, Colt. But Nuestro American Hardware has been in business for nearly thirty years. It's a popular *mom-and-pop* neighborhood store." He shifted his passion back to the table as a whole.

"An American success story begun by immigrants who came to this country with nothing—"

"Not quite nothing," Edna interjected, her wizened voice commanding attention. "Mario's…your father-in-law's aunt and uncle came here with nothing. Mario and I managed to save up for the trip…"

Edna took a sip of water, her hand steady. She'd nearly cleaned her plate, her appetite and elegant carriage belying her health problems. She wore a paisley blouse, her salon-styled gray hair framing the weathered yet refined features of a respected matriarch. I wondered if she styled her own hair; most all salons and barbershops were closed at the mayor's orders during the pandemic. I'd met Edna once before, when Michelle and I visited back in March. She was a studious woman with an extensive library, though her ill health now prevented her from reading as much as she used to; it was hard for her to concentrate for extended periods. And while dignified, Edna was gracious, her accommodating blue eyes smiling as weariness tugged at their corners.

"Aunt and Uncle escaped Franco," I offered, more statement than question. I'd spoken to Edna about this during my last visit. Franco had already died when she and her husband left Spain for the United States in the eighties to join relatives who had escaped Franco's fascist dictatorship.

Edna nodded and winked at me in response, remembering our previous conversation on the subject.

Manny said, "Franco would have these rioters shot, right Ma?"

"Before they even started rioting," Edna answered blithely. "And so would Xi," she added, referring to China's dictator.

"I'll be damned if we need a Franco or Xi," Manny said. "But if the police and mayor can't protect us, we'll have to protect ourselves."

Antonia fluttered her eyelashes at him. "What do you have in mind, cariño? Raising an army?"

Her passive tone suggested a switch in roles with her husband, Manny now the combative one.

Manny downed the rest of his beer in one gulp. "If you consider our *primos* an army," he said. "Those *puta madre* BLM-Antifa rioters are cowards at heart. A few sharks can face them down with shotguns."

"Careful not to shoot your allies," Edna rejoined.

The three of us regarded her in befuddled silence.

"Rioters are not our allies," Antonia said at last.

"No," Edna agreed, a knowing half-smile creasing her lips. "But the protesters are...or should be. Liberty and freedom of speech are wonderful things, though easily abused, even within a civil society."

I frowned. "Not sure I understand..."

Antonia helped me out: "I think she means that the peaceful protestors can't control the rioters, and—"

"I can support the protest," I intervened, "but not the BLM-Antifa rioters." Antonia and Manny cocked their heads at me, searching for clarification. "I know something about police abuses," I added with a quick sip of my beer, the elixir blunting the hate-filled memory of how those feds and local police had exploded my home and life for cultivating an herb. "It's easy to forget as idiot *cabrones* set fire to cities, but I think police abuse is a...

the cause for protest. And I suppose Edna doesn't want Manny to mistakenly shoot an innocent protestor rather than an arsonist…"

Manny grumbled, "It shouldn't be difficult to distinguish between the two."

Antonia focused a narrowed gaze upon me, unsure if I was about to expound on this purported knowledge of mine. She discerned that the "police abuses" I claimed to know something about did not refer to my recent arrest for incitement to riot but the violent SWAT raids on my home and business when I was busted for marijuana a decade ago. I never exactly trumpeted the story of my marijuana arrest, but it wasn't something I was ashamed of or afraid to share, especially with those in the state-legal marijuana industry; the feds could still bust you regardless of state laws legalizing weed, an important factor for those in the industry to bear in mind. Antonia and Manny were privy to the drama—the SWAT raids, the precipitous forfeiture of all my assets, my time in prison—and Antonia was wondering if I was about to make her mother a party to my marijuana story, her wary expression advising me against recounting the narrative as Edna prodded me:

"Have you been abused at the hands of police, Colton?"

I offered Edna a careless shrug. "I had a run-in or two with them, in my younger days…"

Edna dipped her chin and appraised me dubiously, as if over a pair of reading glasses.

She relented, "Bueno," her eyes glinting with arid humor. "Did you commit arson as a result, to seek justice?"

"No more than I'd shoot my neighbor because I got robbed at gunpoint by a stranger."

My remark elicited wry chuckles from Manny and Antonia.

Edna pressed on: "And who would shoot their neighbor because they were robbed at gunpoint by a stranger?"

"No one I know," I said.

Edna brought a finger to her temple, her chin tilted up, as if looking over someone's head. "And that is, most likely, who is responsible for all the destruction."

Manny dropped his gaze to his plate of chicken bones and echoed my words in a hushed voice: "No one I know…"

Antonia reposed in her chair, her lips pressed into a thin line of comprehension.

"I wouldn't be surprised if the principal instigators of the riots, all the riots everywhere, aren't even from the towns they are destroying."

"And their cause célèbre?" Edna prompted her in French.

Antonia responded in English: "I'll bet the store that their real cause is not *célèbre* at all."

"An ulterior motive," I said, and winked at Edna. "It's always hidden or wouldn't be called *ulterior*."

Edna raised her glass of water to me. "Verdad que sí," she said. Yes that's true…

CHAPTER 8

CHARLIE

I like what you've done with the place."

"Organize, organize, organize," Charlie said. "Everything has its face...everything has its place." He followed a worn trail in the carpet towards the kitchen.

"Drink, drink, drink. Something to drink..."

Sounded like an invitation.

"Nothing for me, thanks."

This was my first time inside Charlie's apartment and my impression was similar to the regard with which I held the man—a mixture of sympathy, confusion, and wonder. A sheet hung over the window at the entrance and straddled a humming box air conditioner; sunlight was stifled but the overhead lamp provided decent illumination, its whirling fan circulating relief from a hot June afternoon. I swept my gaze over what I supposed was Charlie's living room. Papers and magazines were piled high on an ample office desk in the far corner, the computer screen surrounded by stacks of books. Books were everywhere, on the dining table leading to the kitchen, on a filing cabinet and makeshift shelves by the desk, standing side by side along the floorboards, and arranged in staggered stalagmites on the carpet. All the books looked to be in good condition, perhaps aged but cared for, and many appeared brand new. A modest flatscreen TV hung on the wall behind the computer screen, as if Charlie worked them in tandem for a double media blast. The rest of the walls were a collage of magazine and newspaper clippings separated by white-boards marked with equations and graphs. A sofa draped in a col-orful Mexican blanket occupied space in the middle of the room and faced the largest whiteboard, about eight-feet tall by twelve wide with a stepping stool at its foot. Small numbers, symbols, letters and signs covered every inch of the whiteboard, in black, red, blue and green, color coding the equation, proof, theory… whatever… I stepped behind the sofa to get an overall impression of it, giving the work the attention of a masterpiece displayed in a museum. I knew how to crunch numbers but could barely recall anything of high school trigonometry. Abstract high math, which I assumed it was, was far beyond my comprehension or desires to comprehend; yet viewing the work in its entirety did provide an odd sense of harmony, a sweeping attraction, like an ocean view from a balcony at sunset.

Charlie shuffled into the room from the kitchen as sailboats and fish appeared within his masterpiece on the wall.

"Ever think of getting a Kindle?" I said. "Might open up some space in here."

Charlie placed a drink resembling iced tea on his desk and opened a drawer.

"Can't locate and keep anything on Kindle. They own it, they can take it away, take it away…"

He pulled a marker from the drawer and rummaged through clutter on his desk.

"You mean they…Kindle owns the books you pay to download?" I knew this to be the case but, as usual, Charlie hadn't been altogether clear on the subject.

He bounced his head and shoulders up and down and approached me, Kindle in hand.

"Yes, yes, yes. And not ideal for research anyway." He extended the Kindle to me, his opaque right eye and lucid amber left averted, drawn to something off his right shoulder. I accepted the Kindle.

"So the books you buy on Kindle really aren't yours, and you want to own them."

"Books belong to everyone," he said, his back to me as he drifted to a whiteboard on the wall opposite his masterpiece. "Everyone, everyone."

"Yes, like music, I suppose they do. Can be shared by everyone at any rate."

I flicked the switch to the Kindle. Nothing. Dead battery.

I muttered, "And Kindle can repo these books whenever they choose," and stepped over to the desk. I placed the dead electronic library upon it and captured a fragrance I'd noticed as a mild scent when entering Charlie's apartment. Reminded me of a camping trip to Big Sur I'd taken years ago, where the redwoods meet the ocean. I located the source, on the floor at the righthand side of the desk. Two tin buckets, each containing their own potpourri—sand and seashells, pinecones and pine needles. I took a deep breath through my nose, my face, like Charlie's, unencumbered by a pandemic mask.

Since the lockdowns and quarantines began, the only home I'd visited was Manny and Antonia's, and I didn't wear a mask there either, generally because we were dining but also due our deepening relationship, the connection and bonds created through shared experiences—dealing with the aftermath of riots during a pandemic. At this juncture we were almost like a family that didn't mask up when isolated in each other's company. And over the past few months I'd discovered a connection with Charlie, not only in conversation on the street but during the rides home I gave him in my car. Like everyone else, Charlie must have worn a mask when buying essentials or his 7-Eleven coffee, but I'd never seen him wearing one. And honestly, I didn't give a damn, not because I thought the threat from COVID was overblown (I did, in many respects) or because I thought myself immune (I didn't but couldn't remember the last time I'd even had the flu and was in a low-risk category as a healthy man well under 60) but because of Charlie himself. Physically, he showed no signs of ill health, yet the principal reason I opted not to wear a mask in Charlie's place was to follow his example as I made a genuine effort to communicate with him. These days were strange beyond belief, from COVID, lockdowns, and riots to my bankruptcy and bogus indictment, and Charlie, it seemed to me, had accurately predicted some of it, perhaps all of it, for all I knew. My bankruptcy wasn't too hard to predict, if you knew the lockdowns were going to last so long. I wished I'd known. If I had I wouldn't have wasted so much time trying to save my business. Yet Charlie knew, had intimated as much to me on the first day of spring when the lock-downs began, and once again a few weeks later. And then there were the riots. Charlie had predicted them as well. He'd told me there was more "hell to raise," that trouble was ahead and down-town would suffer more than businesses in Van Nuys. The man was uncanny, though I had to admit that his predictions hadn't been precise or specific, but maybe that was due to my inability or unwillingness to take him seriously and put forth an effort to really talk to him and understand where he was coming from. I needed all the help I could get, was trapped in a maze of disease, isolation and economic anguish, and if Charlie held any insights or knowledge to help me find my way out of this trap it was time for me to open up and encourage him to share, which, apparent-ly, he'd been trying to do all along.

I scanned a portion of the newspaper and magazine clippings on the wall, stories of gravitational wave detectors, helium com-pounds, the cosmic microwave background, long-distance quan-tum teleportation... But Charlie wasn't all about cosmology and physics. There were also articles on such topics as genetic technol-ogy, artificial intelligence (AI), and Gad Saad's *The Weaponizing of Collective Munchausen*, the latter having to do with a perpetual struggle for the status garnered to those at the top of a victimhood hierarchy. Of particular interest to me were a smattering of pieces on "The Conspiracy of Riots" and COVID as a biological weap-on. As I'd suspected, Charlie did have his conspiracy theories, a state of mind I could relate to given all the dark forces aligned against me and so many others...

I regarded Charlie, his profile partially obscured by his right arm, hand to his graying hairline, fingers twirling his afro at the tip of his forehead, his back curved into that unfailing question mark.

The words "Okay, okay, okay" escaped his lips and he added a couple marks to the whiteboard lefthanded. Then he switched hands, placed the marker in his right and added another few strokes to the top of the board.

"You ambidextrous, Charlie?"

He jerked his head at me and blinked in succession, like he'd forgotten I was there.

"A twang. A bent string. Like a guitar string. That's the secret. And it extends in all directions, in all dimensions, relative to any location and velocity, location and velocity."

I didn't even try to puzzle out his explanation but said, "Fascinating," and joined him at the whiteboard. The numbers and symbols were all in blue, the math incomprehensible to me.

"This a theory or proof?" I asked, and bit my tongue, hesitant to reveal too much ignorance lest Charlie lose interest in enlightening me.

"*Disprove*...falsify, disprove, falsify. If you can't imagine how it might be disproved there is no empirical meaning to clashing branes."

"Clashing...*brains?*"

"Membranes, membranes... Multiverse, yes, multiverse... and primordial black holes."

"Oh, of course. Membranes..."

Charlie refocused his attention on the whiteboard.

"Deductive, predictive, general, causal, meaningful... Meaning, meaning, meaning, empirical, empirical, empirical *meaning...*"

The criteria for a useful scientific theory. I would become familiar with them as I spent time with Charlie, but at the moment they sounded like a disjointed analysis of some sort. Charlie's factions compressed in severe concentration, accentuating the wrinkles etching his forehead and around his eyes, and I shifted my attention to an adjoining whiteboard in grids and sketched with graphs I figured might be easier to comprehend than a conglomerate of numbers and symbols. There were five sets of graphs, the lines color coded, some curved, others jagged, and others straight and angling. The axes were labeled X and Y, but there were no quantities or units of measurement or any clue of referent data. Evidently, Charlie had the quantities, units of measurement, and referent data stored somewhere else, probably in his head, and had developed the graphs as a construct to help him visualize relationships in the data, which was, as I understood, the general purpose of graphs.

"So you think COVID is a biological weapon?" I remarked idly, referring to a clipping I'd seen on his wall.

Charlie's response was lilting and sonorous, like a violin.

"You gather that from those graphs?"

He drew near and examined the work. I had no idea what the graphs represented and remained silent, hoping I'd stumbled onto a truth that might elicit sensible information from Charlie.

Charlie nodded, "Yes, yes, yes. Make the comparisons and the deduction is possible... Compared to what?...compared to what?... Revolutionary France, Russia, China, Ancient Rome, the U.S.A... A country's declining cultural self-worth is directly related to its demise." He pointed his marker at the whiteboard in a sweeping motion. "Clearly, clearly, clearly, China is on the rise, so... And it's modus operandi is in agreement...but..." He twirled his afro between his fingers, lost in thought.

I helped him and myself along: "So China has a higher cultural self-worth. What? Values its heritage? Is more patriotic?'

Charlie cocked his head at me.

"Partly, partly. Values a *heroic* heritage. Heroic, heroic. Without it, there's nothing to defend." He blinked back to the graphs. "Self-loathing is not conducive to survival... But if you know COVID originated in China, then... Originated in...China... And discern China's relative rise from these graphs..." Charlie dipped his chin and shook his head, fingers twirling his afro.

"No, no, no... The key is in the genome.... No natural analogue, no zoonotic origin. Yes...yes...yes... Study the genome, the genome. Genome, genome. That holds the key. The genome."

"I wasn't thinking of the genome. Was simply wondering what you thought."

Charlie lifted his cockeyed gaze to me, a slender, gnarled index finger raised above his head. Charlie was fifteen years my senior, 63, but his hands were older, distinguished by purple blotches and ropy veins.

"It's all a matter of probabilities," he said. "Probabilities. I give it..." His finger drew lines in the air, lines and dots, numbers and calculations. "Odds are...odds are... Eighty-five percent."

"Eighty-five percent of what?"

"An eighty-five-percent probability that COVID is a humanized lab mouse—a lab rat..." Charlie chuckled through his nose. "Or a lab *bat*..." Charlie's chuckles suffused his face, even his beard was smiling.

"Lab rat, lab bat, lab rat, lab bat, lab rat, lab bat..."

He shuffled to his desk, retrieved his iced tea, and took a seat. The drink had a sobering effect, his smiles dissipating within a reverie rich in reflection, his lips fluttering as he twirled his hair between his fingers. He crossed his legs, and I saw he wore no socks to go with his scuffed black Oxfords. Rumpled blue trousers and a multi-hued plaid shirt faded into grayish pink rounded out his attire.

Charlie's opaque right eye seemed to gain color in his sobered state, his reedy voice attaining an acoustic timbre.

"You know," he said, lucid amber eye wandering above my head, "...man's natural governance is authoritarian, even totalitarian. Much like China's fascist-communism..."

I thought he might be referring to the graphs, and as I didn't understand them it was hard to argue the point. Yet I did feel a need to reply somehow, to engage Charlie in the hopes of acquiring useful information I did understand.

"Didn't Jefferson and Madison declare the opposite?" I said, stroking my beard and grasping at straws. "Isn't liberty—"

Charlie cut me off, his acoustic timbre collecting speed: "Locke, Locke, Locke. Yes, yes, yes. But not the natural state, not at all. Not throughout history or today. Hobbes, yes, Hobbes most likely had it right, which makes the U.S. Declaration of Independence and Constitution so remarkable. Yes, remarkable, yes..."

Charlie rocked back and forth in his desk chair, fingers twirling his beard rather than the hair on his head, iced tea clutched in his lap. "It's right there. You saw it. Frankfurt School postmodern deconstruction. Postmodern deconstruction and the beginning of American cultural decay leading to the nation's demise."

He stopped his rocking, and a strange urgency lit his amber eye as it found a spot between mine.

"You saw it. It's right there."

In self-defense I stammered, "Uh…sure…in the graphs. I saw it."

What I really saw was a crazy scientist unable to engage in coherent conversation. Yet I also recognized an opportunity to swerve our dialogue onto a course that might allow me an insight into my future.

"These lockdowns certainly are authoritarian," I said, and had a seat on the arm of the sofa.

Charlie took a sip of tea and waved me off.

"A dry run."

"Dry run?"

"Certainly, certainly, certainly. Now that they know how to do it, there are more to come. Always a national emergency to declare—war, pandemic, global warming… Yes, yes, yes, climate change, man-made global warming—an empirically meaningless emergency; everything proves it!…can't even imagine how it might be falsified… Now they know how to do it, and the people will vote for it. They eventually vote liberty away in favor of Hobbes and Hegel, or Marx disguised as Cleisthenes and Mother Teresa…"

Cleisthenes?

"I see. So these lockdowns—?"

"Into next year. At least the next year. At least next year. But more to come. Certainly more. The unholy alliance the big winners…"

"Unholy alliance?"

"Big business, Big Tech media, China, corporatist oligarchs and political hacks… Political hacks, hacks, hacks…"

Big businesses like Amazon, Apple, Facebook, and Comcast continued to boom through the lockdowns, while small businesses like mine…

I brought a desperate hand to my forehead and ran it through my hair. Charlie was beginning to make sense… Or was his madness contagious?

"The dollar will be worthless…worthless, worthless, worthless, and revived; the economy reconstructed entirely. Entirely, entirely, entirely… Language too. That's always key. Reconstruct language. Control language and you control the future…as well as the past. Obfuscate and obliterate the concept of freedom of speech. New Speak, and destroy the past, all monuments and remnants of a heroic heritage. And destroy dissent as well. Destroy, destroy, destroy…"

"Christ almighty… Destroy… And these BLM-Antifa rioters?"

Charlie released a short burst of laughter, "Ha! Useful idiots."

"Useful to whom?"

"Postmodern deconstruction." Charlie knuckled his eyes, straightened his posture, and rolled his neck, working out kinks. "And China," he added, like an afterthought, "and the statists and oligarchs in their pockets."

Given personal experience, I could think of many derisive ways to describe the activists and rioters, but "useful idiots" had not occurred to me. And I wasn't at all clear on postmodern de-construction. Within the next couple of months my uncle Steven would shed some light on postmodern deconstruction, describ-ing it in part as nihilist, the void filled by a Marxist endgame—tribalism, and "guilty until proven innocent" and "show me the man and I'll find you the crime authoritarian indoctrination." I would finally grasp Uncle Steven's take on the subject, and thus Charlie's, but as things stood right now with Charlie, I had no clue what many of his terms and allusions referred to, yet I brushed off the impasse. The goal was to advance our communication; asking for clear definitions of terms ran the risk of deepening his habit of running off on mystifying tangents. And while I didn't under-stand much of Charlie's jargon, I did see threads with which to weave our discourse and instinctively chose to play a bit of devil's advocate in the hopes of getting him to defend a position rather than babble on about seemingly unrelated topics.

"Don't you think that some of what they say they're protesting has merit? Like racism and pol—"

Charlie burst into shrill giggling, interrupting my advocacy.

"Compared to what? Compared to what, compared to what? Racism in Rwanda, Ghana, Iran?..." His list lengthened with ex-asperated forehead slapping. "Ethiopia, France, China, Russia, Yemen, Saudi Arabia, Italy, Cuba, Brazil, Japan, Mexico, India, Sweden, Canada, Nicaragua, Egypt, Germany, Indonesia, Chad, Angola—"

I snapped my fingers in front of his face a few times.

"Get a grip, Charlie. No need to name all the nations on earth."

Charlie began rocking in his chair again and wrung his hands together as if lathering soap, the veins in his brow beginning to show.

"All are more racist than America," he said. "A million slaves in Africa right now…the Middle East, and far more in China and Asia. Genocidal China. No lives matter. Life is cheap. History has taught us that. Cheap, cheap, cheap…"

No lives matter…

Sounded to me like Charlie giving the back of his hand to BLM. Every now and then I'd heard black spokespeople on TV and radio disparaging BLM as a fraud—hundreds of millions of dollars raised and not a cent given to black scholarships or neighborhoods, and not an office location or company organization chart to be found—but seeing a black man do it for myself was somehow refreshing. That's the way I saw it—Charlie giving the back of his hand to BLM… I repeated the words, "Life is cheap," words I'd heard before which, under these tumultuous COVID circumstances, rang as true as the destruction left behind by rioters and burgeoning COVID deaths in nursing homes due to negligent fucking governance. I regarded Charlie anew, his lopsided gaze unfazed and unfocused on a spot in the ceiling. I shuddered—involuntarily shuddered. His words did ring true, to my state of mind, a state of mind slipping into Charlie's madness.

I can overcome COVID, lockdowns, bankruptcy, and my indictment, and hold onto my sanity. No problem…

Reassuring myself offered little reassurance, but I plowed ahead, eager for some direction.

"So what's next, Charlie? How can I, we prepare for what's coming?"

Charlie placed his tea on the desk, opened his hands and extended them outward with an agile smile.

"Hasten the process, of course."

"Hasten?"

"We're way past the point of no return, so why not? Totalitarian fascist-communism may be a natural state, but liberty…liberty, liberty will, like a geyser, burst forth in revolutionary spirit. Like water seeking its own level, that spirit does once again sink and seek its authoritarian and totalitarian natural state, but it will rise… Rise, rise, rise. The sooner we are re-immersed in inevitable authoritarian and totalitarian rule, the sooner liberty shall reimpose itself."

A bead of sweat trickled down the bridge of my nose. I touched a finger to it and pondered Charlie's soliloquy, baffled at his ability to slip in and out of coherency. Whether or not I agreed with him was immaterial; his capacity to range from nonsense to sense was what struck me, struck me like a slap on the back urging me to action.

"Hasten the process… You expect me to join the rioters?"

"Riot, riot, riot… There is no riot, until you are guilty. Guilty, guilty, guilty…guilty of threatening the city-state powers that be. The *statist* powers that be. Then it will be called an *insurrection*, and the rioters terrorists… Be, be, be… Let the rioters be. Chaos helps hasten the process. See the rioters for yourself. The fascist anti-fascist fascists. Fascist anti-fascist fascists… And if you don't see them, they'll visit you soon enough… Already have…"

I clenched my teeth and released the air from my lungs. Charlie had touched a nerve. I hadn't personally seen the rioters in action but had wallowed within their handiwork. And, evidently, they held a distinct advantage over me: an ability to escape the law and garner admiration from the mainstream media and countless politicians as I staggered and reeled under a piece-of-shit indictment for incitement to riot. What was their secret?

"Been thinking on doing that," I said, "seeing the rioters in action for myself. 'Course it's only a matter of time before their violence, excused and encouraged violence, results in more violence."

"Antipodes will collide... Infiltrate. Double cross. Collide. Infiltrate. Double cross. Collide." Charlie stood abruptly, took a few steps in my direction, pivoted, returned to his desk, and pivoted once again, twirling his hair as he passed me and planted himself before his masterpiece.

"Regardless of biological weaponry, genetic technology, and AI," he said, "future revolutionaries will be quoting Montesquieu, Locke, Madison, and Jefferson, not the utopian claptrap so popular nowadays. Claptrap, claptrap, claptrap...claptrap from activists who claim to fight oppression but have no idea what real oppression looks like."

I stood and took position beside Charlie, staring at the monstrosity of a masterpiece up on the wall.

"Tell me something about your work up there," I said.

CHAPTER 9

JULY

The beaches were open, had been since Memorial Day weekend, except for 4th of July weekend when the governor declared Independence Day, the entire weekend, a time for self-incarceration due to the pandemic. Along with beach closures, firework displays were prohibited. The people, it seemed, could not be trusted to social distance during a time of national celebration. But the governor was late in banning fireworks. The people had stocked up and on the evening of the 4th Los Angeles skies were lit with bombs bursting in air.

A demonstration of patriotism and support of American ideals? A Rebellion against lockdowns? A metaphor for the social-justice upheaval? What was the state of the Union, the Republic? What was the state of the government's case against me for incitement to riot? Would justice really be served by convicting me of this trumped-up charge? Why were blazing, violent riots excused in the name of social justice while the false charges against me stuck like I was presumed guilty rather than innocent?

And if I really was presumed guilty, why hadn't they thrown the book at me an tossed me back in jail already?

Was I guilty? Had I indeed incited a riot? What the hell was a "riot"? Disorder and anarchy? Mayhem and arson? A parade? A ballgame or concert? A church service?

The legal definition of riot was easy to google: *an assemblage of three or more actors in a concerted action made in furtherance of an express common purpose through the use or threat of violence, disorder, or terror to the public resulting in disturbance of the peace.*

I wasn't guilty of any of those things, and had a video to prove it, a video I received from Dan back in June.

I greeted Dan with a "Can't quarantine dolphins" when I found him on the beach in Malibu after he'd finished a surfing session. He and his pals were stoked to see me again. It was our first reunion since our May hijinks, and they welcomed me like I'd just returned from victory at Hawaii's Pipeline Masters Tournament.

"You da Man."

"King Gandolf, lord of surfers' rights."

"Not quite as old as Gandolf," I said, "and certainly not as wise. They're tryin' to rake me for incitement to riot."

Dan banged the heel of his hand off his head a few times, clearing salt water from his brain. "Riot?" he snorted. "Compared to what? Let's haul 'em all down to The Wedge and body whomp 'em if they wanna see a real riot…"

I told my public defender, Mr. Bart, that my surfer buddies would make good witnesses.

He objected: "Those kids in the video you sent me? Good witnesses? Compared to what, dolphins?"

"Dolphins might be better," I conceded. "But they're difficult to corral."

"Try and find someone in the video or who was there that is a little more mature, reliable and believable, Colton," he advised. "And don't discuss your case with anyone."

"How can I find a witness without discussing my case?"

"Use some common sense. Information regarding the charges against you is privileged, and that includes the video… But this case won't be going to trial anyhow."

"I thought I had a right to a speedy trial."

Mr. Bart's nose twitched. He massaged the back of his neck. "Now why would you want to go to trial?"

"Because they have no case. I'm innocent."

"Of incitement to riot…maybe…"

"I'll pay the fine for violating the shelter-in-place order."

Mr. Bart shuffled papers on his desk, his frown penetrating my computer screen. "The state is reviewing further evidence—"

"What? The video? Imaging from my laptop hard drive? Data from my iPhone?"

"Partly."

"Partly? They get something besides what was on my computer and phone when they executed their search warrant?"

"We'll have to discuss this in a week or two, Colton, when I have more discovery, disclosure of evidence."

"I got my computer and phone back a month ago. And they could only search them for evidence pertaining to this case, right?"

"Correct."

"Well, they found nothing, nothing incriminating *outside* this case either. So what about my speedy trial?"

"This is all part of due process, Colton. Just have a little more patience."

I shook my head.

"Due process? Compared to what?"

My marijuana case had dragged on for over a year, but that was a federal felony charge and I faced some serious prison time if my attorney and I hadn't exhausted every avenue of negotiation, including my submission to a polygraph (I passed), before arriving at a plea bargain. In this case I faced a Class 1 misdemeanor state charge that had no merit...or did it?

I needed a second opinion, second *opinions*, and turned to social media. "Is this a riot?" I asked beneath random photos of chanting demonstrators holding up signs protesting the COVID lockdowns. "Or is this a riot?" I asked once more beneath viral photos and videos of angry rampaging mobs engaged in their favorite pastime in Portland and Seattle.

"You're the riot for asking such a stupid question," and, "Are you trying to incite a riot with this post?" were common sentiments. Moral equivalence was also voiced: "Both spread COVID and death and destruction." In several cases, the lockdown protesters were derided as "self-centered racists" and the angry mobs lauded as "working for the common good"—"destruction is construction." This was a contentious point of view and inspired responses like, "Sure, and war is peace," "love is hate," "God is Satan," "red is blue," "black is white," "his is hers," and "boy is girl."

"Boy is in fact girl!" was the irrepressible retort.

After the forfeiture of all my assets and my stint in prison for weed, I not only retained a hatred for The Man and his System but a paranoia that he would come after me again for the slightest real or imagined infraction. I longed to strike back somehow but it had to be done creatively and without exposing myself, so I established my social media accounts and blogs under an alias.

My attractive yet somewhat controversial libertarian and anti-drug-war platform drew thousands of "friends" and followers, a fraction of whom actually knew me and might attend my funeral. The volume of friends and followers I acquired was encouraging for a short time, until I realized that social media is more frequently a battlefield than a platform. If my vision and message were getting through, it was just as often as not to those who would much rather hasten my funeral than attend it. I didn't shy away from social-media confrontations as a result but did regularly find better things to do apart from social media to advance my future or enjoy my free time.

A great portion of my social-media followers and friends were writers and artists, wanna-be writers and artists, intellectuals, and pseudointellectuals who either embraced the differences between a colon and semicolon, a comma and period, a possessive apostrophe and contraction, "there," "their" and "they're," and "he" and "she," or refused to embrace any number of grammatical norms or pronoun identifiers that have developed over centuries and become integral to communication. So it wasn't exactly shocking when comments like "boy is in fact girl" sent my posts into a tailspin. Within the span of an evening my innocent and honest inquiry devolved into a contentious platform for LBGTQ+ activists and those who mocked their claims that males could menstruate, have babies and cervical cancer, while females were indeed in danger of getting prostate infections and could beat men in the Olympic decathlon if not for "sexist social indoctrination."

And my social upbringing and indoctrination prevented me from winning all my Golden Gloves tournaments, Olympic gold, and becoming another Rocky Marciano or Tyson Fury...

Every now and then, I personally entered the fray with sardonic sentiments like that.

Accusations of sexism, homophobia, transphobia, and racism were fired off from social-justice warriors like rounds from machineguns, and I was vilified as a racist toxic male for posting such "divisive and offensive" material.

I couldn't resist firing back:

I am indeed a man, and men are pigs. But that doesn't mean I'm toxic. What have you got against pigs? Are you an anti-pig chauvinist?

The exercise of my speech was violence incarnate, the mere fact that I had used the word "riot" in reference to BLM protests proof that I was a racist bigot. Facebook, Twitter, and Instagram froze my accounts. No explanation was given but the reason was clear: freedom of speech is offensive to woke cancel-culture social-justice warriors and a threat to freedom of speech.

In effect, I'd been canceled.

I was working on a tally of sorts before getting canceled. Felt like sifting through horse manure in search of pyrite—fool's gold. I was impressed with the great number of respondents, not so much with the results. About a third of respondents who referred directly to my posts labeled the lockdown demonstrations "peace-ful protest" and the angry mobs "rioters," a slim majority far from a plurality and not a promising indicator of what my jury pool would look like. Fortunately, it was easy to convince myself that social media did not represent a jury of my peers but a cacophony of riotous blather. After all, if "boy is in fact girl" and men can ovulate and bear children, why not label my imaginary riot mass murder...and looters, arsonists and marauding mobs harmless butterflies?... Better to find other ways to deal with my issues.

COVID, the demonstrations and riots, my bankruptcy and indictment...what the hell was going on? Was anything else hap-pening I should know about? Did I have cancer? A brain tumor? Was my car rigged to explode? Was the tap water toxic? Was bot-tled water toxic? Was a UFO about to rescue me from all the insanity?

More likely I have a brain tumor...

Had the world gone crazy or was I crazy? Both? It was all so perplexing, the puzzle so vexing, I came to the conclusion that a big change in perspective was needed if there was any hope for a favorable resolution. A completely new man would have to come to my aid to make any sense at all of the complexities threatening my life, the lives of millions of others, and return me to prison. So shortly after Independence Day, I shaved. My beard and head. With sheers, not razor blades. I had lots of hair, on my head as well as my face, and made a tremendous mess; but I did feel like a new man afterwards, or a new animal. Like a reptile who had shed his skin I'd been unbound, allowed to grow, although I clear-ly looked younger.

"You look younger," I said to my reflection in the mirror, to see my lips move and reassure myself it was really me. There was an aspect to my features that seemed foreign, out of place. It wasn't the contrast between my newly exposed fair complexion and tan body, or the two white scars in my scalp worming their way through my crewcut. It was something else... My smile. It appeared...toothy. Bright and toothy. An alligator smile.

I snapped my teeth at the mirror. Definitely an alligator, the king of fresh water, which reminded me...

I need to go fly fishing for trout...

The call to fly fish brought me back to reality.

I was the same Colton Candide I'd always been and faced the same vexing puzzle.

"My public defender assures me that I am entitled to due process," I grumbled to Princess one pandemic evening I figured was a Friday, "but has no definitive answer to the state's stalling tactics."

Princess reminded me that I'd prepared myself for the possibility of arrest on that day back in May. She was seated in a corner of the loveseat sofa in my living room where she had a clear view of the TV and was within earshot and my line of vision when I ventured into the kitchen. Her spot on the loveseat wasn't a throne or place of honor but a comfortable pew reserved for a valued guest, a guest who was now my trusted roommate in these maddening times of COVID lockdowns and quarantines and isolation promised to drive me crazy.

Frequent trips to the beach might clear my head, but Princess helped me get my mind right, my thoughts straight. I could share anything at all with her under the strictest confidence, including privileged information related to my indictment, and she'd never tell a soul. And I didn't have to speak out loud to get a response from her, though it often made me feel good to do so. After all, she was the only one at home I could talk to and required less care than a pet, or the goldfish I'd considered investing in. And she was more attractive than a goldfish, or the masked outsiders I encountered when venturing out into the unreal world to shop for essentials, masked outsiders taking on alien aspects, as if none were of the same species as I and were forcing me to wear a mask in public and conform to their alien ways...

I'd brushed Princes' golden-brown fur and secured her bonnet but had not replaced her missing eye and ear...or removed the blood stains. The blood, like her twisted, deformed snout and the scars from her missing eye and ear, was part of her character, proof of her resilience and the wisdom that comes with experience. I'd even stitched her bonnet on at an angle to better expose the inverted crown of blood staining her head...

I sat on the couch adjacent Princess. "Yeah I was prepared to get arrested," I said, "but never thought I'd be charged with a crime that has absolutely no supporting evidence, not even planted evidence, like a weapon or drugs."

Princess had a voice all her own, distinct from my own voice and the thoughts ravaging my brain like a disease. She redressed and pacified those thoughts, allowing me to bring them into focus. At the moment she was silent, but that flying-W smile of hers did shorten into a knowing smirk, nudging me to admit a flaw in my thinking.

"I guess I knew that cops could charge anyone with most anything," I acknowledged. "But the prosecution really has no case against me, certainly not for incitement to riot... Gotta admit I was a smartass to the cops though. It's probably personal for them..."

Princess remained silent, placidly watching and listening to the classic rock video on my TV.

My previous arrest for marijuana had taught me many things, one of which was that DAs are loathe to lose a case, which is one reason there are so many plea bargains. Why was my case dragging on without so much as an offer from the state?

Was I guilty until proven innocent? How about when I got busted for marijuana? A police SWAT team behaved like I was an escaped mass murderer already found guilty of heinous crimes when they arrested me for cultivating an herb. And what about those on that list I'd compiled shortly thereafter, a list of human beings, real people like me actually killed by police in similar raids? Were those victims—men, women, children, black, white, Latino—guilty until proven innocent? And the police themselves, were they entitled to due process? Not according to the mobs bent on anarchy and violence every time there was an officer-involved shooting of a black suspect. The police were always guilty. Why did they bother responding to resident pleas for help in ganglands like Chicago? They could respond with deadly force when attacked by bazookas and the mob would find them guilty and strike back with increased violent destruction, no due process required.

Due process. What a buncha bull. Social-justice warriors mighta been entitled to it but they didn't need it. They were getting away with arson and murder, literally getting away with murder. There was obviously a conspiracy to cancel of the entire concept of due process.

The state's case against me had made me a news junkie, a riot-news junkie, and between TV, the Web, newspapers, and talk radio I could generally find my fix somewhere within a wide spectrum of political perspectives, including the few perspectives that called the riots what they were—*riots*. Businesses, police precincts, and state and federal buildings in New York, Minneapolis, Chicago, Portland, Seattle…they were initial targets of the mobs. Yet no one was exempt from their wrath; innumerable mom-and-pop and minority-held businesses had been ravaged, assaults and shootings becoming commonplace, and mobs were now spreading their upheavals into suburbs. Not surprisingly, the poor suffered the most—more anarchy, more violence and deaths at the hands of BLM-Antifa rioters, and further economic isolation.

"All too often," I said, "those professing to seek justice are themselves guilty of the most vicious, indiscriminate crimes."

Princess nodded and shrugged; perceptibly nodded and shrugged. The effect was not at all disconcerting. Every now and then I reminded myself that Princess was merely a mangled and bloodied stuffed bear, that her voice and movements were tricks of the mind and my mind's eye; but more often than not I allowed myself to be taken in by her. Whether illusions or self-indulgence, my interactions with Princess were therapeutic and helped me maintain a positive attitude, as well as a modicum of gratitude. Overall, my apartment at the far west side of the San Fernando Valley remained a lonely pandemic dungeon without Michelle, yet it was a relatively safe haven, for the time being, and I was grateful for that. I could find the time to read, write, watch TV, play guitar, talk on the phone to Michelle, and work online to earn some money without worrying about an angry mob setting fire to the building. And Princess was always here when I needed to gather my thoughts, vent, or simply enjoy some pleasant company…

As my legal troubles dragged on, Princess became more indispensable the more obsessed I became with my place in this chaotic COVID-infested world. She showed endless patience, was unflappable when familiar disgust and anger roiled within me, and understood my emotions, the roots of my frustrations and how to separate my past troubles and outrage with the law and "system" from the current strange and dangerous days we were all living in.

If not for the wonton, arbitrary destruction of my business, and the damage done to Manny and Antonia's, I would not have been so consumed with the absurd charges against me. I'd simply put up the best defense I could, take my lumps as I had before, and laugh and curse in the face of The Man and his System, even as I faced prison time given my prior conviction. But in light of my bankruptcy, COVID, lockdowns, and the social upheaval, these were exceedingly strange days and I couldn't shake the feeling that some dark forces were aligned against me, people like Manny and Antonia, and millions across the nation.

What to do about it? Well, information is a most valuable commodity, so I resolved to investigate all angles to the real riots in the hopes of discovering my best defense against charges stemming from an imaginary riot. In turn, my information could help Manny and Antonia better protect themselves and their business.

I'd already gathered lots of information from personal experience, the Web, social media, TV network and cable news, talk radio, and Charlie as well, but it was a mishmash of information, everything tangled up in my brain like backlashed fishing line on a reel. I needed to untangle that information and determined to make a list to help me along.

I flipped to a clean page in the yellow legal pad on my coffee table and titled it **RIOTS**, in bold black ink. Then I divided the page into two columns, each with its own subtitle:

Legal | **Illegal**

I reposed on my couch and eyeballed Princess. "Whaddya think?"

"Impressive," she said. "But looks like you may have a long Friday night ahead of you."

"Agreed. This endeavor definitely calls for some fortification."

Jim Morrison was belting out "L.A. womaaan… You're my woman" on the TV as I made my way to the kitchen. I returned with a pint of tequila, two shot glasses, and a beer chaser, extremely pleased with my decisive decision to get down to some serious work.

I poured tequila for us both, winked at Princess and threw back my shot, the elixir instantly warming my diaphragm and firing synapses.

"Reminds me of college," I breathed, and took up my pen. "Fortunately, I have no cocaine. Probably give me a heart attack at my age…"

And after about an hour or so, a half-pint of tequila and laborious scribbling, palpitations did begin to flutter my chest. The song on TV, Billy Joel's *Just the Way You Are*, was not at all one of my favorites, far from it, but nor was it the cause of the numbing *thump thump thump* in my chest. Jacqueline Bisset was the cause of that, and the only reason I didn't change the channel to a different music station.

A brilliant music video producer had converted a sappy, banal love song into an eye-catching stunner by dedicating it to my prepubescent and forever first love: Jacqueline Bisset. Gorgeous still-photos of the English actress and model danced across my TV screen like images of an ethereal goddess transmitted from the heavens. Even my deceased father, stoically framed on the wall above Princess, was drooling over her. The fact that Billy Joel had anything at all to do with this tribute to a true, natural beauty substantially raised my estimation of him and his music, but I barely considered him or the song. Jacqueline held my attention. The lines of her body were finer than those of a classic Ferrari, and her face, that softly sculpted face…sultry, pouty, smiling, luscious, vivacious, mysterious, exotic, enchanting, enticing… The woman had it all, but as the song and slideshow ended, I realized there was something missing. I reached for my laptop beside the legal pad and found the image of Jacqueline I remembered most, the poster my mother wouldn't allow on my bedroom wall till I was sixteen.

A snapshot from the movie *The Deep*. There she was, on a boat, hands lifted to the scuba mask pulled over her head, green eyes cast downward below her long lashes. Her hair was wet, and so was her white V-neck shirt, her raised arms form-fitting the shirt around breasts and nipples that were sure winners in any wet T-shirt contest.

I moaned, "Wow," followed by a drawn-out "oooooooh."

Princess responded with a snarky "Pig. I see you're getting a lot of work done."

I deadpanned Princess and shook my head to clear a vision of her tongue sticking out at me.

Princess was right. I had a job to do. I minimized Jacqueline and began a Web search for several details to add to my lists. Time passed with flourishes of inspiration, pacing gyrations to jazz and rock rhythms, trips to my bookshelves in search of further references, bouts of shadowboxing and bouts of hanging my head in my hands in bemused exasperation over the absurdity of life in the year 2020.

I finally relented and lifted myself from the couch, but paused on my way to bed to retrieve a photograph of Michelle off a shelf below the television. She was knee-deep in ocean water and blooming like a lily in her crimson bathing suit, her native Salvadorian skin darkened to a sugar almond brown, damp raven hair in tassels about her shoulders, her smile and eyes beckoning. I ached for her, suffered and throbbed from my groin to my ears, and released another moan worthy of Jacqueline Bisset. I stared at Princess. Nothing, no reaction.

I repeated myself, a little louder, to garner Princess' attention. "Oooooooooh…"

Princess had polished off her tequila and was dead to the world, as I should be. I might tell her of my wet dreams tomorrow…

CHAPTER 10

SURFING WITH SHARKS

The low and high tides were extreme, low tide opening up lots of space for shore fishing on the narrow beaches north of Zuma and County Line. I was in the water, swimming for long stretches and then floating on my back. The waves were tiny, no wind, the weather clear and hot, the aquamarine water refreshing rather than cold. I could see my feet when standing in six feet of water, along with an occasional fish.

We'd already caught a couple of perch and a corbina and were hoping for bass and mackerel. Charlie was managing the fishing poles, mine planted in the sand, the line as far out as I could cast before jumping into the water.

Charlie was ready to go when I picked him up this morning. I had all the fishing gear, licensing, food and drinks, so he didn't need much more than his clothes, swim trunks, towel, and a hat. And he had everything together, including a few fishing lures.

"Love the beach," Charlie said. "Beach, beach, beach."

Charlie didn't drive but had plenty of time on his hands and often took public transportation to visit beaches from Malibu to Newport, had collected that tin bucket of sand and seashells in his apartment from Huntington Beach—Surf City. Charlie didn't surf either but, aside from the beach, he also enjoyed the woods. That tin bucket potpourri of pinecones and pine needles in his apartment was from Lake Arrowhead, a long day trip from the valley, even by car.

It took us little over an hour to get to this spot from Charlie's place, one of my favorite coves at low tide, just south of Point Mugu, Ventura County.

On our way to the coast, I told Charlie that he'd love the beach we were going to. "It's fairly secluded and there should be lots of fish."

"Mackerel don't like sharks," he said. "But sharks like them, seals too. Seals and tuna… Tuna, tuna…"

"No tuna where we're going, Charlie. And I doubt there'll be sharks. Probably see some dolphins though."

As usual, our conversation wasn't exactly sequential. Yet with patience, I was learning to communicate with Charlie. I knew how to finger snap him out of his occasional fixated ramblings, and otherwise just let him talk and waited for a pause to advance a focal point he might follow for a spell and give us a decent chance at piecing together a coherent conversation. He was an interesting fellow, fascinating in many respects, and I didn't have anyone else to accompany me today. Manny and Antonia were working till their day off tomorrow, Monday, and Princess didn't like the water, her only fault. But Charlie liked the water and, like me, could use some company.

There were advantages to Charlie's method of communication. For one, he didn't ask personal questions. Not that I was unwilling to share with him, but I did have more interest in his background and talents than hashing over any of mine. I held little doubt that Ned, my accountant, had been right about him. Charlie was a tortured genius who'd suffered a tremendous fall from grace, yet he remained extremely high functioning, for a nut case. He was a compelling character who didn't need much impetus to engage me in conversation. You could say he had the gift of gab, albeit at this stage in his life his gab often lacked direction. I had managed to give Charlie enough direction to learn that he didn't generally hear voices, unless he induced and indulged them, and that meds were a "no, no, no...stifle creativity, stifle creativity." I'd also learned that Charlie was an army brat, an only child from Fayetteville, North Carolina, where his father was stationed at Fort Bragg. He'd often gone fishing with his father and had never lost his taste for it. Charlie rarely went fishing anymore but was more than receptive to the idea during my first visit to his apartment.

"I have a fishing pole and tackle," he said, amber eye wide and bright. "They need to be played...played, played, played...

Sounded like he was talking about musical instruments.

Our drive out to the beach was punctuated by comfortable moments of silence while we listened to a variety of music—rock and roll, jazz, classical. Impossible to tell his preference.

"You like this Mozart, Charlie?" or, "How 'bout some Ben Webster?"

"Certainly, certainly, certainly…" was his pat reply, his gaze out the window. I wondered if he was counting telephone poles… or leaves on the trees.

Charlie had the gift of gab, but that didn't mean he constantly blabbered away. Sometimes I found myself initiating conversation, not just to get him to open up but to satisfy my own desires to communicate.

"My father often took me deep sea fishing," I said as we turned off Kanan Road onto PCH. "I used to get seasick sometimes as a young kid. Don't anymore, thanks to those fishing trips, I think…"

Charlie tilted his head at my recollection, fingers twirling his hair, a thin smile creasing his lips.

"Fight, fight, fight a marlin. That will cure seasickness."

"You catch marlin off North Carolina, Charlie? Where? Outer Banks?" Outer Banks was famous for deep sea fishing. I'd always wanted to go there.

"Outer Banks better for tuna. Outer Banks better for tuna… Blue marlin sometimes. Blue, blue, blue…"

I'd caught Pacific marlin, from Cabo to Panama, and sailfish and tuna in the Caribbean, but had never fished the eastern seaboard of the United States. I wanted Charlie to tell me more about it, but imparted another personal detail instead, in the hopes of getting him to reveal something personal about himself.

"Would've liked to return my father's favor," I said, "and take him fishing. But he died when I was twelve. Thirteen, actually. Shortly after my thirteenth birthday."

Charlie's head swiveled around to me, his opaque right eye distracted, lucid amber eye glistened with emotion.

I shrugged, "Car wreck. Dumb luck…"

I was going to elaborate but something painful in Charlie's expression detained me.

"Dumb luck," he echoed, his voice tenuous and fading. "Dumb, dumb, dumb." He let his chin drop to his chest, his lips pressed together and trembling in mournful silence.

I was taken aback, chastened by touching such an affecting nerve in Charlie. Then I recalled something Ned had told me, that Charlie had been driven crazy, in part, by the loss of his wife and child. Had they died in a car accident? I put on some Green Day. Charlie's aspect brightened with the uplifting rhythm and melody, but I couldn't dismiss the interlude and reasoned that we might have something in common, a tragic bond: we'd both lost family in a car accident.

Charles Churchill, PhD. I did a Web search on him later that night. His story, while incomplete on the internet, was amazing. And we did share a tragic bond…

The tide was on the verge of rising too high to fish our cove when Charlie caught something big.

"Keep the tip up, Charlie, and play him. Can you play him?"

The pole was bent at a stiff angle and quivering, indicating he likely had a fish on the line and not a chunk of seaweed. Charlie dipped the tip again and reeled in line.

"If you drop that tip too much you might lose him… Don't reel in too fast. Let the rod and drag do the work…" Whatever Charlie had on the line it was bigger than most fish caught from shore. I extended a hand to the reel to tighten the drag, but Charlie was on top of it and clicked the drag button a few times. He was barefoot in the water, his jeans rolled up at the knees, slender figure all angles as he fought the fish.

"Keep the pressure on him, Charlie."

A broad grimacing smile dominated Charlie's bearded visage, his white bucket hat sloping down over his ears, perspiration staining his T-shirt.

"Having fun, Charlie?"

He glanced at me sideways. "Fun, fun, fun…"

We had a fish story to share on our way downtown late that afternoon.

"At first I thought it might be a halibut you'd dragged off the bottom," I said, "but halibut are more dead weight than fight. You had a bit of a struggle on your hands."

Charlie licked his lips through his grin. "Halibut are good eating. Tasty, tasty, tasty…"

Had we caught a halibut we'd have kept it for a meal. But we threw all our fish back, including Charlie's monster catch.

"Shark can be good eating," Charlie added. "But not easy, not easy to prepare, prepare and cook. Prepare and cook."

"I guess you were prepared, Charlie. You spoke of sharks this morning and, sure enough, you caught one. Over four-foot long."

"Leopard, leopard, leopard. Pretty fish. Pretty fish…"

He looked and sounded like a little boy, despite his beard and graying hair.

"Yes. Leopards are pretty, with their distinctive spots. And we have photos to prove it, not just another story of the big one that got away."

Charlie rummaged through his daypack and fished out his smartphone. We were passing the scene of my "crime," the Malibu Pier coming up on our right. My grip tightened on the steering wheel as a bitter pang of resentment rolled through me.

Charlie said, "No she didn't get away. But she's free now. Free…"

He stared at the photo on his smartphone, his expression fulfilled and at peace. I began to have second thoughts about having Charlie accompany me downtown. He was in a good space right now, had caught a shark. Why go fishing for more? The land sharks I was on the hunt for could ruin his splendid day.

When we turned onto Highway 10 at the Santa Monica Pier, I asked Charlie if I should take him home rather than downtown. "You've had a full day. I can drop you off and head downtown by myself."

"I know my way around. Get around, get around. I get around, 'round, 'round, 'round…"

I overlooked the apparent reference to the Beach Boys hit.

"I know you do, Charlie. But we're liable to encounter some violent action downtown. I have no intention of joining rioters but do need to see them live and in person, and if we get separated, I don't want you to have to take public transport home. We've had fun so far. I'd hate to have it spoiled for you."

Charlie browsed through his smartphone.

"Watch results of deconstruction… Take West 6th Street. West 6th."

Downtown. West 6th was off the 110, but I'd planned on taking the 110 to the 101. I activated my GPS.

Charlie seemed to read my mind: "101 traffic. They marched there today. Best to take West 6th, West 6th. Yes, yes, yes…West 6th…"

According to the GPS on my iPhone, the 101 did look slow, so I got off the 110 at West 6th. I hadn't been downtown in a couple of years; it could be a brutal place to visit. Traffic was a nightmare, less so on a Sunday, a pandemic Sunday, but I did have to keep my wits about me to avoid an accident. And as we made a left onto San Pedro Street, a distinct brutal aspect to downtown blighted the streets like a plague—avenues of poverty-stricken homeless living in tents, cardboard lean-tos, and under canvass tarpaulins, all within view of the financial district's soaring towers, the fading daylight reflected in their glassy exteriors.

Skid Row. Appalling squalor. "Slum," "favela," "ghetto," "shanty town," there were no words to describe it. A crush of bodies, belongings and trash thrown together to form a living organism of filth and penury. Thousands lived here, if you could call it living, some clearly deranged, beyond drugged out, walking spasmodically and talking to themselves, others huddled in groups or sitting off alone abandoned to misery. The majority were men, but women were around, and the destitution was not colorblind; there were more people of color than Caucasian, though all races and genders were well represented and seemed more or less united, for the moment, in their common struggle. I even spotted friendly, animated conversation here and there.

"Make you feel fortunate, Charlie? Makes me feel fortunate… and disgusted."

Charlie had his face pressed against his passenger-seat window, as though searching for someone he knew.

"Fortunate, lucky. Fortunate, lucky."

I chided him: "I don't care what anyone says, Charlie, you're not crazy, certainly not compared to some of these poor souls…"

He sighed and reposed in his seat, fingers twirling his hair.

"Everyone is," he said. "Everyone crazy. Everyone, everyone…"

"Some are probably just way far down on their luck. But it is crazy how these people can endure, even crazier how they are smashed together like this."

The stench of decay and urine penetrated my air conditioned 4Runner, and I mentioned it to Charlie, how the stench and poverty seemed to grow worse down here the more money the government spent trying to resolve the problem.

"No one can waste that much money," I said. "The politicians and bureaucrats must be as corrupt as they are incompetent."

"And crazy. Crazy, crazy, crazy…"

We veered out of Skid Row and headed for Highway 101, where the protestors had marched earlier, looking to catch up to them. General foot traffic increased on Alameda Street, a clutch of police cars and pedestrians gathered four or five blocks ahead, at the Detention Center.

"We better park," I said, recalling images of rioters swarming moving vehicles in Portland and Seattle. I took a right onto a side street and found a spot.

Part of my fishing gear included a waterproof GoPro Action Camera with chest mount. A bodycam that could also be mounted on a boat or moving vehicle. I wore a polo shirt beneath my bodycam and had exchanged my shorts and thongs beach ware for cargo jeans and running shoes. Charlie was similarly attired but wore regular blue jeans and his scuffed Oxfords, without socks. I wasn't looking to immerse myself in violent action but did hope to capture behavior that would clearly distinguish my peaceful protest, my imaginary riot from a real riot.

We approached the Detention Center on foot, and I tugged on Charlie's shirt to prevent him from crossing the street and advancing into the fray. I couldn't be sure that was his intention, but you never knew with Charlie, and I had no desire to have either of us dive headfirst into a conflict with police. It wasn't precisely clear what the commotion entailed, yet an overall view was better captured from across the street anyway. It was nearly dusk, the scene shrouded in shadow. Looked like remnants of the demonstration rather than a full-blown protest. Red anarchist signs—an A surrounded by a circle—were spray painted on the walls of the Detention Center, cops and three squad cars guarding the entrance. There were about a dozen civilians gathered there, a handful of voices raised in petulant profanity. Police took the verbal abuse without reaction. There were seven of them, all in helmets, a few holding shields, none brandishing a weapon or pepper spray. Charlie and I lingered for a moment, just long enough for my bodycam to capture the display. It was theater, a kind of childish exhibition, yet the verbal assaults on police brimmed with more violent overtones than I had been party to in my imaginary riot.

Most pedestrians were moving in one direction, and we followed, paralleled the 101 to North Broadway, and proceeded with a surge in foot traffic towards West 1st Street. The United States Courthouse was on West 1st, a place I was familiar with and had dreamed of annihilating back when The Man busted me for weed. Figures dressed and hooded in black were becoming more prevalent and intermingled with regularly clad folks, many sporting BLM shirts. Twilight was upon us, the streetlamps lit, but the day's heat had not dissipated; there was little reason to wear a thick hoodie, unless, like Antifa anarchists, it was to deepen a disguise and add protection in a brawl. I'd expected to see Antifa. They had left their calling cards at Nuestro American Hardware and were omnipresent at BLM demonstrations in Portland and Seattle. Portland was in the throes of a fifty-day upheaval with no end in sight, while city blocks in Seattle had been invaded and taken over by activists.

Flaming trashcans were scattered about, and shattered windows caught my eye here and there—at the Hall of Records, a café, and gilding parked cars. Furious graffiti depicting dead pigs wearing police caps embellished the street, and red-and-black anarchist-communist stars were painted on walls. The crowd thickened, many of the activists wearing pandemic masks, and a clamor of chants resounded in my ears. Hooded, agile young men pierced me with cruel intelligent eyes as they passed, their eloquent menace lingering, shrouding me in an umbra of doubt and disaffection. I muttered to myself in Spanish, "Where the hell am I?" The foreign language presented a reminder of the humanity I shared with those around me, with those who spoke and acted and looked different from me; ultimately, it provided but a modicum of assurance that I wasn't surrounded by aliens from Planet Zero. I stretched a pandemic mask over my face and extended a packaged one to Charlie, a surge of adrenalin prickling the back of my neck.

Charlie said, "Deconstruction, deconstruction." He accepted the mask but did not put it on.

The main body of demonstrators had to be at the courthouse, around the intersection of Broadway and 1st and a block up the street. Police were at the intersection, about a hundred feet away, involved in a skirmish—stones, cans, bottles, and epithets hurled at them from every direction, accompanied by the chant: "No cops, no walls. No U.S.A. at all!" I raised my iPhone overhead to record an elevated view of the developing chaos. Like at Skid Row, all races and genders were represented, but here white males looked to be in the majority. I stared over my shoulder at Charlie, shuffling behind three young African American women in BLM T-shirts and black pandemic masks. I slowed to let him catch up.

"Recall what the march is for, Charlie?"

"Jacobins devour their own, devour their own. Jacobins devour their own…"

He wore the expression of a man sitting at the station waiting for a train: no expression at all. I didn't know what he was talking about, but that wasn't unusual.

I raised my voice above a sudden din of shouts: "You're marching to see Jacobins?"

One of the women in front of us turned her head to me as she walked, her voice vibrant with youth.

"In support of the Portland protesters," she said, "and to refuse racism."

The young woman beside her chimed in: "Police are killing black men. What do you think we're marching for?"

Both women wore their hair in cornrows, their youthful idealism unmistakable in the passion reflected in their brown eyes.

"How many unarmed black men did police kill last year?"

Like a good attorney, I knew the answer to my question; Charlie had the numbers, lots of numbers of all kinds. But I was not acting in the role of an attorney. I merely wanted a glimpse into where all these activists were coming from, the reasoning behind their motivation. Was it similar to my reasoning behind my imaginary riot? Did these activists have insights that might aid my legal defense against the state?

"Thousands," was the curt reply from the first woman.

"At least fifteen hundred," said her friend.

The three of them joined in outbursts of "Demand a new world today!" as we advanced towards the intersection. I noted that the cops there had dispersed, all of us marching in unison as if to crash and burn a sold-out concert. I also noted that the women were way, way off in their estimates of unarmed black men killed by police last year. The actual number was nine— Charlie's figure supported by my own investigations. This went far beyond faulty reasoning behind motivations, even any faulty reasoning I may have had behind my motivations. I surmised that ulterior motives were at work within BLM leadership, motives reflected in the words "no U.S.A. at all"; yet if most these activists believed like these women, was there much for me to garner here beyond a video to compare to my imaginary riot?

Perhaps there was. And my video did not quite turn out the way I'd imagined.

There was a pause in the chanting, and I took the opportunity to let the women know that I was marching for the Seattle protesters as well as the Portland protesters, just to see if they would confirm the broad reach these activists had. "After all, BLM and Antifa are in Seattle too."

All three of them nodded, raised their fists and shouted, "No justice, no peace!" joining a cacophony of slogans reverberating within the legions. Beyond the hugely flawed genocidal statistics they'd invented or confused with a variable of the number of blacks murdered by other blacks (usually black men), I didn't think much of our exchange. I should have considered the entire picture though, considered the environment, how the young women represented a mindset, and that my comportment might finger me as an outsider.

I glanced at Charlie, just off my right shoulder. He wrinkled his nose, sensing something, his gaze lifted, the crow's feet etching his eyes tightened. He retreated a step, tilted his head to the right, as to beckon me, and then to the rear...and I saw them, several feet to our right. Two men, one wearing a hoodie, both in masks, eyes flickering in my direction and shining with anarchy. Fear flared in my chest, and I flashed on footage I'd seen on the internet of a journalist coldcocked from behind by a violent activist in Portland. I instinctively ducked as a wild roundhouse punch whistled over my head, cleaving air. There were three of them, white thugs, the two I'd seen, bulging hatred in their eyes now, and the brazen coward who'd likely shoot a man in the back under less constraining circumstances. He was stumbling now, off balance from his wild punch. I helped him along with a shove that sent him sprawling to the pavement at the feet of his two comrades, hands outstretched to break his fall. He wore tactical gloves, knuckles hardened with fiberglass.

"Fucking racist fascist spy," the taller comrade growled. A lean growl, like his figure. "We're gonna shove that bodycam up your ass."

Were they armed? Maybe. I had no intention of hanging around to find out. But running free within this swarm of activists was not an immediate option. A bulge-eyed maniac had begun his leap from a martial-arts stance to wheel a Bruce Lee kick at my head.

I was no cage fighter, or street fighter for that matter. I'd had a few good scuffles as a teenager but learned at an early age that I could always avoid a fight...generally avoid a fight. This was a definite exception. Yet I did have some training as a boxer and, as a boxer, was nonplused at how often cage fighters appeared off balance and vulnerable by leaving their feet, a big no-no in boxing. In boxing, you kept your feet; once you raised a foot beyond positioning for stable footwork, you were off balance and open to attack. It was tough enough to keep well balanced with both feet planted, let alone with one or none, yet cage fighters did leave their feet to throw kicks. I had no pretentions of being able to take on a pro cage fighter with my limited ability and experience, but I did have experience, distant experience but experience nonetheless. And my experience and training had taught me that, once you have your man off balance, charge; he's sure to fall under a barrage of punches. So once I saw that bulge-eyed maniac lift a foot off the ground to throw a kick, I charged him.

Retreating would have given him a good chance at landing his kick, but my charge closed the distance and floored him, floored him like a block from a 300-pound offensive tackle; I was about 90-pounds shy of that but my charge had a similar effect, leaving all three of them in a heap, no punches required. My flaming fear had been doused by rivers of adrenalin, adrenalin urging me to press my advantage and tear these assholes apart like a wild animal...or get the hell out of here. Fight or flight. Fight *and* flight. My mind raced and time slowed to a crawl as I shifted my weight from attack mode to escape mode, my senses heightened to a preternatural state. I was feeling no pain, but that condition could change if I became a rabid wolf foaming at the mouth to devour his prey. Rabid wolves get shot. Activists thronged around me and the fallen thugs, their eyes and voices and emotions wild and confused, torn between helping me out against the odds— odds that appeared to be shifting—and seeing to it that I got my ass kicked for being a "fucking racist fascist spy" which, to my racing mind, was analogous to an underground journalist looking to dig up dirt on BLM and Antifa. Dashing to escape through this gathering horde seemed as futile an exercise as sprinting in a jail cell. The three maniacs were collecting themselves for another round. I had to run, wasn't sure I could outrun them or any allies they might have within in the crowd, but I had to bolt, my escape aided by a flurry of cracks detonated in staccato.

Gunfire? Was I the target? Howls and screams swirled in the air, flocks of activists ebbing and flowing and parting, leaving holes for me to dart through like a halfback. If I was the target, I hadn't been hit or seriously wounded. Last time I ran like this was on a sandlot football field twenty-five years ago. Fear consumed me, a result of the flight response and the sound of gunshots. My fear had been doused in the throes of battle but literally lit a torch under my ass now. I didn't run over anyone or get tripped up but did bounce off several heedless shoulders and torsos. The court-house was to my right, beyond a white gaseous cloud rising above the heads of a multitude. I cut left, looking to do some open field running away, away, away from the throngs and maniacs on my heals, a scintilla of acumen needling my brain: the sounds weren't gunfire but flashbang grenades set off by police, accompanied by that cloud of tear gas. 1st Street opened up like a green-ribbon field. People were around but I'd left the vast bulk of demonstra-tors and rioters in my dust. I tore the mask from my face and let it fall to the pavement. The unrestricted air rejuvenated me and I chanced a look behind. If I had pursuers, they appeared to have given up the chase and were enmeshed somewhere within the wash of light and darkness and a mass of unrecognizable human-ity. I slowed my pace to a jog and hopped onto the sidewalk to avoid an oncoming vehicle, Los Angeles Street dead ahead, the quickest route back to my car. I wiped sweat from my face with my shirt collar, the brief respite liberating my thoughts...

Charlie...

I thumbed his contact number while walking, my heart slam-ming against my chest. No answer. I tried again. Someone picked up but didn't say anything.

"Charlie? You there? That you, Charlie? Can you hear me?"

"Yes, yes, yes... You get around as well..."

CHAPTER 11

NED

I ran into the accountant who could have been a doctor in Nuestro American Hardware early one morning shortly after it had reopened in late July. His black pinstriped tie was loosened in deference to this morning's brewing summer heat, his gray gabardine slacks and short-sleeved white dress shirt draped over his pear-shaped figure like linens pressed and creased for a formal toga party.

Ned greeted me with a "Nice haircut. Do it yourself?"

"My teddy bear helped me."

Ned chuckled, "Ho-ha ha," and tugged on the edge of the pandemic mask sliding down his imperial Roman nose. "A trained bear could help you earn some extra money… How'd you know I was here?"

"I didn't. Wasn't looking for you. Our business with my bankruptcy is over."

"You get your federal COVID relief?"

"Yep. I can stay in my apartment for a while."

Ned bounced his beetled eyebrows, his effusive dark eyes amused. "Still teaching English online to Chinese kids—?"

"And preparing them for world conquest."

Ned tapped a finger off his temple with a "Ho-ha ha! Yes indeed."

That bit about preparing Chinese kids for world conquest was Ned's line. He'd chided me with it when I told him how I was making some money. Ned enjoyed having his witty refrains repeated.

Antonia sniggered, "*Ho-ha*. As if China needs Colton's help to conquer the world." She was standing behind the counter opposite Ned, her floral dress, winged eyeliner, and pink pandemic mask in harmony with the rebirth of her hardware store.

Ned brought a hand to his heart in feigned offense. "Just droll hyperbole, *señorita,* which draws truth to your observation. Of course China doesn't need Colton's help to conquer the world, that's what makes it exceedingly appropriate that they pay him for it."

"They pay me a pittance," I said, "and give me COVID, and a brain tumor."

Antonia's eyes grew big as saucers. "COVID?" she said. "When?"

I tilted my head from side to side, as though on a spring.

"Don't you care about my brain tumor?"

Antonia's eyes narrowed into a gaze of calculated appraisal. "Clown," she said, and turned her attention to Ned, her voice and eyes a duet of embracing charm. "Here to make a purchase, señor? You're our first customer today."

Ned ran a pensive hand over his balding pate, dropped it to the meerschaum pipe in his breast pocket, and pointed the stem of the pipe at me. "Might be you're suffering from RF enigma syndrome," he advanced in all seriousness.

"RF—?"

"Radiofrequency... Been feeling alienated and confused, as if trapped in a riddle within a puzzle?"

"More like a puzzle wrapped in a riddle."

"That's it. Ho-ha ha!...that's it..." Ned shifted his beetled brows back to Antonia. "I shoulda been a doctor, but I'll have to be a plumber this evening. My garage suffered a minor flood this morning. I'll need some PVC pipe, couplings..."

His list of items to purchase trailed off as Antonia guided him to the far end of the store. I'd come to check out the store and was impressed. The place was immaculate, with sparkling new inventory and a lemon disinfectant scent in the air. A complete turnaround from the disaster that had struck at the hands of the mob. A pang of jealousy prodded my chest. Fisherman's Shore Bait and Tackle was in immaculate condition as well before I was forced to close shop. I remembered the spiders and drifted further into the store, eyes focused on the ceiling. The plaster had been refinished. No sign of spiders or the hole they'd dropped from to ambush me. I swung around at a commotion at the entrance. Manny, accompanied by three young men in boots and construction garb. I recognized two of them as Manny's primos—cousins. Litteral cousins. Manny had plenty of amigos who were also "primos." Manny gave me a fist bump and they passed in a beeline towards the rear of the store and the storage garage.

"The place looks splendid, absolutely splendid."

Ned. He placed a basket of pluming knickknacks on the counter while Antonia made her way to the cash register.

"Just like new," I said.

Ned pulled his wallet from his back pocket. "Yes it does look brand new. Impressive, very impressive. As good if not better than any of the rebuilding I saw after the riots of '92."

I arched my eyebrows and blinked at Antonia. She offered me a knowing nod from behind the cash register.

"That what they called them back in the day, Ned?" she said. "*Riots?*"

"A rose by any other name would smell as sweet, señorita. And a riot by any other name still stinks of violence and anarchy." Ned placed a credit card on the counter, his pear-shaped figure swaying to an interior rhythm. "Of course, unlike *rose, riot* is a legal term." He winked at me.

As Ned helped me through bankruptcy, I'd shared a few of my imaginary-riot details. "*Riot* is a legal term," he pointed out during our last Zoom meeting. "I doubt the modifier *imaginary* will win you points with the judge, though, ho-ha ha...I have to admit it gives me a chuckle." Ned lit his pipe.

"*Riot* is not just a legal term," I told him, "but a descriptive noun, like its Spanish translation—motín. But, lord almighty, I saw a so-called social-justice leader on TV justifying looting and arson as *reparations*, and two politicians urging the mobs to be more confrontational, the word *riot* never mentioned, like there's a goddamn conspiracy going on between rioters, the media, and politicians... Is it necessary to have a massacre before a riot can be declared? And how would that work to my defense?"

I screwed up my face for my laptop camera and added a pleading whine to my voice: "I can't be guilty of incitement to riot, Your Honor. After all, there was no massacre or intent to massacre…"

Ned pointed the stem of his pipe at me.

"He'd throw the book at you, not only for incitement to riot but for sheer, unadulterated idiocy."

Antonia ran Ned's credit card. I said, "The riot I'm accused of inciting smelled much more like a rose than violence and anarchy."

Ned swayed to his rhythm and signed for his hardware.

"Maybe so. But best you don't have to prove that in a court of law."

My brow stiffened into a hard, uncertain line.

"The burden of proof lies with the prosecution."

Ned retrieved his bag of hardware off the counter.

"Ho-ha ha. That's what they say…"

Ned gave Antonia a short bow. "Gracias, bella," he said, and offered me some advice as he left:

"Might want to check with Charlie about your RF enigma syndrome, before it becomes chronic…"

"Already is chronic," I said to his back out the door, and shook my head at Antonia. "He's a bigger clown than I am."

"Quite the character, but a good accountant."

"He was a great help with my bankruptcy, saved me money. Not such a great help with my imaginary-riot case though."

"Well, he's not an attorney."

I rolled my eyes at her. "But he—"

Antonia finished my thought, "Could have been."

Antonia's phone pinged. She retrieved it from under the cash register, her eyes amused as she answered the text. "Imaginary riot," she said, and looked up at me. "Sounds delusional."

"Maybe I am. But the so-called *peaceful* BLM protest I recorded last Sunday was far more violent than mine in Malibu."

"Where?"

"The downtown courthouse. Nothing sensational. Smashed windows, melees, general vandalism, all to show support for the Portland activists."

Antonia hummed, "Hummm. Maybe I saw something about it on the news or social media… Or that might have been one in Huntington Beach. Didn't see reports of violence."

"The media can be very selective."

"Any arrests where you were?"

"I looked it up Monday. There were several, but they made bail right away. Some sort of political national bail fund project for rioters. Doesn't apply to imaginary rioters. I spent four days in jail back in May."

Antonia shot me a quizzical look. "Why'd you expose yourself to that crap downtown?"

"I'm conducting my own investigations, to aid in my defense. By chronicling real riots I should be able to draw clear distinctions between those and my peaceful protest."

"I see. Swimming with sharks. Careful you don't get bit…"

CHAPTER 12

AUGUST

Searches for RF enigma syndrome turn up an acronym: ENIGMA. Something to do with neural genetics and meta-analysis—studies of brain health. No mention of a radiofrequency syndrome."

Princess released an attentive grunt from her spot on the loveseat sofa.

"And you tried searching just radiofrequency syndrome?"

"Radiofrequencies are used to treat pain. Nothing on radiofrequency syndromes."

"You can't always trust the internet," Princess stated flatly. "And something's clearly going on that isn't right...even when you return from the beach you've been moody lately."

I slouched and paused my pacing.

"Isolated...alienated... Everyone at the supermarket looks like they're from outer space. I've seen aliens in space suits, or maybe hazmat suits, and yesterday two female-voiced aliens in white Star Wars face shields warned me to step back from them or I'd be vaporized by a Death Star superlaser."

Princess scowled at me.

"Surely you exaggerate."

"Yeah, well... They probably meant ion blaster. It's portable. Death Star superlasers can destroy an entire planet. Aliens wouldn't destroy the planet they inhabit, would they?"

"They might. But not just to vaporize you."

I stroked my thickening beard.

"I'm more likely to get vaporized by an ion blaster, or maybe a Star Trek phaser."

"Or maybe you think too much of yourself. You're probably not worth the trouble to vaporize."

"Oh yeah?" I pointed an accusatory finger at Princess. "You try stepping too close to an alien, or the alien security guards at a bank. See how quickly they vaporize you."

Princess shifted in her loveseat.

"I'd like to give it a try but I never get out. Try taking me out sometime. We never go anywhere together."

"You don't like the beach."

Princess huffed.

"I don't like the water and all that sand. But that doesn't mean you can't take me somewhere. Could help us both."

So we went for a drive that morning, before the afternoon August heat dropped its anvil upon the valley. I had the windows down and sunroof open, Princess in the passenger seat. Reseda Park was nice. Princess didn't like the water but appreciated the pond and ducks. I walked with her on my back, in my backpack, her head above the rim. The tennis courts, basketball courts, and ball fields were empty, ball games still prohibited during the pandemic. Bipeds were around, strolling here and there, some in couples, most keeping their distance, avoiding one another.

"I could use some coffee," I said.

"Starbucks?"

"Too bitter. Let's head to Charlie's 7-Eleven. Might find him there. We can ask him about RF enigma syndrome."

"Enigma, enigma, enigma." Charlie twirled his hair. "Lots of concurrent symptoms in an enigma. Yes, yes, yes…could be a syndrome…"

He dropped his hand to his heavy lower lip and stared down at Princess, seated between us at the bus stop adjacent the 7-Eleven. Charlie wasn't waiting for the bus when we found him, just resting and thinking.

"Are you the one suffering from enigma syndrome, Princess?" he asked.

"*RF* enigma syndrome," I clarified. "Radiofrequency enigma syndrome. And Ned said I might be suffering from it."

"Oooh…Ned." Charlie rocked back and forth, his askew gaze lifted to the piercing blue sky. "Ned, Ned, Ned. Radiofrequency, radiofrequency, radiofrequency. Ned, Ned, Ned. Radiofrequency, radiofrequency, radiofrequency. Radiofrequency, radiofrequency, radiofrequency. Radiofrequency, radiofrequency—"

I snapped my fingers by Charlie's ear a few times. He stiffened and wrung his hands together in that lathering motion of his, his eyes narrow slits.

"Havana. That's the answer. Havana, Havana, Havana."

"Havana? Cuba?"

"I prefer Roatán, Honduras. Let's go. Beautiful beaches and snorkeling. Beautiful, beautiful, beautiful."

"You said something about Havana."

He brought a hand to his forehead.

"Oh yes. Yes, yes, yes. Havana. Havana Syndrome. Pulsed microwave energy. Pulsed radiofrequency energy. Weaponized RF energy. Dozens of US diplomats and government workers afflicted in Cuba…Asia and Russia too. Russia denies any involvement. Cuba denies any involvement. China denies any involvement. China, China, China… American corporate oligarchs support China's claims. *Every* China claim. Shocking, shocking, shocking… But they do profit…"

I massaged my temples to a sudden pain behind my eyes.

"So you're saying that RF enigma syndrome could be related to this Havana syndrome? What're the symptoms?"

"Psychogenic illness."

"Psychogenic?"

Charlie fixed me with a bright ironical stare, chin dipped, eyebrows arched, his afflicted right eye closed.

"Shell shock."

Sounded about right.

"Where can I get it? My phone? Computer? A pulse directed at me from space or through the air?"

"And China, Russia too. Not to mention the US government."

"Aliens?"

Charlie rocked back and forth, nodding in cadence, lips pursed, hands on his knees.

"Possible," he said. "Anything is indeed possible. Possible, possible, possible."

Anything was indeed possible. But probable? Believable? The possible, probable, believable and unbelievable were all becoming indistinguishable within my brain. Yet one thing was clear: everyone was out to kill me...or torture me. Torture me and kill me. Well...maybe not everyone. Manny, Antonia, and Edna weren't out to kill me. Princess wasn't out to kill me. Michelle wasn't out to kill me. And Charlie, I was convinced, couldn't kill anyone. So who was left? Everyone...

"Everyone's out to kill me," I told Michelle on FaceTime.

"Everyone?"

"Sure seems that way."

"You talking about COVID?"

"Maybe. Not particularly."

"COVID affects us all, Colton, not just you."

"What difference does that make?"

Michelle was skeptical about RF enigma syndrome, said that my feelings of isolation, confusion, persecution and alienation were most likely due to my economic troubles, my bogus indictment, the lockdowns, and, well...isolation.

Within a couple weeks, after I'd recorded another riotous L.A. melee, Dr. Bolton had a different take on RF enigma syndrome.

Dr. Bolton dressed as though ready to hit the links. She liked polyester but lacked a golfer's tan, her complexion soft and pasty, reddish hair done in a pageboy. Dr. Bolton's hands looked to be carved from soap—slender and white with agile fingers that multitasked between the files on her desk and on her computer screen—and she had a placid sanctimonious smile I couldn't see behind her pandemic mask but matched her nasal voice and the air of superiority expressed in her gray eyes. I was a COVID hardship case with few resources, so her counsel didn't cost me personally; and while state-appointed her supposed function was to aid my defense against the state, at the request of my state-appointed public defender, as she analyzed my mental condition. We always met in her office, she at her desk behind pandemic plexiglass while I remained seated eight feet away, practicing social distancing.

"This syndrome you describe," she said evenly. "Looks to me like it's an excuse for you act out rather than a medical condition."

"Act out how?"

"By recording those demonstrations and risking confrontation."

"I did that to aid in my own defense against charges of incitement to riot."

"So you say. But there are lots of sources for similar videos that you can draw from rather than making your own. Why the obsession…the compulsion?"

I rocked back and forth in my seat, consumed by yet another danger that had descended upon me like a bird of prey. There were lockdowns, riots, an indictment, aliens, a brain tumor, RF enigma syndrome, and now this, OCD—obsessive-compulsive disorder. COVID was on the list as well, but I'd come to view it as one of many Chinese-inspired tools of oppression rather than a distinct danger or disease designed to torture and kill me, though it certainly retained all the characteristics of a distinct danger or disease designed to torture and kill me.

I muttered, "Maybe a symptom of RF enigma syndrome."

Dr. Bolton said, "Pardon me?"

I stopped rocking in my seat and sat up straight, as if startled awake from a lucid dream.

"OCD. Could be another symptom of RF enigma syndrome."

"I never said you had OCD, Colton."

"Looks like I might have it," I retorted boastfully, inspired by my insight.

The good doctor released a heavy sigh.

"Let's stay focused here, Colton. Please. I'm more concerned about why you feel compelled to act out, why you are drawn to those demonstrations and the people you record when you know it can invite conflict with others."

I looked at her askew, uninspired by her misplaced concern.

"Those people I record don't need an invitation to conflict with others."

"But why expose yourself—?"

"Expose myself? I've been exposed and targeted anyway. After all, I am under indictment. And I'm not drawn to the people I've recorded in those demonstrations any more than I'm drawn to the people I see generally when I'm in public. Unless I already know a person I might be with or talking to, I can't relate to anyone and feel alienated and trapped just about every-where I am. Don't see how a need to act out would be a reason for me to do or not do or record or not record anything. If I am drawn to record certain events it's to aid in my own defense, not to *act out*."

Dr. Bolton gave me a minute nod and made a note in my file on her desk.

"Ingenious. Is filming or recording public activities a hobby of yours? Does it help you escape from…how do you call it…?" She flipped through my file.

I saved her the trouble: "The puzzle wrapped in a riddle—life in the year 2020. But I can't look to escape. There is no escape."

"So you are indeed trapped…"

"Mostly, except when I escape to the ocean."

"Ahhh. So there is an escape." She raised an index finger for emphasis.

"I suppose so, for short periods."

Dr. Bolton made another note on a sheet of paper in my file, and reposed in her chair, fingers tented at her nose.

"That's an important realization, Colton."

"What?"

"How you have now admitted you do have an escape from your turmoil."

"Admitted?" I puffed my cheeks, stretching my pandemic mask. "I may have contradicted myself but I'm not sure what I admitted."

"If there is escape that means—"

"It's not uncommon for me to contradict myself," I interjected. "Opposing ideas can often reveal a truth, though nowadays everyone is offended by an opposing idea…"

Dr. Bolton cocked her head at me, eyes studious, as though examining a rare reptile. The expression mirrored in her eyes reminded me of the look a prison counselor had given me when I responded to his claim that weed is a gateway drug, that "all drug addicts start with marijuana."

"Actually," I told him, "they all start with milk."

Dr. Bolton said, "So opposing ideas reveal a truth. And what is that truth, Colton?"

I slouched in my chair, elbows on knees, fist curled under my chin—The Thinker.

"I'm not sure. That I contradict myself?"

"The truth," Dr. Bolton resumed, "is that you feel trapped without escape, yet you find you can escape. Now we just have to determine what those binds are that have you feeling trapped."

"Lockdowns, bankruptcy, RF enigma syndrome… I'm sure I can name others."

Dr. Bolton leaned forward, hands folded on her desk, and appraised me with a look of targeted concentration, one eye closed, as if staring down the scope of her rifle.

"The ties that bind you run deeper than that, Colton."

I cleared my throat and shrugged agreeably.

"I'm sure they do, Doctor. We have a lot of digging to do to get to the bottom of Colton Candide…"

I'd known that for quite a while. There was a lot of digging to do period if I were to get to the bottom of or make any sense at all out of most anything going on since the COVID pandemic broke out here in the States and California. An underlying concern was to mount a convincing defense against the state as they tried to railroad me for incitement to riot, an unbelievable charge totally believable, under the circumstances. And my primary method for gathering evidence in my defense was to record mob behavior during social-justice demonstrations here in Los Angeles, for comparison against the exemplar peaceful protest I'd inspired in Malibu. But that didn't go deep enough. If I really wanted to swim and surf with the sharks, Portland, Oregon, was the place to go.

I wanted to go to Portland but decided it was best not to violate the travel restrictions imposed upon me with my indictment. So I opted for the next best thing: a phone interview with my cousin in Portland. Steven was from my father's side of the family, a former prosecutor turned high-priced corporate negotiator. Twelve years my senior, Steven was looking forward to retirement and, given our age difference, in my youth I'd typically referred to him as Uncle Steven rather than Cousin. Something of a crazy uncle. My most vivid memories of him were back in his college days here in Los Angeles. With a wink and a nod he'd blithely confirm family rumors about wild rugby parties at his frat house, and his girlfriends sparked my nascent puberty with their glistening shanks, punk hairdos and makeup. Steven was a trickster—could still fool me with sleight-of-hand magic—and a fast, calculated talker, yet a good listener, always quick with an addendum, anecdote, or retort. A conversationalist. And his admonitions at the ice cream parlors tickled me: "Don't tell your mom I brought you here."

Mom died of cancer a few years ago. When I was a kid, she was not a big fan of allowing me to eat sweets at all hours of the day. The death of my father in a car accident left her alone to raise me and my older sister, Candice. Candice lived in New York and had helped paint the streets in BLM slogans. The one phone conversation I'd had with Candice this summer ended in a tiff when I told her that I made a habit of removing BLM graffiti.

Back in the day, Uncle Steven would visit a couple times a month, on a drive with one of his girlfriends, or to play football with me and my friends, and to spar with me in preparation for one of my upcoming matches. I hadn't spoken to him much since Mom's funeral but had often called him during my marijuana legal troubles. This time around, my legal problem did not seem such a big deal at first, nothing to bother Steven about. But the case was dragging on, so why not call him and ask for some legal advice as a segue into gleaning information about the Portland riots?

It was a Wednesday evening, and Steven sounded upbeat. "Voluntary early retirement," he said. "Always something to look forward to."

Steven and his wife were sitting on a plot of land they bought in Maui, in preparation for the leisure times ahead. I told him about my arrest in May and the imaginary riot. He chuckled and repeated the term, "Imaginary riot." I went over several details—the trumped-up charges against me, the *real* riots in L.A. and the vandalism and destruction at Nuestro American Hardware and my shop, the lockdowns and my bankruptcy—and Steven assured me that the charges would probably be reduced if not dropped altogether, if my public defender was "worth a damn."

"I'll tell ya, Kid" he added briskly (he'd called me "Kid" since my childhood days), "ain't nothin' imaginary about the riots here in Portland."

"Riots or upheaval?" I asked, without effort at masking my interest. "And who's behind them?"

"Behind them? You kiddin' me? This is the birthplace of Antifa—the anti-fascist fascists. Been doin' this kinda crap for years. Put those anarchists together with BLM and a gutless mayor, and we got an interminable insurrection downtown. Most of the media and politicians gloss over it with their propaganda but it's a war zone, replete with armed belligerents, firebombs, and Antifa women disguised as *moms*—a wall of moms to be used as human shields. I haven't been downtown in weeks and weeks. Been avoiding it, like most all who can."

"What about other elements—?"

He cut me off, like he'd heard my question before: "Shiiit, Kid. Once trouble starts there're always shitheads looking to take advantage. But it sure as hell isn't skinheads, the KKK, or Proud Boys burning down buildings and looting businesses, I'll tell ya that. And it wasn't the Proud Boys who tried to burn those people alive in the police precinct. That's Antifa, their calling card. The Proud Boys may add to tensions with a counter-protest—an anti-Antifa demonstration—but anyone who thinks they're the ones actually destroying downtown has their head up their ass."

"Sure are a lotta people with their heads up their asses nowadays."

"They've grown in numbers, but many have been around for decades."

"Not the ones I've tangled with. Young fucking punks."

Uncle Steven's pause bristled with apprehension at my bitter tone. "Tangled with?"

I shared my personal encounter with BLM-Antifa thugs in downtown L.A., how I was labeled a "racist fascist spy," and my motives for recording "the *real* destroyers and rioters," a note of pride entering my voice as I described my ability to emerge unscathed.

"You sure about that?"

"Not a bruise or scratch," I said. "Left those thugs in a heap, and my legs moved faster than when I was chased by a swarm of bees as a teenager."

"Impressive, for an old man."

"You should know."

Uncle Steven grunted, "Unh-huh… You know, it wasn't all that long ago when you would have liked to destroy that federal courthouse."

"I thought about that at the time."

"What's changed?"

I reminded Uncle Steven that my hatred for "the system" had abated not long after my release from prison, when I came to the conclusion that America offered many roads to success, as long as I didn't allow myself to be blinded by hatred.

"And I did open my own business."

"Good job. But then you were screwed by the lockdowns."

"Yep. And the lockdowns are so indiscriminate, so unjust."

Steven chuckled.

"So you justify yourself and your actions with a concept of justice. You're starting to sound like BLM and Antifa."

"I may sound vaguely like them, but there's no comparison."

Steven baited me: "A man of contradictions."

I didn't rise to it.

"So was Jefferson. And I don't label everyone I disagree with a racist fascist, and my contradictions don't lead me to riot, despite what the state alleges."

"Where do they lead you?"

"James Madison," I replied without missing a beat. "I appreciate where my concept of justice comes from—western culture and American heritage. Shoulda seen me utilize the Bill of Rights against those cops that arrested me during my imaginary riot."

Steven snorted insipidly. "I'm sure you were brilliant."

"The strategy seemed preferable to creating a war zone."

"You don't have the funding to create a war zone. But you might become a casualty of your own firebombing."

I raised my voice an octave, "Who am I firebombing?"

"Relax, Kid. It's an implied metaphor. I'm not accusing you of anything." Steven's tone acquired that of an attorney reviewing the facts of the case with his client. "You're in a jam and trying to come to grips with what's happening with the riots and all. Okay. I'll enlighten you some so you don't feel the need to fly around looking for trouble like some kinda war correspondent. These movements—BLM, Antifa—have been brewing for a long, long time, back to before Martin Luther King Jr. threw a wrench into the violent tactics of the Black Panthers, Weather Underground, and Black Liberation Army…and Marcuse. This is their opportunity for a comeback, a comeback long in the making."

"Okay. I see that. I never did believe they were spontaneous uprisings. My imaginary riot…now *that* was *spontaneous*."

Uncle Steven quickened his pace to make a point. A technique of his I'd grown accustomed to over the years.

"I first experienced their kinda bull rhetoric back in college. Postmodern deconstruction crap, nihilism that spawned identity politics, intersectionality, the *woke cancel culture*—"

I muttered, "Postmodern deconstruction," recalling Charlie.

Uncle Steven hesitated, to let his tongue catch up with his brain, and spelled out postmodern deconstruction: "PMD my buddies and I in prelaw used to call it. Parasitic Mental Disorder—the denial of any kind of objective truth."

"Doesn't sound compatible with the study of law."

"Not Madisonian law, but it does compel laws to be implemented. If human beings were angels there'd be no need for any laws or government, to paraphrase Madison. But humans are far from angels."

"You're tellin' me."

"PMD demands that all constructs of law and justice, particularly western constructs of law and justice, be viewed as baseless and only benefiting those in power, as if the framers of the U.S. Constitution were morons and hadn't developed a separation of powers and mechanisms to *form a more perfect union*. Never has been perfect...what is?"

Steven didn't wait for an answer.

"America's academic elite think they know perfection, but first they must deconstruct and destroy our concepts and constructs of law and justice and remake or erase our entire history with PMD. The void created is then filled by another western construct—Marxism, Frankfurt School Marxism which, conveniently enough, demands that the past be annulled so history may start anew. In America, the Marxist endgame is executed via the conscious shift from class struggle to identity-politics racial warfare—intersectionality—tribalism that pits citizens against one another, erodes the unifying notion of American citizenship and serves as a means to politicize everything, from Comparative

Literature and engineering to the color of your skin and the style of your clothes and hair. It's show me the man and I'll find you the crime authoritarian indoctrination, and all of America, particularly white America and western culture, is guilty until proven innocent, never can be proven innocent. Fealty to the collective—the State—is paramount, the concept of *individual rights* as posited in the Constitution obliterated and trashed as a white-western capitalist invention, and feelings rather than facts adjudicate disputes. Didn't believe it would catch on so much back when I was in college. Maybe my wits were addled by the beer and 80s cocaine, but I just thought postmodern deconstruction and identity politics were stupid fads that would burn themselves out. I've known I was wrong about that for years now. Amazing. The Marxist power play is relentless, its utopia only perfect for elites in the politburo. How the philosophy can continue to gain followers after Mao, Stalin, Pol Pot and the rest slaughtered well over a hundred million last century is baffling…"

He paused, and so did I, trying to internalize what Uncle Steven was saying. Did he speak the truth or have an axe to grind? Both? I'd find out soon enough that he did have an axe to grind, was dealing with the consequences of PMD and intersectionality in his work, a principal reason he'd retire early. Nonetheless, in many respects his monologue accurately described some of what I had encountered in college years ago. But Steven was difficult to follow when he got on a roll and my immediate response was, "Not sure I under—"

"It's the *New World Order*, Kid. Here in the U.S.A. and in general the movements are Jacobin in nature, Maoist at heart.

Read up on the French and Russian revolutions, and Mao's cultural revolution…"

Uncle Steven's clipped tone indicated it was time to disconnect. "I'll do that," I said with forced enthusiasm, torn between the respect I had for Steven and what sounded like an incomprehensible equation he'd given me to solve and live up to his expectations.

Steven sensed my uncertainty and offered to solve for a variable or two.

"I'll email you a few references and notes on the subject," he said, his pace relenting. "And…uh… How long has it been since your arrest for incitement to riot?"

"Almost three months now."

Silence, accompanied by a bit of cell-phone static. "And no offer by the state yet?"

"Nope."

"Been a couple of continuances."

"Yep."

More silence.

"Have you submitted to a mental evaluation of some sort, like with your marijuana case?"

"That was more of a one-time thing. They've got me visiting some kinda shrink semi-regularly now. Seen her a couple times."

"What's her certification?"

"Certification? You mean PhD or something?"

"That and maybe a specialty or another degree. Should be letters on her card accompanying MA or PhD."

"I think I have her card right here, with my intake forms." I rifled through papers on the kitchen table…and read Dr. Bolton's name and the letters following it out loud.

Steven grumbled, "IME."

"Mean something to you?"

"I'm afraid it might… Say, uh…Colt… I gotta run, but I'm stopping over in L.A. for a night or two on my way to Miami next month. Keep me posted and maybe we can meet up."

"Sure thing. Thanks Steven."

"Anytime."

CHAPTER 13

FALSE INFORMATION

I texted Michelle a photo of my "new girlfriend"—Princess clutching a glass of wine between her legs.

Michelle texted back:

Looks like you're getting desperate.

Indeed.

"I'm desperate," I confided to Princess on a hot and smokey August afternoon. The sky outside drooped gray from wildfires fifty miles south of here, in the San Gabriel Valley, the miasma infiltrating my pandemic dungeon.

Princess responded with a coquettish giggle.

"At least you have me."

Princess and my air conditioner. Both provided respite, but the beach was better, and so was Michelle. Yet the tone of my international exchanges with Michelle had shifted since June. A typical June conversation between us went something like this:

Me: Will you marry me, Sugar Plum?

Michelle: Always and forever, Honey Bunny…

We'd add dirty talk now and again to enhance the torture of separation, and dream of escape together. But how, and escape to where? There wasn't a corner of the globe uninfected by the COVID Chinese virus, and the Salvadorian government, U.S. government, U.K. government, French government, Canadian government, Ecuadorian government, Australian government… every government was full of false promises when it came to easing international pandemic travel restrictions.

By August, my communications with Michelle were becoming dispirited, even fatalistic at times:

Michelle: COVID has a 99% survival rate, and many who get it show few if any symptoms.

Me: It's not precisely designed to kill but to sew fear and demand compliance to government mandates.

Michelle: Designed? I've heard it might have escaped a lab but supposedly that's a fringe conspiracy theory.

Me: If you believe China, their propaganda and American Big Tech media and political hacks.

Michelle: Isn't COVID more likely an accident of nature?

Me: Sure is a convenient accident. Best excuse ever invented to implement authoritarian and totalitarian rule. For activists and power-hungry government statists looking to dominate our lives, COVID is the best thing to ever happen.

Michelle was unconvinced but admitted there might be some truth to my caustic reasoning. Salvadorian bureaucrats and their henchmen seemed to take a "sick pleasure" in closing down restaurants and small businesses and tossing those in violation of COVID quarantine mandates into containment centers. And when Michelle's elderly aunt came down with a debilitating case of COVID the first week of August (she was getting better), government authorities reacted "like they relished the opportunity" to intensify quarantine restrictions on all who had come into contact with her, including, naturally, Michelle and most the rest of her family, though Michelle and those she was holed up with— her parents and sister—tested negative for the virus.

When I informed Antonia of Michelle's latest COVID predicament she said, "Then it's up to you, *pinche cabrón*. Find a way to her. Love will find a way, if you put your heart and soul into it…"

Antonia had a singular talent for inspiring and deflating me all at once.

I always dreamed of escape to El Salvador and stealing Michelle away with me. At the beach I dreamed of it. When playing guitar or shadowboxing I dreamed of it. As I put gas in my car or interacted with masked extraterrestrial beings at the supermarket I dreamed of it.

Fuck my indictment, travel restrictions, COVID, and border police. Just pick up and go. Run! Go on the lam…

Trouble was, I'd likely get busted and die of an RF-enigma-syndrome brain tumor while awaiting extradition in a Mexican or Guatemalan prison before ever seeing Michelle again.

I sent my public defender, Mr. Bart, a desperate email:

Is the state's goal to add desperation to desperate times? Why not just find me guilty already and end the misery?

It was a Saturday, but Mr. Bart replied promptly. We met on Zoom.

"The state made an offer," he said. "My secretary is sending it to you."

"Tell me about it."

Mr. Bart shuffled some papers and perused one of them in bookish, lawyerly fashion.

"In a nutshell, you plead guilty to disturbing the peace and providing false information to police—"

I leaned into my computer screen. "False information? What the—"

"Your name, for one."

"Puddin Taine? They wanna bust me for saying *Puddin Taine?* What if I'd told 'em I was Santa Clause or the Easter Bunny? They call that false information too?"

Mr. Bart paused, lower lip extended, mulling over the question.

"Come on Mr. Bart. That's not information at all, much less false information."

"You also told them you were homeless."

"I was about to be, would be now if not for the COVID relief I received... *Jesus.* If only I'd gotten a mob together to break some windows, loot and set fires in the name of social justice they'd a let me off."

I collapsed on my couch and muttered, "Fucking hijos de puta..."

"The fact that they're willing to drop the incitement to riot charge is a step in the right direction, Colton. Read the offer, review the evidence, and get back to me on Monday."

"How 'bout if I wear my BLM shirt to a looting party? They give me a break then?"

"You got yourself a BLM shirt?"

"Sure. Best way to blend in and record the action."

Mr. Bart's nose twitched.

"Try not to make matters worse, Colton. I'll see you Monday afternoon. My secretary will send you a Zoom invite. Have a good rest of your weekend."

Mr. Bart signed off.

I clicked to my email and opened the latest communique from Mr. Bart's office. The offer made me sick, especially the part about eight months in county lockup.

I shook my head at Princess, in her spot on the loveseat adjacent me.

"Makes me sick," I said.

"Review the evidence," she replied.

So I did. It was attached to the offer. Bullshit officer testimony, and nothing at all about the big nothing they'd found on my laptop and iPhone.

"*All* the evidence."

I stared at Princess and parroted her words, "All the evidence…"

Is something missing?

The videos. Mr. Bart and the prosecution knew I already possessed videos of my imaginary riot and the real riots, so I didn't expect them to be attached to the email. But it occurred to me that I hadn't thoroughly studied the video of my imaginary riot yet.

So that's what I did. And after about an hour I did discover something. Something that wasn't there but should be, according to officer testimony...officer testimony and my constitutional rights.

I needed to compare and contrast the video and officer testimony to be sure, but I had a party to attend first. A Saturday evening get-together. A small celebration that would have been a big bash if not for the pandemic. Nuestro American Hardware was rebounding thanks to loyal patrons and Antonia's radio spots promoting their "smashing comeback." We'd have barbeque and champagne...

CHAPTER 14

DOXED

The wildfires were under control for the time being and
lingering smoke swept across the descending sun to turn
the sky into a prism of color. I had a celebration to attend at
Antonia, Manny, and Edna's house but slowed my 4Runner a
few blocks away to appreciate the sunset spectacle. Below the sky,
the hills blushed and shimmered, and in the foreground I saw
a small group of people milling about as if to play soccer in the
street. I advanced cautiously. They were in front of Antonia's place
and were not playing soccer. A few of them, dressed in black and
matching pandemic masks, stood their ground in the middle of
the road; I swerved to pass them on the left, their sneering eyes
triggering a heart-skip of apprehension in my chest. I parked my
car around the nearest corner. Something in those sneering eyes
had looked familiar. Dangerous and familiar. What were they doing here instead of downtown where I'd last seen them pelting
police with flying objects and shouts of "Assassins," "Killers," and

"Racists"? (To police of color, "race traitors" was the preferred epithet, along with "assassins" and "killers.")

I called Antonia. My call went straight to voicemail. I left a quick message—where I'd parked and to call me right back—and took off on foot, assuming the role of a jogger. My khaki cargo shorts and polo shirt didn't fit the part, but my running shoes served the purpose. The small group gathered in the street had grown into a scrum of bodies jostling for position along the edge of Antonia's front lawn. I jogged at a relaxed clip, my heart thumping at a sprinters pace, those sneering eyes I'd seen stamped on my retina. Bad elements had targeted Antonia and her family. Extremely bad elements. Rioters.

I needed to record them, preferably from inside the house, from the perspective of those being harassed and attacked, and considered calling police, when my phone chimed. A murmuring chant arose from the crowd as I passed at a brisk walk and pulled my phone from my pocket. Antonia.

"I'm here," I said before she could get a word out. "Open the front door when you see me coming."

"Don't park—"

I cut her off. "I'm on foot, ready to make a break for your place. Be ready."

"Wait!" she pleaded, panic rising in her throat. "Find Mom."

I slowed down, Antonia's house about fifteen yards behind me. "Edna? What—?"

"She left for her walk an hour ago and…oh, wait. That's her… Ma! Don't!…"

I could hear Antonia open the door, her voice a muffled cry of help and vicious warning. I stuffed my phone back into my pocket and pivoted just as a van arrived to deliver five or six more people—young men—to the developing mob. The mob faced Antonia's house, their cacophony of voices rising and falling in search of a chant. I advanced guardedly from the rear, keeping my distance and hunting for Edna through a maze of psychotic figures. A violent screech pierced the madness: "Let her pass you fucking animals!"

Antonia. She was on the front lawn gripping a baseball bat she swung indiscriminately, arms extended, as though waving it at swarming insects. Shouts of "Racists shall die" answered her. My mind reeled, the scene unfolding in slow motion, like a traffic accident you see coming and know you can't avoid. Within a nanosecond I wished I had Antonia's baseball bat so I could show her how it's best used as a weapon against aggressive adversaries—gripped two-fisted like a lance and jabbed like punches. And I wished I had my own weapon, not necessarily a gun but a knife, a knife gripped in my right fist so I could both punch with the fist and hammer these thugs and terrorists with the knife, leaving my left free to jab at will. Antonia's wild swings threw her off balance and she slipped and fell from sight on the lawn. The mob swirled and surged forward, but detained itself instead of rushing the property, as if awaiting orders to charge. Should I shout my own orders, reasoned pleas? Was there any chance at all that this cyclone of hatred and brawling rage could be pacified, that my calls for calm could soothe these vengeful hearts? Warlike chants and seething malevolent eyes said no way. I spotted Edna, off to my left, within the edge of the mob, her styled gray hair disheveled in spokes about her pale skull. I dove headfirst into the fray. My legs weren't all they had been twenty years ago, but my arms were strong, my body solid and hefty. The mob of young men, mostly men, perceived the power pushing and plowing through them and fell away for a moment. Edna was within an arm's length or two when the maniacal frenzy regained strength, the violence tearing at my shirt, shouting in my ears and flailing at my head and back. Oddly, the sheer number of gouges and blows directed at me worked to my favor; many blocked each other and didn't reach their marks. I took Edna in my arms and shouted, "Let her pass! She's old and frail! Let her pass!"

Edna felt as light as a rag doll, or Princess. The throngs simmered at the sight of her in my arms. Antonia screamed, "Get away from them! Get away!"

An invective bellow within the horde responded: "The old lady is just another racist pig!"

The mob found these words hugely inspirational and broke into chants of "Raaa-cist. Raaa-cist. Raaa-cist..." Once again I wished I had Antonia's bat; these skulls deserved to be bashed, even at the risk of my own. But the mob had ceased its physical assault, opting instead for their creative fit of rage-filled race baiting. I wrapped an arm around Edna's waist and hefted her; Antonia and I fought our way to each other, scrambled across the lawn, up the porch and into the house.

I slammed the door shut behind us and deadbolted it. "What the fuck is going on?"

Antonia dropped her bat, sat her mother on the living room couch and kneeled before her.

"You okay Ma? You okay?"

Edna was pale, her eyes glazed and confused. She twisted her mouth to speak, but nothing escaped her lips.

Antonia spoke in Spanish and caressed her mother's head, the tears in her voice blunting an underlying fury at the mob outside.

"Say something, Ma. Say something…"

Edna's face drooped, mouth agape, incoherence suffusing the domes of her eyes.

I hustled to the kitchen and returned with a glass of water. Antonia held the glass to her mother's lips. Edna swallowed water with effort, eyes closed, her complexion regaining some color.

I retrieved the baseball bat off the floor and glanced out the window. The property line had been breached but no one advanced beyond the edge of the lawn. I returned my attention to Antonia.

"What the hell is going on outside? You call the police?"

Antonia ignored me.

"Mejor, Ma?"

Edna nodded feebly and blinked, her expression distorted and palsied. Antonia kissed her forehead and whispered in her ear. Antonia's pinstriped blouse stretched over her back, grass stained and muddied from her slip and fall, and I could see her lungs expand with a deep breath. I took a deep breath of my own, through my nose, and released the air in a muffled growl of seething impotence. Outside, a woman had gotten ahold of a bullhorn. "Silence is violence," she said again and again, inviting imitative chants. My head was swimming with emotions—anger at the insane mob, fear for Edna, and a dull helplessness.

"You call 9-1-1, Antonia?"

"Before I called you back. Who knows when they'll show…"

I tightened my grip on the bat and stepped over to the window for another look outside. A streetlamp and orange sunset hue burnished raised fists and galvanized zombies. BLM shirts were prevalent, and most wore pandemic masks, all of them crushed together in a phalanx of diseased passions oozing inchoate slogans, the latest "silence is violence."

I grumbled, "What the fuckin' hell does that even mean?… There is no such thing as peace unless I support your asinine social-justice bullshit? Even then there would be no peace…"

Speech you disagree with is violence, and silence is violence. So your violence in response is always justified…

What in God's name possessed these people? Were they evidence that life was actually so good they had nothing better to do than terrorize this family? Or were they proof that those seeking "justice" for past wrongs are just as capable as anyone else of committing hateful, indiscriminate acts of violent vengeance? And why had they chosen Antonia's house in particular?

I leaned the baseball bat against the wall and began recording the scene with my iPhone, mindful to keep a record of yet another example of destructive mob behavior at odds with my imaginary riot.

Edna said, "Ahora mejor. Sí te oigo. Ahora mejor." Better now.

I swung my phone around to record Antonia caring for her traumatized mother.

"You have a firearm in the house?"

Antonia rose from her kneeling position, eyes steady on her mother, the soft contours of her oval features pinched and grimacing.

"In a safe in my bedroom closet. We'll take it with us. But emergency rooms are a pandemic nightmare." Antonia retrieved her iPhone off the coffee table and drifted towards the window. "I'll find an urgent care that's open for Ma."

Edna lifted her chin to me.

"Gracias, Colton. Muy valiente. El Príncipe Valiente."

I slid my phone into my pocket and sat next to her. Edna's hands were clammy and cold, and the left side of her face drooped, but her expression retained a serene quality, serene and grateful. I told her that I was no prince but simply a friend aiding another friend in distress. Her eyes welled, and tears pricked the corners of mine. Edna gave me a crooked smile and brought a hand to my neck, just below my right ear.

"Sangras."

Edna had a delicate touch, her hands silky, adorned by her wedding ring, nails manicured, the fingers she'd touched to my neck stained with blood and giving me a start.

"Let's see."

Antonia dropped onto the couch beside me and dabbed at my wound with my torn shirt collar. The clamor outside droned with monotony.

"Not too bad," Antonia said unconvincingly. "Looks like someone with long sharp fingernails got to you."

"Don't even feel it. Felt a few body shots but didn't—"

"First aid's in the bathroom. Clean up and we'll take Mom to urgent care."

Edna objected, "No, no. Estoy bien… I'm okay… Estoy bien…"

She looked better but definitely not "okay"; the small effort of her objection appeared to leave her exhausted, perspiration glistening her forehead. Edna must have been a knockout thirty or forty years ago, and age could not mask her attractive nature and elegant carriage. When I first met her she seemed regal, a woman who commanded respect and was not given to idle pleasantries. Yet she turned out to be quite pleasant, disarmingly friendly with an engaging smile and subtle wisdom and wit that invited interaction without fear of being judged. Like her daughter, Antonia, Edna's charms were embracing, yet she'd left behind Antonia's combative aspects, if she ever had them, aspects Antonia figured to have inherited from her deceased father. Edna was the essence of civility and grace and to think that those detestable assholes outside had subjected her to abuse was infuriating, made me want to forget all civility and mow down the motherfuckers with my 4Runner.

"Just a precaution, Ma," Antonia said in soothing Spanish. "You've been through a trauma. Remember, we have to monitor your health."

Antonia sounded calm and composed, but I sensed the electric tension in her body as we rose in unison from the couch.

"The bathroom in the hall?" I said.

"You'll find what you need there."

I took a step for the hall but stopped in response to renewed confusion in my brain.

"Where's Manny?"

"At the store…" Antonia took me by the arm and guided me toward the bathroom, out of earshot from Edna. We paused before the bathroom door.

Antonia hushed her voice: "Manny is facing something similar at Nuestro American Hardware."

I stiffened and scowled.

"What—?"

"He has help—primos with him…" Antonia glanced over her shoulder as if expecting an ambush. "We've been doxed."

My confusion deepened.

"What? How?"

"Remember that morning we were scrubbing graffiti…those putas in the SUV?"

"They record us? They couldn't have. No phone or camera or—"

"No, but someone did. It's gone viral."

CHAPTER 15

MISTER BART

I told you not to make matters worse."

"We were recorded back in June, the day after riots in Van Nuys and downtown. And it's not me who's making matters worse. I'm not the one doing the doxing, searching for the addresses of those I disagree with and gathering mobs together to disrupt and destroy lives."

Mr. Bart's pearly smooth complexion grew rough around the edges, conforming to his prematurely gray hair and the years he seemed to have aged these past months. His image on my computer screen flickered, but his voice remained clear.

"Who made the video?"

"How the hell do I know? Everyone's got a phone to make a video."

"You have been identified as one of the people in that June video."

I wanted to say, "No shit," but held my tongue and nodded, "Uh-uh." Remnants of a mob were gathered in front of my apartment complex when I returned home late last Saturday night. I parked my car around the block and snuck in through the back entrance. I half-expected my place to have been vandalized, maybe looted, but the social-justice thugs did not breach the secure building. Unable to sleep, I retrieved my 4Runner at four in the morning, relieved it hadn't been discovered, identified, gutted and torched.

Much of that morning was spent blocking numbers from nasty calls and texts:

racist scum

rid the world of white supremacists like you

you'll meet your racist maker in hell

Mr. Bart said, "This changes things, Colton."

"You're tellin' me."

I was seriously considering acquiring a pistol from Manny. Firearms would have been no help at all in rescuing me from bankruptcy, were of no aid in my defense against charges of incitement to riot, could not cure a brain tumor or provide immunity to COVID, were useless against RF enigma syndrome and OCD, and extraterrestrials would likely vaporize me before I managed to get a shot off against them. But the mobs were nothing more than galvanized zombies, and I knew damn well that zombies could be blown away with bullets and mowed down by my 4Runner. They represented yet another threat to my life but, unlike the other threats, there were ready made defenses against zombies, a gun one of them.

As a convicted felon, I was prohibited from possessing a firearm, further proof that the dark forces aligned against me really were out to torture and kill me...or have me killed.

"The prosecution has withdrawn its offer."

"Oh yeah? Well, so have I."

Mr. Bart's nose twitched.

"What offer are you talking about, Colton?"

"Any offer." I rocked in my seat on the couch. "Review the evidence, Mr. Bart. Contrary to officer testimony, the prick cops did not read me my rights when they arrested me."

Mr. Bart cocked his head as to a strange noise chirping in his office.

"Look at the video of my arrest," I said. "Then compare it to officer testimony. They said they read me my rights when they arrested me, but it sure as hell ain't in the video. My verbal sparring had the sonsabitches so flustered and pissed off they forgot to read me my rights."

Mr. Bart rubbed his chin, brow furrowed and lower lip extended in the expression of a professor examining the intricacies of a new proof.

"If true, this puts us in a much stronger position."

"Stronger position? I want all charges dropped. Plain and simple."

Mr. Bart pursed his lips and nodded, eyes shifty, calculating a strategy to get me off...or fuck me over...

"Do your job please, Mr. Bart. Review the evidence I've described, present it to the prosecution and get back to me asap."

"I'll do that, but the state has a tendency to take their time in responding. And in the meantime, please do me a favor."

"What's that?"

"Don't make matters worse..."

CHAPTER 16

SEPTEMBER

I began a rigorous training program. Despite the pandemic and lockdowns, frequent trips to the beach had kept me in decent condition, but now I stepped up my activities. Swimming, surfing, fishing, and shadowboxing were augmented by pushups, pullups, handstand pushups, core workouts, and soft-sand running. I cut out the TV dinners and junky fast food as well. Time to get serious. I even resolved to limit my drinking to a few beers on weekends.

A zombie apocalypse was upon me. Ever since we'd been doxed, I'd spied the zombie enemy shuffling about in front of my apartment complex daily. Faceless, colorless creatures I avoided by always using the back entrance. They knew where I lived, my apartment number, and had managed to breach the secure building on at least one occasion, the evidence an arrow shot into my door. These were not run-of-the-mill lumbering zombies but galvanized zombies; armed and weaponized zombies who'd already drawn my blood with a neck wound that required a few stitches.

I didn't tell the manager about the arrow and have her call the cops. Cops wouldn't have done anything anyway; maybe end up searching my place and busting me as a felon in possession of a firearm.

"Untraceable," Manny had assured me.

The night we were doxed, Manny and his primos defended Nuestro American Hardware with shotguns. Not a shot was fired, but the show of force prevented vandalism and looting, or worse.

Manny had called 9-1-1 but police did not respond. They'd finally responded to Antonia, just as I pulled her Infinity out of the garage to take her and Edna to urgent care. Mighta pummeled a few galvanized zombies with the car had cops not showed… Law enforcement was hamstrung, from L.A., Portland and Seattle to Minneapolis and New York. BLM demands had left police defunded, deflated and undermanned. My Glock 9mm was stashed in a heating duct in my apartment, and I never went anywhere without my spring-loaded Browning pocketknife.

My old baseball bat had a new home, from the closet to a spot against the wall next to the door to my apartment.

Self-defense was my main concern, yet I did yearn to take the fight to the enemy. My 9mm was an effective weapon, but zombie skulls crushed like watermelons with each swing of my bat was a recurring dream, replete with all the gore of a typical zombie TV flick.

"To kill a zombie, you have to destroy their brains."

Princess sniggered. "Aren't zombies already dead?"

"*Undead*. Zombies are undead. There's a difference. Unlike a corpse, zombies respond to stimuli, their movements triggered within neural pathways. Demolish the brain and zombies are dead."

"Best for you not to go out in public feeling like this."

Sage advice. Behaving like a crazed zombie killer would give the state all the evidence it needed to throw the book at me and sentence me to death. And no matter how many zombies I killed, there were more out to devour me. If I wasn't careful, I might get ambushed by them out in the unreal world; yet galvanized zombies generally traveled in groups and could be avoided, if I kept my wits about me. It was imperative to stay cool when venturing outside during the day and not draw attention to myself as I took tortuous routes in and out of my neighborhood and apartment complex to dodge the undead.

At night, I removed my 9mm from its hiding place and slept with it by my bed. I heard noises—low growling voices, scraping and dragging sounds, and creaks and squeaks and occasional thumps. My apartment was located next to a park and busy boulevard, so I'd grown accustomed to a certain amount of noise at night, but not in the middle of the night, and not these kinds of noises. It was becoming routine for me to be startled awake sometime after midnight, grab my gun, and slink from my bedroom to the kitchen and living room, aching to pull the trigger and blow away intruding zombies, only to find my apartment empty, but for Princess.

"I'm going zombie hunting."

"Don't leave a blood trail. And lock the door behind you."

I didn't go zombie hunting every night I was startled awake, but the darkened and abandoned late hours did embolden me on occasion and I'd slip out of my apartment, gun at the small of my back, and search for them, expecting some to have breached the expansive building. The parking garage downstairs offered a challenge. Lighting was scattered and sparce and shadows appeared behind every parked car. I gripped my 9mm at my side, trigger finger itching. Usually I cleared the parking garage without incident, but one 2 a.m. morning a clang by the trash bins and screeching tires out on the boulevard sent me scurrying for cover behind a concrete post, pistol raised to a cat leaping from a trash bin and through the iron gridded gate. Sweat bloomed on my brow, the ensuing silence thick with my fear and hot throbbing panic in my head. My fear was maddening, intolerable and infuriating. Infuriating. I seized upon the anger, swallowed my fear and fingered the stitches on my neck, dull animal rage simmering to a boil within me. Someone or something was going to have to pay for my torment.

I let myself out of the parking garage through a door that opened to the side street bordering the park. A warm late-summer night illuminated by streetlamps and a full moon. All tranquil, but the zombie enemy was out here somewhere, hiding amongst the trees in the park, or lurking in the alley separating my home building from the neighboring apartments. I determined to clear the surrounding area, beginning with the alley. I'd then circle my apartment complex, kill any intruding zombies, and head for the park to continue the hunt.

I'd left the light on in my bedroom, could see it filtering through the slatted window shades up on the second floor. Much of the noise I'd been hearing in the middle of the night originated from this alleyway, an ideal hideout for the galvanized zombies out to devour me. A tall wrought iron fence bordered my apartment building to my left, the alley divided by two trash bins, their metallic finishes reflecting a smattering of moonlight. I pulled the 9mm from the small of my back and held it at a 45-degree angle from the ground, my ears sensitized to the sound of my cautious footsteps and level respiration. An animal was in here. I could sense it. An animal larger than a cat. Zombie size. A muffled carnivorous growl from just beyond the first trash bin gave it away.

I shielded myself against the near edge of the trash bin, the growls and snorts clear, like a bear gnawing on a bone. The moonlight revealed nothing down the alley. The creature was hidden at the opposite end of this trash bin, engrossed in devouring remains, perhaps human remains. I approached with stealth, my gun leveled, ready to fire. The growling stopped abruptly, and so did I, afraid I'd given myself away somehow, that a galvanized zombie would jump out into the alley and pounce on me before I got off a headshot to destroy its brain. I remained still, breath silenced, my instincts paralyzed by internal conflict, a second or two debate on when to seize the initiative and attack, wheel myself into position for a clear shot. The growling resumed. Now was the time to act, while the creature was immersed in its meal. I leaped forward, into the middle of the alley…and held my fire at a figure that was more orangutang than zombie.

"What the fuck," I snarled, out of frustration rather than anger or fear. I really wanted to blow away a zombie. The simian figure stirred in its prone position, its growling snores punctuated by snorts and grumbles. A jacket served as a pillow, and a shopping cart filled with junk was just beyond its feet—*his* feet. Zombies don't travel with shopping carts, and didn't sleep, as far as I knew, so I had to admit he was human; not exactly a fine specimen of a man but he was, most likely, human, his body odor more pungent than the stench from the trash bin. A filthy dirty, hairy and liquored-up human beast, an empty bottle of Jim Beam whiskey at his side. I nudged him with my foot.

"Hey. Asshole. You the one making that racket in the middle of the night?"

He shook himself awake and rolled to his back. "Huh?"

A long pink scar creased his forehead, his nose flattened at an angle from punches and falls. His brown wiry beard was thick but not long; he'd found the time and place to trim it, as well as the tangled mop of hair on his head, but not to clean it, or the rest of his body. Grimy from head to toe, his camo clothes tattered and worn, but his black sneakers looked fairly new. He was mid-30s, ruddy and heavyset, fattened from junk food and booze, his blue eyes big as shot glasses as they alighted upon the gun in my hand.

He slid on his back in retreat, hands up, his head banging carelessly against the trash bin.

"I didn't do it. I swear it wasn't me."

I regarded him cynically, certain he was guilty of something. Until the zombies arrived to torment me, this was a relatively peaceful San Fernando Valley neighborhood, especially as compared to parts of Van Nuys and large swaths of Panorama City. Vagrants and homeless were around but they didn't congregate, and violent crime was uncommon. Things had changed. Everywhere things had changed, and I was changing as well. Adapt or die…

I hacked and spit, the phlegm sticking to the empty Jim Beam bottle and distracting the hairy beast's eyes for a second. He propped his head up against the trash bin, and my trigger finger twitched. I thumbed the safety lever from the fire position. Galvanized zombies were my target, not this pathetic son of a bitch.

Pathetic, and maybe armed. I glared at him and raised my 9mm to a 45-degree angle from the ground, the barrel pointed at his feet.

"What didn't you do? You swear you didn't do what?"

He jerked his feet from my line of fire, knees bent, hands shaking, his voice a quavering plea.

"N-nothin'. I didn't do anything."

"Don't gimme that crap. You done plenty…and know plenty."

I narrowed the gap between us, gun aimed at his midsection, and kicked at a bulge in his front pocket.

"What the fuck is that…drugs?"

He gulped audibly, beads of sweat prickling his forehead.

"You want it? You can have it."

He reached for his pocket and froze, unable to move with the muzzle of my 9mm pressed between his eyes. I was on a knee and knuckled the lump in his pocket, feeling for something solid resembling a weapon. Nothing…maybe drugs, but that didn't interest me. I patted down his left front pocket…and prodded his temple with the gun muzzle to get him to move off his jacket.

"What the hell you got in there?"

I snatched the jacket out from under him, sending a utility knife skidding into the alley. I searched the jacket and retrieved the knife.

"Use this for hunting squirrels and carving roadkill?"

A cheap knife. Fixed 4-inch blade. A little rusty, but deadly.

The beast stammered, "J-just found it. The other day."

I stood and pocketed the knife, gun at my side.

"Whaddya know about the fucking zombies prowling around here?"

The beast blinked in succession, eyes darting from side to side. "Zombies?"

"Yeah. You know. The motherfuckers who began congregating out on the boulevard here last week."

"I never seen 'em here before."

"Where have you seen them before?"

"I dunno. I mean...I...maybe—"

He choked on his words and my gun pointed at his mouth. I had no desire to shoot the bastard but could envision pistol whipping him to get information.

"Maybe where?"

He gasped, struggling for air.

"Maybe downtown."

"Downtown? When? You recognized them from downtown?"

"No... I mean...they all look the same. But I seen 'em. A couple months ago, when they started those riots."

"Riots, huh..." I lowered my weapon, pleased to hear him use the accurate descriptive noun avoided by so many media and political hacks. "Bet you took advantage to loot."

"No, no. It wasn't me. I swear. I didn't do anything."

"I don't give a shit what you did or didn't do but what you know about those motherfucking galvanized zombies that have invaded this neighborhood. You said you recognized them, that they look familiar, like others you've seen. Where are they now?"

His hands remained up at his shoulders; he clinched and un-clinched them a couple times.

"Gone."

"Gone? Gone where?"

He pursed his lips, brow furrowed and eyes cast down at his ample belly.

"Wherever they want."

I echoed his words, "Wherever they want," struck by their simple truth. The galvanized zombie mobs did go wherever they wanted. They could be killed with bullets and clubs, runover by cars and trucks, and even intimidated by superior firepower and shows of force, but no one had the balls to stand up to them, or very few, like Manny and his primos, had the balls to stand up to them. I tucked my 9mm inside my waistband, mildly miffed by the truth coming from the mouth of a bum: the zombies were gone, for now.

"And how do they get to wherever they want?"

The beast lowered his hands, relieved to see my gun holstered, and hoisted his back up against the trash bin, his defensive pos-ture now one of accommodation.

"I seen 'em in pickups and Jeeps." He glanced over his shoul-der, like someone might be eavesdropping, and dropped his voice a notch. "And vans supply them tools and shit to throw. Weapons too. I seen 'em with weapons—bats, knives, and guns. They got money. Must have money. You planning a hit?"

I eyed him suspiciously.

"Why? You wanna piece of the action?"

He worked his jaw, a glint of avarice in his eyes dimming as he considered the question.

"No…uh…maybe. I don't want no trouble."

"Tough shit. You got trouble. We all got trouble. Nothing but trouble." I ambled back the way I came, towards the park. "Trouble, trouble, trouble…"

CHAPTER 17

DOCTOR BOLTON

Dr. Bolton mentioned my growing troubles in a transparent attempt to perforate the cool veneer I maintained during the day and get to the bottom of Colton Candide.

It was a special day, so I spruced up a bit before visiting Dr. Bolton and picking up some champagne.

"How do I look?"

"Chino shorts. Bahama deck shoes. Nice nautical shirt. But I like you better with a beard."

I winked at Princess, behind me and to my right, her image on the loveseat sofa reflected in the living room's full-length mirror, and ran the back of my hands over my smooth cheeks.

"A little sunburned, but my face more or less matches the rest of my body... My crewcut has grown out. Might get a trim in a month or two."

"You're tanned almost as dark as an Indian."

I straightened my collar and snapped an alligator smile at myself.

"Funny you should say that. My great-grandmother was part Navajo."

"Which part?"

I snorted a laugh.

"The Navajo part."

"No kidding. You know, most Native American tribes revere the bear."

I blew Princess a kiss through the mirror.

"And so do I, Princess. Don't know what I'd do without you."

"You're just partial."

I faced her. "Yes I am."

"Y guapote." Handsome. "But why the getup? Your birthday's not till tomorrow."

I snatched my keys off the coffee table. "Last day as a 48-year-old, Princess. Thought I'd dress for the occasion. Tomorrow I enter my fiftieth year. Nearly a half century on this blue marble out on the edge of one of a couple trillion galaxies."

"So you're not just trying to impress Dr. Bolton?"

I dipped my chin and lifted my eyebrows at Princess.

"You jealous, Princess?"

Princess scoffed and focused on the TV—Nirvana's *Come as You Are* video.

"I know more about you than Dr. Bolton ever will."

True. But that didn't prevent Dr. Bolton from assuming she knew all about me and my motives as she dug to get to the bottom of Colton Candide. She was in top form, recalling a bevy of memories I had of prison counselors—clinical professionals and their unyielding tortuous mind games and logic:

Counselor: You're contributing to the horrors and violence of the black market by producing marijuana.

Me (thinking): *Make Pepsi illegal and you'll get more of the same.*

Counselor: When did you first embrace criminal behavior?

Me (thinking): *Like when did I stop beating my girlfriends?*

Counselor: Your criminal activity is indicative of an antisocial ethos.

Me (speaking): I was sociable and ethical with everyone.

Counselor: The first step in breaking your cycle of criminality is to admit you have a problem.

Me (speaking): I got a state license to produce marijuana so I wouldn't have a problem with criminality.

Dr. Bolton's mind games and twisted logic easily rivaled those of the clinical professionals I was subjected to in prison. All pretended to have science on their side, yet thanks to Charlie and the criteria for a useful scientific theory, I'd become more adept at picking out bullshit and concluded that well over ninety-percent of the "scientific theories" I'd been exposed to inside and outside of academia, prison, or anywhere else didn't actually explain a damn thing; and that's what a useful scientific theory is: an explanation of phenomena. Both Newton's and Einstein's theories, for example, are deductive, causal, general, predictive, and empirically meaningful, the difference being that Einstein's general theory of relativity explains phenomena that Newton's theories do not. That doesn't make Newton wrong; his theories are falsifiable, which makes them empirically meaningful, but he isn't wrong. Newton can land you on the moon, he just can't explain the perihelion precession of Mercury (amongst other phenomena) like Einstein can. As I spent time with Charlie, the realization that most every blabbermouth expert I'd heard in my life who claimed their theories were scientific really was full of crap, especially social- and political-science idiots, bolstered confidence in my instincts. I'd suspected it all along: they were just spouting off pseudoscientific theories that rarely conformed to a single useful criterion, much less all of them, to further political ends and advance a conspiracy, a conspiracy to control my mind and behavior.

All along my instincts had told me that Dr. Bolton was full of it. But she'd been recommended by Mr. Bart to help bolster my case against the state as she analyzed my mental condition, so I tried to play along with her best I could. I should have known my efforts were doomed from the start. My instincts failed me in that regard. Overall, I didn't know how to play along with bullshit...

Dr. Bolton opened with an unsurprising statement: "I understand you had some trouble with doxing."

"Nothing outta the ordinary considering the way the rest of the year has gone."

"How do you feel about it, and the way the doxing might affect your case?"

As a potential expert witness and my state-appointed shrink recommended by my state-appointed public defender, Dr. Bolton was privy to privileged information regarding my case. But she didn't know everything, her sustained sanctimonious demeanor a sign she had no clue I'd gained the upper hand, that any day now I expected my attorney to inform me all charges had been dropped due to the cops' failure to read me my rights and the fact that the state had no case anyway.

I remained willfully ignorant to the fact that facts didn't matter, and garnered strength from what amounted to an illusion of having gained the upper hand against the state. Yet it was a powerful illusion and I clung to it like a self-satisfied drunk nursing a fresh bottle of whiskey, my disposition carefree as I leaned back in my chair and crossed my legs.

"If the state needs me to be doxed to bolster their case, they have no case anyhow."

"The video that led to the doxing demonstrates a pattern of behavior, Colton, behavior indicative of anger, rage associated with white fragility."

White fragility.

I recognized the term. Uncle Steven had included it in a plethora of sources and notes he'd emailed me. The assumptions and theories associated with "white fragility" were manifold and empirically meaningless, not to mention noncausal and nonpredictive, but I saw no advantage in getting into a pissing match with Dr. Bolton over the issue. And Antonia believed that her radio spot promoting her hardware store's "smashing comeback" had triggered the doxing and revelation of the video, had suggested to those who possessed the video that now was the perfect time to fuck us over, but there was no reason to mention that either.

"I felt more amused than angry at the time. And look rather amused in the video."

"Appearances can be deceiving."

"And feelings?"

Dr. Bolton's mouth was concealed beneath a white pandemic mask, but I could see the pretentious smirk mirrored in her eyes. She reached down into a desk drawer and withdrew a stack of cards the size of 8" x 10" photos.

"We're going to have you take a little test. Many are usually completed on a computer, but space is severely limited due to pandemic regulations and our computer lab is occupied."

I leaned forward in my chair, hands folded across my knees.

"I'm ready when you are."

"Tell me what you notice or are reminded of when you see these images." She held up a card.

"The Deschutes."

"The Deschutes?"

"A river in Oregon I've fished on several occasions."

Dr. Bolton glanced at the colorful circles and lines printed on the card and showed me another—a multi-hued inkblot.

"A closeout."

"Closeout?"

"Hydrodynamic wave action that crushes a surfer if he tries to ride it."

Dr. Bolton wrinkled her nose and fingered through her cards before holding up the next one.

"The Smith."

Dr. Bolton shook her head, her gaze narrowed.

"Another river?"

"Up in northern California."

"But unlike the Deschutes card, this image is all blacks and grays without distinct forms."

"I can see some purple. Like fishing the Smith at twilight."

Dr. Bolton added a note to my open file on her desk…and searched through her cards.

"How about this one?"

"Water."

Dr. Bolton stiffened, her nasal voice frigid, "How the—?"

She was about to say "hell" but checked her emotions and pressed the card against the plexiglass guarding her desk from pandemic droplets, to give me a definitive view of the figures.

"You telling me you don't see two human faces?"

"Sure. Cartoon faces."

"And?"

"Profile. Kinda resemble Charlie Brown faces, the comic strip."

"And what do you notice about the faces?"

"Like you said. I suppose they're human."

"In addition to that. Anything else strike you?"

I reflected for a moment. Evidently, Dr. Bolton wanted some kind of pat answer, but the only pat answer I could think of was an explanation of my original answer.

"Well, humans are over sixty-percent water, so I said water."

The doctor's pale forehead reddened with a spark in her gray eyes; the card she pressed against the plexiglass trembled.

"Differences," she breathed. "Differences in the faces."

I clapped my hands together in singular applause of comprehension.

"You mean the colors, that it? The different colors?"

"Yes, the colors. What do the colors that distinguish those two faces indicate?"

"In this case, could be brack."

Dr. Bolton cocked her head at the unfamiliar term, so I went ahead and expounded upon a subject I knew something about:

"Could be natural, the brown caused by the breakdown of organic material in the water, like leaves, roots and bark, the yellow a result of oxidation. In humans it's different. Melanin—"

Dr. Bolton interrupted, "Okay, okay," and raised her hand like a traffic cop, the card sliding carelessly down the plexiglass.

"Why do you think," she asked deliberately, "you have a natural aversion to discussing race?"

"Race or skin color?"

She deadpanned me, eyes hooded, hands folded upon her desk.

"One and the other."

"If I do have an aversion, it's not natural. Naturally, I don't have an aversion to discussing most anything."

"But you do admit you may have an aversion to discussing race."

"It's not exactly the focal point of every conversation I have."

"How do you feel about our discussion about it now?"

"Is that what we're discussing? I haven't had time to feel much of anything about it."

Dr. Bolton steepled her fingers and pointed them at the Charlie Brown cartoon card.

"Most people notice the colors that distinguish those two faces right away."

"I might have noticed the different colors right away, just wasn't thinking about it. Didn't interest me."

"Ingenious." She made another note in my file. "I suppose we'll get to the bottom of this soon enough."

"I was about to mention melanin though, natural skin pigment. I've read up some on the subject, so I do find it interesting at times."

Dr. Bolton straightened her posture, chin lifted to me.

"First you said it didn't interest you, now you say it does at times. You're contradicting yourself again."

"I guess the things I find uninteresting at times interest me at others."

"But we're engaging in conversation, Colton. Your propensity to contradict yourself can be a hindrance to communication."

"I thought I was taking a test."

"The test was paused."

"Oh. Sorry. I'll make an effort to advance conversation then."

I kept my tone modulated and sincere, though I did have a sneaky hunch that Dr. Bolton was trying to entrap me somehow.

Dr. Bolton set the cards aside.

"I suppose we'll get to the bottom of your contradictions soon enough. Let's try something different. I'll begin a sentence and you complete it."

"Another test?"

The doctor brushed imaginary lint from the shoulder of her polyester blouse.

"Yes. A test."

"Okay," I said, unconvinced that the good doctor wasn't deliberately commingling her tests with conversation to catch me contradicting myself again.

"Finish this sentence for me: When faced with frustration I usually…"

"Swim and fish."

Dr. Bolton brought a hand to her brow and scratched her forehead.

"My father rarely…"

"Tacks anymore."

"Tacks?"

"Come about—turn the bow of a sailboat into the eye of the wind."

"Your father is deceased, so I don't think he tacks at all."

"Maybe not. But he enjoyed sailing and every now and then I envision him tacking…and jibing."

Dr. Bolton squeezed her eyes shut and blinked in succession, to gain a new perspective of me.

"You're fixated on one thing, Colton. You've got water on the brain."

I massaged the base of my skull.

"You think so? What're the symptoms?"

Dr. Bolton crossed her arms, and I could hear her foot tapping beneath her desk.

"Let's try another *tack,* Colton. I'll say a word and you say the first thing that comes to mind, whatever you're thinking about that's not related to water. Think you can do that?"

I planted my elbows on my knees and clasped my hands under my chin, assuming a studios position.

"Okay. Shoot."

"Gold."

"Quarterback."

"Thunder."

"Linebacker."

Dr. Bolton hesitated…

"Black."

"Punt."

"You're fixated on one thing again, Colton. Football."

"I like football."

"But I want you to let your mind roam. Free your thoughts and tell me what you think about when you hear the word."

I nodded in agreement, "All right," eager to comply yet doubtful of the doctor's motives. Like the suspicions I had about Mr. Bart, I wondered if Dr. Bolton was bound to aid my defense or fuck me over.

"Let's try again… *Leader.*"

"Band."

"White."

"Mexico."

The doctor's nasal tone sharpened. "What made you say that?"

"It's what I thought about. The nearest border."

She reached for her pen to make a note in my file, thought again, and shifted her attention to her computer screen, clicking the mouse and typing. The printer behind her beeped and whirred.

"Under normal circumstances, you'd be enrolled in group." She brought her attention back to me. "But these are not normal circumstances. Group sessions have been suspended. We're all stretched rather thin here at the clinic and it's difficult to dedicate the time needed to each individual…client."

"I appreciate your time, Doctor," I said, careful to sound sincere.

"Take a look at these." She slid a couple of freshly printed photos beneath the plexiglass. I retrieved them and returned to my seat.

"What do you see in the photographs?"

"Looks like demonstrations or protests."

Both photos were letter size, the one in my right hand a shot of what appeared to be my imaginary riot in Malibu. I searched for my face.

"What differences do you see in the photos?"

"More people holding signs in this one," I said with a lift of the picture in my left hand. "And more raised fists. And I don't see any American flags like I do in the other."

"Anything else?"

"This one with the American flags is in Malibu, I think. Might be the protest I was involved in. The other..." I took a closer look. "Can't tell where it took place."

"What do you see in the demonstrators themselves?"

"They all seem animated, energized. And if this one is of the protest I was involved in, their motives are different than the demonstrators in the other picture."

"How so?"

"We were protesting the COVID lockdowns and beach closers. From the looks of the signs held in the other..." I looked again. *Stop racism. No justice no peace.* BLM is on a sign in the background. This is a BLM demonstration. So I'd say that the motives behind the two protests are different."

"Okay. Good. What else?"

I lifted my gaze to Dr. Bolton. Her demeanor had changed, her voice softened and gray eyes complaisant. I went ahead and humored her.

"There are people of color in the BLM demonstration. The protestors are white in the other, or mostly white."

"And what does that indicate?"

"Spontaneity."

"Spontaneity?"

"If I had organized my protest beforehand, publicized it on social media and with fliers, people from all over probably would have attended. But the demonstration was purely spontaneous, and those visiting or living around there are mostly white."

"Are you saying that the BLM demonstrations are not spontaneous?"

"Not from what I've seen and heard."

"Your experience is anecdotal, the deduction a specious argument."

Deduction? I didn't make a deduction.

"Specious? Okay. I guess they're just always prepared to…"

I was about to say "riot" but sensed that the term might alienate the good doctor. To my mind there remained a 50-50 chance that she was bound to aid in my defense or fuck me over, and I saw no advantage in alienating her outright.

"…always prepared to *protest*," I enunciated, "whether or not the demonstrations themselves are actually spontaneous."

Sounded like I'd just contradicted myself again, but Dr. Bolton didn't seem to notice.

"They are prepared to seek justice. And the power structure and justice system are white. The fact that your unlawful gathering consisted of whites is proof of its racist origins and goals."

I slouched in my chair and grumbled, "Proof," my gaze unfocused on my deck shoes.

Dr. Bolton perceived vulnerability in my posture, an opportunity to dig deeper into my psyche.

"Does the realization that your motives are racist upset and anger you?"

I squinted at her. "Realization?"

"The first step to seeking a cure. You must get your mind right."

I massaged the base of my skull, feeling for the water on my brain.

"Inherent racism," the good doctor said, "is something all whites have to remedy within themselves. And the realization, acceptance of the condition is the first step in treating the malady."

Dr. Bolton's pale arms seemed translucent, her figure ghostly.

"I suppose you know this from experience..." I said, "...and not just anecdotal experience..."

"The white hegemony of social and power propinquities requires a new conception of structural justice tonalities and a restructuring of the asseveration of power itself."

Anyone who talks gibberish like that must be brainwashed...or have something to hide...

"Sounds simple enough. A preamble to some kinda theory?"

Dr. Bolton gave me a skeptical look, her brow scrunched up, uncertain if I was genuinely interested or mocking her.

"Social Justice Intersectionality," she said. "A key component to Critical Race Theory."

"Any way to imagine how the theory might be falsified?"

Dr. Bolton stifled a snort. "The futile effort would not be conducive to your treatment, Colton. The science is irrefutable. Denial of your racism is evidence of racism and will deepen your racism."

"I see... Guess I can't argue with that."

"There's no need to argue, Colton."

The water on my brain began sloshing back and forth, a small-scale seiche caused by Dr. Bolton's gibberish and circular reasoning—*denial of my racism is evidence of my racism.* I rubbed my forehead to cushion the oscillating wave action, unsure if it was the water on my brain, Dr. Bolton herself, or both that represented yet another danger designed to torture and kill me.

"Don't look so despondent, Colton. Your affliction infects all whites, not just you."

I jerked my head at her. "What difference does that make?"

"Take comfort in the fact that you're not alone. And this is an opportunity to heal yourself."

I muttered, "I'm not alone," and glanced at the photo of what I assumed was my imaginary riot. I held it up for the doctor to see.

"So all the white people in this photo are racist?"

"They are a product of a complex system of racial hierarchies—structural racism—and, at the very least, suffer from internalized racism."

"And you can tell all that by looking at a photo."

"And by taking into consideration the circumstances under which the photo was taken."

"Circumstances? We weren't wearing white hoods and burning crosses."

Dr. Bolton wrote a note in my file. I rose from my chair and placed the photos on the edge of her desk, beneath the plexiglass.

"Amazing," I said, and resumed my seat.

Dr. Bolton nodded affirmatively, her pause an invitation for me to elaborate:

"I've always found it challenging to see into a person's heart and determine the content of their character. Your theory certainly cuts through the crap. All I have to do is see their race and the color of their skin and all questions are answered."

Now the doctor shook her head, disappointed in me.

"You're getting cynical and defensive, Colton. Inherent racism is in your DNA. Accept the fact and work to better your condition."

"Get my mind right and cure myself."

"In a matter of speaking. Yes."

"Have you studied my DNA? The government has samples."

Dr. Bolton chuckled, a self-conscious chuckle.

"Oh my no. But it's evident you are white, Colton."

"I'm a lot of things, including Navajo. And my maternal grandfather was Jewish."

Dr. Bolton stiffened. Something in my words or attitude had given her a start.

"What matters," she said at last, "is how you self-identify. And your actions and associations indicate—"

I interrupted, "How *I* self-identify or how others identify me?"

The good doctor ran a hand through her reddish pageboy hairdo.

"Okay, Colton," she said, her voice oozing feigned patience. "I'll play along. Exactly how do you self-identify?"

I gave the question careful consideration for several seconds, and recalled the last image I'd seen of myself, in the mirror at my apartment, Princess reflected behind me. I smoothed my hands over my tan legs, adjusted my collar, and snapped an alligator smile at Dr. Bolton sharp enough to cleave my pandemic mask.

"Un metro caimán negro," I said in Spanish, except for the word "metro."

Dr. Bolton frowned.

"Sorry. I don't speak Spanish."

"You don't speak Spanish?'

"No."

I channeled Antonia and released a string of Spanish expletives at the ceiling, mindful to sound carefree and confident, agreeable and nonthreatening as I called the good doctor an arrogant brainwashed whore worthy of my 9mm stuck up her ass.

"Eres culpabale de todo lo que acusas a los demás." You are guilty of everything you accuse everyone else of.

"Express yourself in English, Colton."

I fluttered my eyes at her patronizing tone.

"*Metro* is English. As in a meticulously groomed and dressed metropolitan. *Caimán negro* is black alligator." I stretched out my arms, as if awaiting an embrace. "I'm a metro negro alligator."

CHAPTER 18

NEW DISCOVERY

I'm a white supremacist."

Michelle giggled.

"Sounds kinky."

"Will you be my slave-girl?"

"If you let me tie you up after…"

Michelle's giggles devolved into choppy FaceTime sneers and jeers when I related my recent interlude with Mr. Bart and brought her up to speed on my evolving conflict with the state.

I had connected with Mr. Bart on Zoom shortly after my last meeting with Dr. Bolton.

"I don't think they ever read me my rights, much less in the car."

"It's your word against theirs, Colton," Mr. Bart said.

"And they're the ones who are lying."

"Failure to read a person their rights when arrested does not automatically result in the dismissal of charges. The facts of the case do not rely on when, or whether or not, you were read your rights."

"Which facts? The fact that I did not incite a riot because there was no riot?"

"And your guilt or innocence does not hinge on whether or not a riot was actually prevented. The state contends, and is prepared to prove, that your actions on that day in May constitute intent as specified in California Penal Code 404.6 PC."

I was familiar with the Code. It helped me characterize every "protest" I'd personally witnessed these past couple of months and the vast majority of nationwide demonstrations I'd seen on television and the Web throughout the summer:

Every person who with the intent to cause a riot does an act or engages in conduct that urges a riot, or urges others to commit acts of force or violence, or the burning or destroying of property, and at a time and place and under circumstances that produce a clear and present and immediate danger of acts of force or violence or the burning or destroying of property, is guilty of incitement to riot.

"How can they hope to prove my intent to cause a riot and sentence me to three years in prison when there was no immediate danger of acts of violence or the destruction of property?"

"You presented a health hazard due to COVID."

"We've gone over this. No way they can prove—"

"But now," Mr. Bart intervened, "the prosecution also contends that your past and present behavior, your state of mind constituted and continues to constitute a clear and present danger and that you objectively desired a specific result to follow your actions in Malibu—a riot."

I pinched the bridge of my nose and closed my eyes.

"Objectively?"

"That's the state's contention."

I cradled my chin in a hand, elbow planted on a knee, and stared sideways at Princess in her spot on the loveseat sofa adjacent me.

"All the evidence," she said.

"You mean they have new evidence?" I asked Princess.

Mr. Bart replied, "They think they do. Yes."

I looked at him askance.

"What do you mean they *think* they do? You talkin' about the viral video that preceded the doxing?"

"Along with expert testimony."

"Expert? Who, what expert?"

Mr. Bart's phone pinged. He retrieved it from his desktop and thumbed the screen.

"I have another meeting to attend, Colton," he said. "But I expect new discovery from the state any time now. I'll have my secretary forward it to you."

Upon reading the new discovery my suspicions were confirmed: Neither Mr. Bart nor Dr. Bolton were bound to aid in my defense but fuck me over.

CHAPTER 19

ANTONIA

Michelle and I got into a squabble over my BLM shirt. At first she said she didn't like the colors, then admitted that my intentions behind wearing the shirt were what bothered her.

"What do you mean it helps you blend in?"

"It helps disguise my motives when recording their riots."

"You've been doxed, Colton. They know who you are."

"But between a pandemic mask and the shirt, I'm disguised."

"No, you're not. Not anymore. And at this point you have plenty of video evidence at your disposal. I think you're just looking for trouble."

Maybe so, but I didn't admit as much to Michelle. Told her I'd burn the shirt when we signed off FaceTime, which was indeed my intention. I didn't need it anymore, had no further desire to blend in with the mobs or disguise myself, or hide at all. Tortuous routs in and out of my neighborhood and apartment complex to avoid bloodshed were out. It was time to stop living in fear and confront the enemy head on.

If they accosted me or threatened me in any way anywhere around my home, I'd start shooting. But the galvanized zombies had disappeared from my neighborhood, for the time being, and I opted to leave my 9mm in its hiding place at my apartment rather than fall into a state-sponsored trap by traveling with it and getting busted as a felon in possession of a firearm before I even had a chance to use it. I always carried my spring-loaded Browning pocketknife though…and had placed an eighteen-inch wrecking bar under the seat of my car for easy retrieval.

"Ultimately," I told Antonia, "force of arms will be the only way to stop them."

Edna said, "Or you can simply watch as they eventually devour their own."

I'd dropped by Antonia's place for an afternoon chat and to check up on Edna, my first visit with either of them since we'd been doxed. Edna's speech now slurred a little, but her palsied grimace so evident on the evening we were doxed had all but dissipated. Antonia was taking time off work—a morning or afternoon—to care for her mother. Edna tired far more easily than she had before enduring abuse at the hands of the mob, and while her mental capacity didn't appear to have declined too much, her hands shook, her teacup trembling as she brought it to her lips.

Edna had suffered another stroke and had spent twenty hours in the hospital under observation. COVID restrictions prevented Antonia from visiting her mother in the hospital, and she was still seething over it when I spoke to her on the phone several days later:

"Marauding social-justice warriors are allowed, even encouraged to loot and set fire to cities and I can't visit my mother in the hospital? What a bunch of hypocritical political bullcrap."

Our visit together this afternoon began with idle pleasantries followed by my remark that Edna looked good. She certainly looked better than she did when I'd last seen her, perspiring on the couch, palsied and disoriented.

Edna always impressed me with her acuity and regal yet accommodating bearing. She took pride in herself and despite her stroke at the hands of brutal, mindless galvanized zombies who knew exactly what they were doing as they victimized her and deserved to have their brains exploded by bazookas, she'd taken the time to beautify herself—maybe with Antonia's help at this stage—and I appreciated the effort and didn't think it was due to my visit. My compliment on her appearance—eyeliner, a splash of makeup, her grayish hair done in a layered bob—was sincere. Even her nails were manicured. She raised a hand to the scar on my neck, below my right ear, and thanked me again for "rescuing" her. I flushed, and told her it was nothing, that I'd do it a million times over, but maybe bring a weapon next time. She gave me a crooked smile and knowing nod that allowed for more direct discussion on the topic.

I repeated her words, "Devour their own," reminded of Charlie's reference to Jacobins—the primary movers behind the reign of terror during the French revolution—and some literature Uncle Steven had sent me.

Edna set her tea down and reclined on the couch.

"Por Dios. Son tan voraces. Insaciables…" They're so voracious. Insatiable.

"But they haven't been back since?" I asked Antonia.

"Not here, no." Antonia had mentioned to me over the phone that Manny and his primos continued to confront vestiges of them at Nuestro American Hardware. And shortly after Edna's stroke, Antonia paid police a personal visit to report the nasty, threatening texts, phone calls, and tweets she was receiving.

When Antonia called me and relayed the results of her visit with police, I imagined her comportment at the station—her charms dissolving into hushed sobs of pleading outrage that registered sharp in my ear pressed against my phone:

"Those barbaric terrorists gave my mother a stroke for Christ's sake. And cyberstalking is a crime, but looks like police won't put forth the effort to trace the bullies until they have a dead body on their hands...*pinches putos*..."

Edna said, "Los matones no han vuelto, gracias a Dios." The bullies haven't returned, thank God.

Antonia released a frustrated breath.

"My Twitter account and Facebook page were cancelled."

"Because you've been doxed? That doesn't make sense. The doxers are the ones who need to be cancelled."

Antonia lifted her palms and deadpanned me, her twisted smirk sparking a flare of comprehension in my brain.

Lemme guess," I said. "Your freedom of speech is offensive and a threat to freedom of speech."

Antonia sniggered, "I suppose so. Your video I posted of the BLM mob outside my house and my traumatized mother must be hate speech, while China's Chairman Xi, Farrakhan, Antifa, the Taliban, BLM and woke hate of America all get a pass. Since

Facebook and Twitter not only own the platform and soapbox but the public square as well, they can—"

Edna distracted her with a heavy sigh and head list.

"Vamos a cama, Ma?"

Edna sat up and sighed once more. Antonia helped her off the couch and into the adjoining bedroom. I nursed my tea and waited patiently.

"She needs naps every day," Antonia said upon return. Her pregnancy was showing, delineated by her rainbow striped body-con dress and a slackened pace. She took her mother's place to my right on the L-shaped sectional couch. Antonia had her blond-streaked hair tied back in a ponytail, her oval features creased by fatigue. She stared down the bridge of her pixie nose at her tea, her hazel eyes retaining a remote flame through a weary expression.

"I could use something stronger than tea," she said. "But I'm pregnant."

"So I see."

"You like a beer?"

"I been cutting back. Part of a new training program."

Antonia appraised my figure and cut me an approving smile.

"So you're preparing to do something other than apologize."

"Why the hell would I apologize?"

"That's what these dictatorial pricks on Facebook and Twitter...the woke cancel culture always demands of those who have or ever in their lives violated their speech or comportment edicts."

"That what they expect you to do, apologize?"

Antonia took a quick sip of tea.

"Fat chance, like paying the bastards to kill my mother. Never pays to apologize to bullies. You ever seen how those pitiful celebrities and students and journalists look apologizing to their cancel-culture masters?"

I opened my mouth to speak but Antonia answered her own question.

"Like hostages," she said. "Whipped dogs…"

"Cowering wimps," I added, recalling a few I'd seen grovel to woke cancel-culture tyrants on social media and television. "Terrified of being labeled racist by a league of racists and their vigilante justice. Goddamn pussies."

Antonia shifted in her seat, hand to her rounded belly, a twinge of distress contorting her expression.

"The baby kicking?" I said.

"Should be. I…" Antonia shook her head, eyes downcast.

I placed a hand on her arm.

"You okay?"

She lifted her gaze to me, her voice distant.

"I suffered some unusual discomfort after."

"You mean from your slip and fall out on the lawn? When we saved Edna from the mob?"

Antonia slouched, elbows on her knees, and pursed her lips. She had a heart-shaped mouth when her lips weren't pressed between her teeth, and it flickered at the corners, dimpling her chin with emotion.

"I"—a hiccup—"think so."

I held her gaze, a glistening gaze, pained yet indefatigable.

"Anything serious?" I asked.

"Doctor doesn't think so. I have another appointment next week."

Antonia reclined on the couch, assuming the position her mother held moments ago. Her chest heaved with a deep breath.

"You know," she said, "you may be right. They might only be defeated by force of arms…"

CHAPTER 20

MCCARTHY

I'd been radicalized. I used to wake up in the morning delusional, filled with false hopes, envisioning a new day, a new year, a new era. These past months had been but a bad dream and I would soon regain my life as an entrepreneur, marry Michelle, and live happily ever after. Well, that new era had finally arrived, but not in the form I'd imagined.

Princess recognized my radicalization as a natural defense mechanism.

"You're under attack," she said, "economically, physically and mentally. It's only natural for you to feel the need to defend yourself."

"At this point, my best defense is an offense. It's time to take the battle to the enemy. And It's not all about me but people like Antonia, Manny and Edna as well, not to mention the culture and precepts expressed in the nation's founding documents and Bill of Rights."

"You looking to defend yourself or become some kind of martyr?"

Good question.

"This is war," I said, and borrowed from General Patton: "No bastard ever won a war by dying for his cause but by making the other poor bastard die for his cause."

"Sounds good. But how can you possibly kill them all?"

"One by one."

"if you leave a blood trail, you will die for your cause…"

A key point. The law protected the enemy, my tormentors, allowed them unalienable rights even as they destroyed mine and the lives and rights of millions of others. If I was caught killing them, I'd find myself on death row. Like a sniper in warfare, I had to strike without leaving a blood trail. But unlike a sniper, I was not an expert marksman; and for a convicted felon, obtaining a high-powered rifle could be tricky…

Manny might be able to find me one…

No. Assuming the role of American Sniper and dispatching my targets from a quarter-mile away was out of the question, mostly because I didn't have confidence in my marksmanship. I could pick off a buck at seventy-five yards but anything farther than that was a dubious proposition. And who were my targets? Those galvanized zombies for one, especially any doxer lingering in the valley and at Nuestro American Hardware.

Contrary to the conclusions represented in the state's new discovery and supported by Dr. Bolton's Critical Race Theory, my radicalization and offensive had nothing to do with white supremacy. This was a matter of self-preservation, not aggression stemming from a sense of racial superiority, white supremacy, or "white fragility" and white rage. I didn't give a shit what color the enemy was, be it Dr. Bolton, the prosecution, Mr. Bart, BLM-Antifa leadership, oligarchs and political hacks, or galvanized zombies. Hell, I didn't care what color I was, though I did self-identify as a metro caimán negro. And caimanes negros are killers. Hunters and killers.

Dr. Bolton would've pointed to my denial of racism as behind my radicalization as proof of my inherent or internalized racism. Dr. Bolton could point to most anything, everything, and call it a result of racism, caused by racism, evidence of structural and inherent racism, or outright racism; and like Charlie had mentioned to me during one of my visits to his place, "If everything is racist, nothing is racist."

"Result, result, result...cause, cause, cause. Racism is the cause of everything...God is the cause of everything. The blue genie in my closet is the cause of everything. Not an explanation, no, no, no. But it is a mindless, empirically meaningless answer to every question..."

"You have a blue genie in your closet, Charlie?"

"Sometimes..."

They'd been getting some more publicity lately, those maniacal undead motherfuckers. Two sheriffs were ambushed in Compton, shot in the face, and throngs of galvanized zombies blocked the entrance to the Lynwood emergency hospital to cause mayhem and demand they "fucking die." When I saw the display on the news, I did have a desire to drive to Lynwood and plaster their brains with my 4Runner, but I hadn't been thoroughly radicalized yet; a trip all the way to Lynwood to smashup my car and take out galvanized zombies did not strike me as a sensible plan of action. And my 4Runner would leave a blood trail.

I was thoroughly radicalized now though. It wasn't my last meeting with Antonia that had finally done it, or those galvanized zombies at the Lynwood emergency hospital. Each had an effect upon my radicalization but the state and its obtuse intransigence and obsession with prosecuting me for a crime I did not commit but BLM-Antifa social-justice warriors routinely got away with played a large, active role in making me a killer, as did Dr. Bolton and Mr. Bart's collusion with the state, Dr. Bolton's Critical Race Theory and the assumption that I was racist, the galvanized zombies out to devour me, and those dumb-shit politicians, media talking heads, and moronic social-justice spokespeople on TV who continued to justify BLM-Antifa and galvanized zombie aggression as legitimate peaceful protest. All were part of a grand conspiracy to take over the nation and played key roles in my ultimate radicalization. Some politicians even called Antifa a "myth," proof that they were the delusional ones, not me; delusional or, more likely, attempting to coverup the conspiracy they were managing, a conspiracy and coverup facilitated by all-too-convenient COVID lockdowns—Chinese COVID Virus lockdowns that served to isolate and silence all but the activists and rioters and zombies allowed free reign to devour me and millions of others.

A wished I spoke Mandarin and could afford plastic surgery to blend in and kill those mainland Chinese hijos de la gran puta madre. All 1.4 billion of them. They were the ones who started all this, with their world-conquest obsessions and COVID labs.

And they had American conspirators on their side. It was obvious! Nike, Coca Cola, Comcast, Facebook, Google, Microsoft, the L.A. Times, New York Times, politicians, Bank of America, Apple, Amazon, AT&T, the NBA, NFL, MLB, NBC, CBS, Twitter, Disney, the National Institutes of Health, CDC, WHO…the International Olympic Committee… All profited from their ties to China, remained silent in the face of the Chinese Communist Party's atrocities and enslavement of millions, often lauded China and parroted woke and Chinese vilification of the United States, and then virtue signaled with donations to woke outfits like BLM to obfuscate their support for China's genocidal dictatorship.

Charlie had the list, an endless list of what amounted to Chinese proxies—American slave holders. That's what they were. Every NBA player and team owner, every political hack, every manufacturer or Big Tech media and corporate oligarch CEO and employee who had any ties at all to China were nothing more than Simon Legrees acting in concert with China's totalitarian regime to torture and kill me and dominate the lives of every person on earth.

A Chinese inspired conspiracy, aided and abetted by Americans, to install a totalitarian new world order. That's what it was—a conspiracy. Definitely a conspiracy.

I'd quit my job teaching English online to Chinese kids and preparing them for world conquest, opting instead to teach South Korean and Japanese kids for a different company that paid about the same yet distanced me from the Chinese aggressor…

Washington, Jefferson, Madison, Adams…all risked their fortunes and lives against all odds to create a constitutional republic, and the democracy they established was now rife with cowardly oligarchs, politicians, and bureaucrats hungering to sacrifice it all to make a buck and Chinese yuan.

Antonia was right when she said I might be right. The only way to defeat the woke cancel-culture and zombie enemy and their corporate-political allies was by force of arms. And I'd make the start. One by one.

The totality of it all, the aggregate, is what forced me to face the truth and become radicalized. I was under attack, plain and simple, the conspiracy against me clear, and I embraced my radicalization and focused it, determined to use it as a tool to strike back at the enemy. Aliens were hard to identify out in the unreal world, which figured. Aliens could shapeshift; yet classifying everyone (or every*thing*) conspiring against me as an alien could make me paranoid and lead to feelings of helplessness. Aliens held unfathomable technological advantages and were difficult if not impossible to kill. And not everyone conspiring against me was an alien anyhow. Galvanized zombies, for example, were easy to kill. Aside from aliens, political machinations, Big Tech media, corporatists, and weaponized radio frequencies (alien radio frequencies?) resulting in RF enigma syndrome, a brain tumor, OCD, and water on the brain, many of the dark forces aligned against me—galvanized zombies, social-justice warriors, the state's legal lackeys—were not so dark at all. I could see them, identify them and find them, and get close enough to kill them. Just had to come up with a modus operandi that would not leave a blood trail.

Jack the Ripper and the Zodiac Killer. I thought about them, again, as I drove to Nuestro American Hardware early one

Saturday evening before closing time. Two examples of serial killers able to get away with their crimes. Jack used a knife, a weapon Zodiac generally eschewed in favor of a pistol. Both weapons were used in close proximity to their victims, although Zodiac's pistol allowed him to keep some distance. And contrary to Zodiac, Jack was a stalker, targeting the prostitutes he killed before striking. Zodiac did stakeout certain locations, like a lover's lane, but in general his homicides appeared more random than Jack's. And Zodiac taunted police with phone calls and cypher-laced letters after his kills while Jack never gave himself away in the least. The modus operandi of both killers retained an indispensable talent to facilitate escape: the ability to strike without detection and then completely disassociate themselves from the murder, blend in with associates, family, coworkers, and the public as they went about their daily lives.

Given computer-age forensic advancements, particularly DNA forensics, a knife seemed an inadequate weapon when it came to avoiding capture. My Browning could easily penetrate a zombie temple or brainstem, but I'd have to get close, real close to ensure death. I was bound to leave some DNA behind. My baseball bat was a lovely weapon. Gory and effective. And it would allow me to keep my distance as I pulverized zombie brains. But a bat would be difficult to conceal both before and after the kill.

That left one option: my 9mm.

Like Jack stalking prostitutes, I had specific targets, and my preferred weapon would be Zodiac's: a pistol.

I parked my car a couple blocks away from Nuestro American Hardware, poised to stalk any vestiges of the galvanized zombie doxers I might find there. The days were noticeably shorter now, a scent of autumn in the air, the setting sun reluctant to surrender its heat to a change in seasons. I fantasized as I walked, imagining BLM-Antifa zombie brains splattered on sidewalks, in hallways and bedrooms. And the media furor after my kills: "A serial killer is targeting peaceful activists!"

Peaceful my ass. Dozens had been killed already due to those "activists," this summer's BLM-Antifa riots directly responsible for more deaths of black men alone than police had killed during arrests all of last year. And few politicians or anyone in the main-stream media seemed to take note or care; all were either in favor of the anarchy as a method to achieve political ends or afraid of being labeled racist, petrified to the point of allowing plunder, arson and murder at the expense of law-abiding citizens too cowed to make a stand themselves. Well, I'd take a stand, and relished images of zombie activists and their leadership cowering in their caves and homes, fearing for their lives and a serial killer targeting them; this was but part of the restitution they'd have to pay for the lives they relentlessly destroyed.

I planted myself at the edge of the office building across the street and kitty-corner from Nuestro American Hardware. From mid-March through June and into July, these streets and side-walks were nearly deserted. Things had picked up a bit as folks struggled to regain a semblance of normalcy within unremitting pandemic restrictions. Cars were lined up at red lights and pe-destrians milled about, most wearing pandemic masks. I wore a black pandemic mask, blue cargo shorts, running shoes, and a flowing gray collared shirt—untucked to conceal the Glock 9mm tucked under my waistband at the small of my back.

Jaime McCarthy guarded the door to Nuestro American Hardware, one of Manny's primos who was actually an amigo. I recognized him despite his pandemic mask. A strapping young man who'd been a customer of mine at Fisherman's Shore Bait and Tackle, and we'd fished together once on a boat I charted as part of my business. Jaime was the product of a mulatta Columbian mother and Irish American father, affording him handsome chiseled features, a rugged nose, and a natural complexion darker than my Indian tan.

Jaimie and I shared a tragic past. Both our mothers had died of breast cancer, his when he was nine-years old. Jaime's father cared for his wife while raising three young children, and the older Jaime got the more he admired and respected his father and what he'd gone through.

"The older I get, the more I appreciate him," Jaime had confided.

I didn't have children but had seen the ravages of cancer and could imagine the struggles Jaime's father must have endured, the pain and anguish no drug could alleviate.

According to Critical Race Theory (CRT), Jaime's white father was the privileged oppressor, his mulatta mother a victim of the white oppressor and his "psycho-existential" mania—one of a multitude of superficial, absurd, destructive, brutal, empirically meaningless, noncausal and nonpredictive premises of CRT I might discuss with Jaime some time.

Thanks to Dr. Bolton, as well as Uncle Steven's emailed docs, I'd studied up on CRT—another dark force that had contributed to my radicalization—and fumed over it now while observing Jaime. Like so much scholastic bullshit, CRT claimed to have science on its side but was really just a bunch of psychobabble designed by elites to divide and conquer the masses, devious totalitarian elites and academics who indoctrinated youth and had direct ties to BLM-Antifa, the galvanized zombies, and China.

China was a huge contributor to the politicalization of U.S. academia, with their Confucious Institutes, Chinese Scholarship Council, and their billions of dollars donated to universities in gifts and contracts. After Nuestro American Hardware, I'd stalk USC and UCLA college campuses to target the academic elite dedicated to destroying my life, the entire country, yet had never created a damn thing in their own lives apart from communist youth.

Jaime spoke Spanish and English growing up, had majored in Spanish and English in high school and community college, and now taught English as a Second Language to augment his construction work with Manny's real primos. He also taught civics to those seeking to become U.S. citizens. I held no advantage over him when it came to citing the Bill of Rights, and his bright chestnut eyes and affable smile belied a brawny figure you wouldn't want to tangle with. A shade under six-feet tall, Jaime had been an All City wrestler at Birmingham High in Van Nuys, but a handful of years ago.

Along with his sky-blue pandemic mask, Jaime wore Levis, work boots, and a plaid shirt, sleeves rolled up at the elbows. At first glance you might think he was loitering, but he waved to passing pedestrians and opened the door for two customers as I watched, screened by the corner of the office building across the street. Jaime's role was not easy to discern for those who were not in the know. He stood alone outside the entrance to Nuestro American Hardware but had been part of concerted effort to thwart picketing doxers looking to shut down the "racist" hardware store. I wasn't sure if Manny continued to post guards with shotguns after closing time, but Antonia had informed me of a daytime strategy that, by the tranquil looks of things right now, appeared to have worked some magic.

"It's really quite simple," Antonia had told me. "These cancel-culture-BLM-intersectionality assholes are a bunch of hypocrites and are guilty of everything they accuse us of. And I'm convinced that individually they're cowards at heart. When confronted with their own racism and bigotry they'll backdown."

"Or intensify their attacks," I said.

"Maybe. We'll see. But gathering dark-skinned Latinos together to shout 'racist' right back at them seems to have lessened their intensity."

"Just a matter of time before they label Manny and his primos race traitors and are back with a vengeance."

That's what I was counting on, the reason I was here. I expected some kind of confrontation and, as the galvanized zombie doxers practiced their specialty, I'd pick out one or two to stalk and kill.

As usual, they arrived in a group. A small group of five males that didn't exactly constitute a mob but was sufficient in numbers to cause trouble. The zombies appeared like specters at dusk, their jackbooted strides benighted and imperious, and I noted that one was female, shorter than the others and with a bustline hard to conceal. They were dressed in black with smatterings of red and white BLM insignias, three in hoodies and one with cardboard signs tucked under an arm. The zombie gang crossed the intersection opposite me on their way to Nuestro American hardware, their faces concealed behind pandemic-riot masks.

Jaime marked them as quickly as I did, was on his cell phone and eying them while they were in the crosswalk. I picked out the largest one as a potential target, aching to bash the brain of a big galvanized zombie, one with a cranium the size of a watermelon. I reminded myself that I'd be using bullets, not a baseball bat, and that the leader of the pack should be my preferred target, not the biggest, unless the biggest zombie was also the leader. He didn't look to be. He walked tall in the middle of the pack—a couple inches taller than me—and tilted his head to defer and ask a question of the female zombie behind him, an attitude inconsistent with leadership. She pointed dead ahead, indicating the hardware store, and advanced to the head of her troops in a posture of command. I focused on her and her red bandana. A couple of the others wore red bandanas as well but hers had more black in it, distinguishing markings I could pick out in a crowd.

Three customers exited Nuestro American Hardware, two with bags of goods. Three of Manny's primos followed, shut the door with authority, and posted themselves astride Jaime.

This is gonna be good...

The curb along the front of the store was a loading zone, off-street parking in the back. The loading zone remained clear and three of the zombies stationed themselves there and held up cardboard signs, their backs to me across the street. The signs fluttered, revealing they were two-sided, the words I could read from the rear presumably mirrored by those in the front:

Say No to Racism

Cancel Racism

Racists Work Here

Much like when I recorded the galvanized zombies outside Antonia's home, I wondered again what possessed these undead scumbags. Did they sit around all day with nothing better to do than find racism in everything? What other country on the face of the planet could possibly afford them such a luxury? They'd found their utopia, a place where they could wallow in their endless search for racism…and then hunt and destroy their perceived enemies. Hunt and kill…

That's what these galvanized zombies were doing—hunting and killing—and the hunters would soon become the hunted.

Jaime and his primos were unmoved, arms crossed as they guarded the entrance to Nuestro American Hardware. I couldn't quite discern her words at this distance, but the female zombie was trying to make some kind of point, her index finger pointed at Jaime as she railed about something or other. When the zombies finally abandoned their vindictive demonstration, she would be my target. A bullet to the brain would present her, all of them, with the utopia they deserved.

Most pedestrians gave the zombies a wide birth, yet a handful did pause in curiosity and to witness the brewing confrontation. The zombies began to chant "racist, racist," and the scene took on a surreal quality, the figures, signs and chants blending together under the scattered light of streetlamps to form a singular organism—a blob that ebbed and flowed and searched for sustenance. I was screened by the corner of the office building, biding my time, conscious to remain undiscovered. If I was marked, I could be fingered as a potential suspect in a zombie killing. Neither Jack nor Zodiac were ever identified as they targeted their victims, and I couldn't afford to be either. My plan depended on concealing myself, my identity, until I struck.

A blithe laconic voice echoed in my ears from behind my head:

"Marvelous bastards, those activists, aren't they? McCarthy should be proud."

I stiffened and held my breath. I recognized the voice, but did he recognize me, or was he offering idle chat to the back of an unknown pedestrian?

"Ho-ha ha. McCarthy couldn't have figured on something like this, but he might be proud to see improvements in his tactics utilized by descendants of those he obsessed over and tried to ruin. Ho-ha ha...history certainly has a funny way of turning itself on its head, even as it repeats itself."

I'd been made, marked. Even Ned wouldn't prattle on like that if he didn't know who I was. He knew me well enough to recognize my stature and physique, my shorts, running shoes...and the back of my head. I grumbled inwardly and turned to him, my plans for the evening shattered now that I'd been identified as present at this zombie demonstration.

"Working late tonight, Ned, or did you come to see Jaime McCarthy?"

"Jaime McCarthy?" He looked past me, at the demonstration across the street. "Is there a Jaime McCarthy out there? That would be ironic. Ho-ha ha, ironic indeed. Is he related to Joseph?"

"I don't know. Never met his father or—"

"Joseph died well over a half-century ago, and only left a daughter, so I doubt your friend Jaime is related to him."

My head and thoughts were spinning, had been torn from a specific goal and were now in rebellion against Ned, an intruder who'd spoiled my flawless strategy to strike back at the enemy. Yet I had to play along with Ned, act natural and not give myself away as a zombie killer on the hunt.

"Jaime is closer to Manny than he is to me. He's out there guarding the store right now… Who's Joseph?"

"I always thought you a well-educated man, Colton. Have the lockdowns clouded your brain? Certainly you recall learning something about the McCarthyism of the early fifties…"

The spinning tempest clouding my brain stabilized for a second. I did recall learning about Senator Joseph McCarthy and McCarthyism—the practice of making unsubstantiated accusations of subversion and treason and communism, and then blacklisting enemies, preventing them from working or earning a living. Yet I couldn't quite fathom Ned's reference to Joseph McCarthy; my mind strained in rebellion over his intrusion and this sudden turn of events and I missed the obvious congruences between McCarthyism, woke cancel culture, and the galvanized zombies I'd resolved to hunt and kill.

"I recall learning about McCarthyism," I said, careful to maintain my calm, "just not so sure what it has to do with these aggressive demonstrations by *marvelous bastards*."

Ned tugged on the pandemic mask slipping down his imperial Roman nose and raised an index finger up by his head, assuming the pose of a lawgiver.

"Are you now or have you ever been a racist or associated with racists?" He chuckled and shrugged, "Ho-ha ha. Substitute the word *racist* for *communist* and you have the perfect McCarthy attack on character."

I finally got it. Woke cancel culture did represent a contemporary form of McCarthyism, with one crucial exception that instantly came to me:

"Except woke cancel culture and their *marvelous bastards* don't ask the question, they simply find you guilty and attack."

Ned swung his pear-shaped figure to an interior rhythm. He was tieless, his pinstriped shirt flowing in eddies and tucked into his gray gabardine slacks.

"That's to be expected," he said, and pulled his meerschaum pipe from his breast pocket. "After all, they're totalitarian activists, not senators in a democracy. And McCarthy himself was eventually vilified and ruined for his tactics."

"Wish I could expect the same fate for woke cancel-culture tyrants."

"On the other hand, some totalitarian woke activists are indeed in congress. Ho-ha ha...maybe they will suffer McCarthy's fate."

Ned paused his swaying and knitted his beetled eyebrows at me, a strange glint revealed in his effusive dark eyes—a sagacious glint, like he knew something I didn't. He shifted his gaze and pointed the stem of his pipe over my shoulder. I swung around and focused on the demonstration. Jaime and primos had been joined by another primo, this one with a shotgun. He stood with military precision, at attention against the wall where we had scrubbed graffiti, the weapon gripped across his chest in a present-arms position. Zombie chants and clamor had subsided some, the shotgun and a new sign, a tall one leaning against the wall next to the armed primo, a plausible cause:

Immigrants Own This Store

Ned's voice reverberated in my ears, his words putting a new spin on the tempest in my head:

"They'll either suffer McCarthy's fate or get shot."

Was he referring to the shotgun?...or had he spotted a 9mm bulge beneath my shirt at the small of my back? I faced him, mindful of a surge of adrenalin convulsing my heart and pulsing my temples—a flight response. I had to get the hell outta here before Ned discovered my intentions, if he hadn't already.

He bounced his eyebrows at me, his eyes retaining that sagacious glint.

"I imagine it'd be difficult to shoot them all. There are many more where these marvelous bastards came from. Ho-ha ha…yes indeed, both inside and outside of congress. And shooting them would simply make them martyrs for their cause, unless, like your friend Jaime might, you could prove self-defense—protection of life and property."

The tempest in my brain began spinning out of control, on the verge of becoming a Category 5 hurricane. I shifted on my feet, and my eyeballs sucked back in their sockets, staring at Ned as if he himself was an alien, an alien who knew of my plans to go on a killing spree.

"You okay, Colton? You look as though you're about to have an intestinal emergency."

"That's it," I said. "When you gotta go you gotta go." I shouldered my way past him, quickstepping it back to my car like a Paso Fino colt, Ned's ensuing words a distant buzz within the storm in my head:

"You're welcome to use the bathroom in my office…"

CHAPTER 21

UNCLE STEVEN

If Ned was an alien, he had to be a friendly alien. First off, his accounting prowess had been tremendous in helping me through bankruptcy. Thanks to him I was able to squirrel away a good portion of money, far more money than the meager federal COVID relief I'd received and all the wages I'd earned thus far teaching English online. He'd also given me a heads-up about RF enigma syndrome; and then, last night, Ned jolted me into the realization that killing my enemies would simply make them martyrs for their cause...

Unless, somehow, I can kill them all at once...

I wasn't even a practiced marksman, much less capable of targeting and blowing up all my enemies at once. If I were at the helm of laser-guided missiles and a nuclear arsenal I wouldn't have been able to do it without killing millions upon millions of innocents like me, Charlie, Jaime, Manny, Antonia and Edna. Aliens could accomplish the feat, without nuclear weapons or conventional earthling weapons, but I couldn't, unless aliens allowed me use of their technology. If only I could identify friendly aliens with certainty, the ones who weren't out to colonize the planet and utilize woke cancel culture, China, political and corporate greed, COVID, statists, social-justice warriors and galvanized zombies to implement totalitarian rule, I might be able to collude with them to eliminate all the forces aligned against me and millions of others. But aliens didn't need my help. They could do whatever they wanted anyway, including shapeshift. I could divide them into friendlies and un-friendlies but honestly, I had no idea what their goals were or if and how they worked together, or if they'd swoop down today, scoop me up and rescue me from this madness...

My hand found the wetsuit zipper strap dangling down my backside. I zipped up and stared out over the ocean, the offshore breeze and early morning sun nuzzling the nape of my neck. The waves at Zuma Beach are famously powerful, thick and speedy with a heavy undertow. Every day is different, naturally, but it might be flat at Malibu while ten miles up the coast the sound of the waves pounding the long Zuma shoreline could be heard from the hilltops, the foamy white-water spray visible from the highway. It's a beach break, ideal for body surfing but boarders love it too, if it's not too big and brutally closing out from every direction. It was a little rough out there today but glassy, the breaking waves forming and holding their tubular shapes into thunderous closeouts. If an alien spacecraft were to emerge from the ocean depths and levitate into the sky, there'd be plenty of witnesses. The surfers paddling out or sitting on their boards in anticipation of a set would have a better view of the alien craft than the body whompers, their heads just above the surface. And from where I stood now on the shore I'd have a great view of it, would extend my arms and hands and cry out, "Take me! Take me!"

Was that really Ned I'd run into last night, or an alien shape-shifted to look and sound like Ned? Either way, it didn't matter. Ned himself mighta been an alien and it wouldn't have mattered to me. Professionally, he had proved himself more than competent, not only to me but as Antonia and Manny's accountant as well; and while he did have his amusing, at times exasperating personal quirks he was in no way malicious and seemed a good judge of people and character, to my mind had been the first to codify Charlie as "extremely high functioning..."

It didn't matter if the man who'd spoiled my plans last night was an alien who knew all about me and my intentions or if earthling Ned, draped in his wry ebullience, had unknowingly stumbled upon my intentions, or had seen the 9mm bulge beneath my shirt at the small of my back and accurately presumed my intentions. What mattered was that I trusted Ned—Ned the human or shapeshifted Ned. I couldn't trust him (or anyone) to keep my identity a secret while I went on a killing spree, but I did trust his judgment enough to credit his insights and devise another strategy to overcome and eliminate the enemy, a strategy that wouldn't make them martyrs for their cause.

What that strategy might entail I couldn't yet fathom. I remained radicalized, the killer instinct simmering within me, but had no clue how to proceed after ruling out the Jack and Zodiac modus operandi.

The pounding I took body whomping cleansed my mind, body, and soul. With the aid of my fins, I utilized all my tricks to have fun and keep from literally getting pounded and wounded, but I did take a decent beating. Exhilarating. Maybe not as exhilarating as escape in an alien spacecraft, but I'd been rejuvenated…and racked facedown on the sand till noon. I checked my email on my iPhone when I awoke. I'd been remiss in checking it the last twenty-four hours and there was a lot of junk, but one email did stand out. I responded right away:

See you there.

I had an afternoon date with Uncle Steven tomorrow. An early dinner date at 4:00.

"Another date with Dr. Bolton?" Princess said in reference to my pleated Tommy Bahama shorts, Meridian collared shirt, and Topsider shoes.

"Bolton's written her report. Think I'm done with her, and Mr. Bart as well."

Princess raised her voice an octave, "Really? Mr. Bart too?"

"I'll get another public defender if I have to. But I have a feeling that Uncle Steven has something to offer on the subject. He's stopped over in L.A. on his way to Miami. A business trip."

I'd sent Steven the state's new discovery and latest offer a week ago, the body of my email a single sentence:

I think I need a new attorney.

Nothing but the best for Steven; he had a suite at Shutters on the Beach, stumbling distance from the Santa Monica Pier. The hotel was operating at half-capacity due to COVID, the pier and its parking lot closed completely. As per Steven's instructions, I left my 4Runner with hotel valet parking and took the elevator to the top floor.

Steven pinged me with a text the moment I stepped out of the elevator:

make yourself at home. I'll arrive soon

Had he left the door to his room unlocked, or was someone there to greet me?

The swing latch held the door ajar. I let myself in and had a look around. Fireplace, stocked bar…dining table and chairs before lengthy French doors open to a balcony, patio furniture and an ocean view. Appointed furniture and a rattan coffee table occupied space adjacent the fireplace, a glass armoire and capacious entertainment center against the opposite wall. Elegant cream and red-floral throw rugs protected the wood floor, and a low scent of beeswax hung in the air, like the floor had been polished recently. Bedrooms and bathrooms likely adjoined the hall to my right, but I headed straight for the balcony to check out the view.

I pulled off my pandemic mask and savored the ocean air. In less than three hours the sun would set on the first day of autumn, 2020. I'd have liked to be happy to see summer go and welcome autumn, consider the equinox a harbinger of better times ahead, but my delusions of a new day—a new era—were, I now readily conceded, nothing but delusions, the friggin' zombie-infested statist-corporatist Chinese Virus cancel-culture woke-social-justice conspiracy as endless as the immaculate horizon before me. I resisted an impulse to hack and spit over the balcony's handrail, unwilling to sully the hotel's classy environs, and grumbled out loud:

"Gotta be a way to beat these motherfuckers…"

"There is, if you're referring to the prosecution."

I turned on my heels to the unfamiliar feminine voice and found an attractive middle-aged woman standing at the French doors, a glass of chardonnay in her hand.

I stammered, "Uh, yes… Excuse me… Yes, I am referring to the prosecution. Mostly."

Her chic white blouse complemented her smooth mocha skin, her arms taught but not particularly muscular. A tilt of her head and the amused smirk in her deep brown eyes disarmed me, relieved my embarrassment at the profanity she'd heard me utter. I toyed with the pandemic mask in my hands, uncertain if I should put it back on. She wasn't wearing one. She had a generous mouth—full lips painted the same rare shade of violet as her eyeshadow—and a dimpled chin beneath an inquisitive aquiline nose, her high cheek bones and almond-shaped eyes suggesting Asian and Native American descent, kind of like Michelle.

Her complexion was darker than Michelle's, and she'd lived longer, how much longer I couldn't be certain but she was not a woman self-conscious of her age, the character lines at the corners of her eyes and mouth candid beneath a minimal makeup look somewhere between shimmer and smokey.

"Would you like something to drink, Colton? A beer perhaps?"

"Okay," I replied rather lamely. The woman had caught me off guard. Considering Uncle Steven's penchant for magic tricks and anecdotes, I should have expected her—something like her—to greet me here, and the fact that she knew my name did not surprise me. Her poise was sublime, a commanding allure that she didn't flaunt, like a thespian aware of her charisma but holding it in reserve for the stage rather than giving a performance in a hotel room.

She gestured to the rattan and wooden patio furniture.

"Make yourself comfortable."

She made her way to the bar. She was of average height, her silver-black hair done in ringlets, and wore sensible office shoes, her knee-length navy-blue skirt hugging a figure that remained shapely, especially for a woman I judged to be well into her fifties. I took a seat on a cushioned wicker chair and kept a surreptitious eye on her, pouring a cold beer into a frosty mug at the bar inside the room. She knew about my troubles with the state's prosecution and had intimated that there was a way to beat the mother-fuckers. I surmised that Uncle Steven had enlisted her to aid in my defense. Was she an attorney? She looked as though she could play any role she chose, and play it well, but I couldn't imagine why she'd take an interest in me...unless...

What's her connection to Uncle Steven...?

She returned and presented my beer to me.

"Thank you." The beer was delicious. Dos Equis.

"You're welcome."

She placed her wine on the coffee table and sat opposite me, legs crossed at the ankles, hands folded over a knee. A pearl shine beautified her nails, the large diamond on her wedding finger matching her teardrop earrings.

I wanted to say something, ask her name, anything, but felt tongue tied and falling into her brown eyes as I looked at her.

"I'm Anselma," she said through a half-smile, "an old friend of Steven's."

She had a husky voice, not hoarse or notably deep but sultry and smiling, like she might release a throaty laugh at any moment.

"Pleased to meet you." I really was and raised my beer to her. We clinked glasses and drank.

I cleared my throat and found my voice.

"Appears you might know something about the state's case against me."

"A little something. Steven understands that much of the information you've allowed him to access is privileged."

She sipped from her wine and sat back in her chair. I willed my gaze to shift between her captivating eyes and the middle of her forehead, afraid her eyes would allow no escape if I stared into them too long.

"So you think there's a way to beat those...uh..."

"Motherfuckers." She grinned. A canny grin, sharp and white.

Somehow the profanity didn't sound so profane coming from her mouth. I chuckled and nodded. Once again she'd disarmed me, her plain speaking allowing for a sense of camaraderie between us.

"Seems there are a lot of them aligned against me, including my public defender."

"There doesn't need to be a conspiracy for there to be collusion. The collusion may be unintentional or inadvertent, often a result of cohesiveness in thought and action. People trained to think the same might end up working in sync to reach similar goals, whether or not they make the conscious, conspiratorial effort to do so."

"I see. Well, if that's the case, I need to go after the sonsabitches who train those MFs."

Anselma's chest heaved with a deep laugh, from the diaphragm. She had a full bustline, a slice of cleavage running its course up the lace V-neck of her blouse; I idly wondered if they were real.

"One step at a time, Colton," she chortled. "One step at a time."

"And the first step?"

As if on cue, the door to the hotel room swung open.

Anselma said, "To eat."

The door to the room was within my line of vision, the server's backside to me as he wheeled the meal cart over the threshold.

I said, "Don't they usually knock first?"

Anselma snickered, "Not this guy."

The server had a husky build and nimble feet, did a pirouette and skipped to the other end of the meal cart to push it rather than pull. He wore a black pandemic mask, his dapper gray suit appropriate attire for the manager of the hotel.

He was not the manager, seemed unsure of himself as he halted before the dining table, fidgeting on his feet.

Anselma said, "Out here is fine."

He wrestled with the meal cart's length and wheeled it around the table and chairs.

"Excusez moi," he said. "Sa nourriture."

Anselma replied in kind, "Merci beaucoup."

It had been a few years since I'd seen him, but I'd have recognized him in another five seconds despite the pandemic mask and his hotel-server routine. He wore his salt-and-pepper hair in an unfamiliar coif side-swiped over his widow's peak, and had gained a couple pounds or so, but the telltale scar cornering the right eyebrow of his steely blue eyes left no doubt—Uncle Steven.

"Nice theatrics," I said, and rose from my chair to greet my cousin who, due to our age difference, I'd referred to as uncle in my youth.

When I was four years old, Steven was sixteen, a mature sixteen. He could grow a full beard at fourteen and was a terror at middle linebacker against kids certain they were playing against a ringer from the L.A. Rams. By the time Steven graduated high school, most those kids had caught up to him in physical maturity, and in college he gave up football for a stellar academic career... and rugby. He played fly-half, a man who could run with the ball and marshal his team on the field. Uncle Steven was a rough customer, and extremely bright. You don't go from the Portland DA's office to high-priced corporate negotiator without having a lot on the ball upstairs. To me, Uncle Steven always seemed to have it all. Sure he worked hard for it, and he must have suffered setbacks I wasn't privy to; but he and his wife were grandparents now, both looking forward to Steven's early retirement. As usual, Uncle Steven's life was right on track... My life, on the other hand...

Uncle Steven raised a hand to me.

"Attendre, attendre," he said, and wheeled the cart astride the coffee table, leaving space for him to attend us.

My French was rusty but I recognized the word, the gesture easy to interpret. I resumed my seat and waited.

A white tablecloth draped the meal cart, a bottle of red wine, carafe of water, glasses and silverware on top. Steven opened the bottle of wine without flourish, let it breathe atop the meal cart, and laid out the glasses and silverware wrapped in napkins on the coffee table for Anselma and me.

"This how you plan to spend your retirement?" I said. "I can see you've practiced."

"Regardez."

He reached beneath the tablecloth into the meal cart and retrieved two dinner plates covered by stainless steel lids—cloches, a French word utilized in English that, I remembered, also meant "bells."

Steven placed our plates before us and removed the cloches with a "viola."

I stared incoherently at the food—kale for me, steak and lobster for Anselma.

Anselma said, "Parfaite," and laid her napkin over her lap.

"Parfaite for you maybe," I said, and stared up at Steven, standing between us at the coffee table. "In your email you told me to bring an appetite. My appetite for kale is severely limited."

"Ahhh… *Pardon, pardon…*"

Steven turned to the meal cart, retrieved two more covered plates from behind the tablecloth and set them on the table, one aside the steak and lobster, the other aside my kale.

This time he added a flourish while uncovering the food.

"Viola!"

Anselma gave him quick applause.

"You think of everything, Steven." She winked at me and drew up her fork. "Sauteed calamari. My favorite."

I frowned at the dinner plate beside my kale and hovered my nose over it—two shriveled shrimp smothered in something other than cocktail sauce. Probably ketchup.

"Is this some kinda joke?"

Steven poured me a half-glass of water. "Une blague? Non, non, non…" He filled Anselma's glass. She rolled her eyes in extasy and chewed her calamari.

Steven studied me, the blued steel in his eyes above his pandemic mask softened.

"Vous n'êtes pas satisfaits?"

"Am I satisfied?" I glanced at Anselma, her fork poised to spear more calamari. "The company's good…"

Anselma looked up at Steven. "Shall I share with him?"

Steven switched to English: "I'm afraid that wouldn't conform to the laws, *Madame*. But perhaps we can bend the laws."

He covered three of our plates with cloches, leaving the calamari uncovered for Anselma. Steven then pulled another plate from behind the cart's tablecloth, rested it in the palm of his left hand and extended it over the coffee table. He uncovered the food and held the plate there, over the table, to make sure Anselma and I got a good look at the steak and lobster.

"That more like it, Colton?" Anselma said.

I nodded. "I'm a fan of surf and turf."

Steven reset our dishes, placed the new plate before me, cloche back on top, and slipped and stumbled, catching himself on the edge of the coffee table. His smartphone tumbled out of his jacket's breast pocket to the tile decking beside my chair. I picked up the phone.

"Clumsy of me," he said.

I handed him his phone, and thought nothing of it, till I uncovered the food before me.

"What the fu—?"

More kale…or the kale originally served me instead of the surf and turf Steven had presented.

I eyed Steven suspiciously.

"That was quick. But you had to slip to pull it off. You must literally be slipping." I surveyed the three remaining covered plates on the table and made an instant calculation. Two had to be steak and lobster—Anselma's and the plate Steven had held out for us to see—the other my shriveled shrimp. I reached to uncover the plates, but Steven waved his hand over the cloches, interceding mine.

"Autorise moi."

"Be my guest."

I blanched as he uncovered the food: Anselma's steak and lobster and two more dishes of kale.

"Best to get rid of the shrimp," Steven said. "Even cocktail sauce couldn't have made it edible."

I chuckled, and would have laughed and applauded but, "I'm too hungry to laugh and applaud." My eyes narrowed on Anselma, relishing her calamari. "You his helper?"

Famulus," Steven clarified. "A magician's helper is called a famulus, and Anselma has much better things to do than practice that profession."

He set the bottle of wine on the table and flipped the tablecloth over the food cart and cloches. Food was in there, uncovered. A big bowl of salad, steak and lobster, and what appeared to be seared ahi.

"Voila," I said. "The shrimp has disappeared."

Steven loosened his tie and slid a whicker chair over to the table.

"Just an illusion, Colt." He placed the other two plates of kale before me. "A trick."

"*That,*" I said, finger pointed at the kale, "is not an illusion." I shifted my gaze between Steven and Anselma. "The theatre going on here looks like collusion to deliver me some kind of message, and this kale for my dinner is not an illusion."

"We can give you the steak and lobster," Steven said, "but then the ahi would have to go to Anselma, along with the rest of her food. Would you like the food to go, Anselma? I don't think you could possibly eat it all."

"Let's take a vote," Anselma suggested between bites of calamari.

Steven agreed. "Okay. All those in favor of allowing Colton his steak and lobster raise their hand."

The two of them were definitely colluding on something, some kind of farce or lesson or… I started to object, but Steven stripped off his pandemic mask and flashed me an encouraging grin through his square jaw, motioning me to raise my hand along with his.

I sighed and raised my hand.

Steven said, "Good." We lowered our hands. "All those opposed?"

Anselma raised hers.

"Really, Anselma?" I said, a twinge of disappointment tainting my voice.

"That makes it a tie," she replied. "We can vote again when I finish my calamari."

"A tie?" I blinked at Steven. "We're two to one in favor."

"Anselma gets two votes." He served himself salad with the ahi and sat down with us, fork in hand.

"This act of yours would be funny, if I wasn't so hungry."

Anselma tried to concentrate on her food but noted something in my tone—a hint of desperation—and broke character with a giggle.

"Now you've done it, Anselma," Steven said. "Colt will never take you seriously again." He smirked and shook his head at me. "She just can't control her emotions sometimes."

Anselma rose from her chair, swept up two plates of my kale— one on top of the other—and replaced them with her steak and lobster.

"Eat before it gets cold," she said, and returned the kale to the meal cart.

I dove into my food. Steven remarked, "Your charity is admirable, Anselma."

"Charity rarely tastes this good," I said.

Steven poured the wine, an equal portion for us all. Anselma retrieved the steak and lobster from the meal cart and resumed her seat.

"Sorry, Colton," she offered. "But your cousin is a fan of theatrics and metaphors."

Steven savored a bite of ahi.

"Goes to motives," he said. "Did you feel singled out, Colt?"

"No one else around to suffer through it." I dipped lobster in melted butter.

"That's equity," Anselma said. She stabbed a slice of fillet mignon to go with the calamari on her fork.

"Equity?"

Steven sipped from his wine.

"As distinct from equal opportunity. Anselma is black and you're the white oppressor. She's the oppressed and requires two votes to your one, along with your food, property, assets, tax dollars, bank dollars, and the elimination of academic standards...to make up for past and present injustices and allow for comprehensively equal economic and socio-political outcomes. And much of the population will be equal—a permanent, poorly educated underclass surviving on handouts and kale, and serving elites steak and lobster."

"For these purposes, I'm black," Anselma said. "My grandmother was Chinese. A political refugee."

I pointed my fork at Steven. "You're white. Why not sacrifice your food?"

"I'm different," Steven said. "As an elite member of the politburo and Race Czar, I make the laws." He raised his wine to me, "And profit from them, naturally..." He drank.

I tried the wine. Red and dry with a savory bouquet.

"This some kinda new philosophy, two wrongs make a right? And what's it got to do with me?"

"More like three, four...ten wrongs make a right," Anselma said, "or more. Never enough. And racist wrongs can only be righted by more racism...against whites, since they're born racist and have to pay for the sins—real or imagined—of their fathers. Glad I don't have to pay for Mao's and Xi's sins...or Mugabe's; they make Confederate slave holders look like saints... The concept of *equity* as a racialized socio-economic construct and remedy is a relatively recent phenomenon here in the States, bolstered by mostly white academic elites and parasitic white guilt, and it's infecting the fabric of the country, including the justice system… Damn government prosecutors have too much power as it is, imagine what they can do with *equity* in their arsenal."

"You have personal experience in a DA's office, Anselma?" I had a hunch she did, so she could aid in my defense. Why else would Steven invite her here?

"I received a helping hand up the ladder in Portland." She raised her glass of wine to Steven. "I have a private practice here in L.A. now."

They clinked their glasses together and drank…

Steven said, "No *equity* for you, Anselma?"

"Don't insult me. I worked my ass off, before and after I met you." Anselma brought her attention to me, her voice acquiring an eastern, soft-black accent. "Nothing wrong with having mentors, Colton. But there's no replacement for hard work. Throw equity and wokeness into the equation though and…my lord… the concept of hard work is disparaged as white racism and oppression." She leveled her attention at her food. "Even math is considered racist nowadays, as if blacks can't live up to standards and achieve in their own right…"

"I've always found math oppressive," I said. "And I'm white, so I don't think it has much to do with race."

"The corporatist-political powers that be," Steven rejoined, "the fascist powers that be—the marriage of government and corporate power—would love to treat us all, not just minorities, like needy children. But some of us prove more resistant than others to their machinations and propaganda. You've been singled out by the state, Colt...that's how it appears. Anselma would say there's unconscious collusion going on, a result of training and an equity mindset, but I wouldn't be surprised if there's an outright conspiracy. You probably feel the same."

I paused, a steak and lobster combo lingering on the fork below my chin.

"I do feel the same. But I'm a little surprised that you—"

"I've seen it," Steven interposed, "and experienced it."

Anselma stood from her chair and swept an accusatory finger over the two of us, her attractive features contorted in inexplicable fear and anger.

"You make me feel unsafe. Both of you! Now line up against the handrail here. It's time for a line-of-oppression exercise."

I was taken aback, flabbergasted, and dropped my fork onto my plate.

Steven said, "Not the line of oppression, Anselma. Not again."

Anselma's expression transformed into a blinking look of inquiry.

"Really? I thought you liked theatre."

"Now what's happening?" I said.

"Anselma loves theatre just as much as I do. Should see her in court."

"I'd enjoy that, long as she's on my side." I drank from my glass of wine.

Anselma sat down to her meal.

"I apologize," she said. "Just felt a sudden urge to reenact Orwell's Two Minute Hate with a demonstration of a corporate antiracism session, or a scholastic antiracism session."

"You coulda been a movie star, Anselma." I really meant it. She had the looks and talent for it. "Scared the hell outta me for a second there."

"And I could 'a been a Beatle," Steven said with a Liverpool accent. He played guitar and was an accomplished pianist. "I'll be playing more when I retire."

Anselma hummed, in reaction to the taste of her succulent lobster…or Steven's reference to retirement.

"Sure did pick a good time to retire, Steven." She dabbed her mouth with her napkin. "Beats the hell out of putting up with woke corporate-government inquisitions against *whiteness*."

Steven shrugged. "Just another control mechanism. Corporate pricks can virtue signal and acquiesce to their *infallible* woke constituents to make a buck…and have their lackeys berate me and white employees as much as they like during their antiracism sessions…doesn't affect me personally. I don't let it."

"That's 'cause you're one step away from retirement," Anselma said. "Others aren't so lucky, especially the grammar school kids next on the woke indoctrination agenda. Hope you give the corporate bastards hell before you leave."

"I have a few tricks up my sleeve."

Steven stripped off his suit jacket and rolled up his sleeves, to demonstrate he had nothing hidden up them. He reached behind my chair.

"Voila," he said, a photo the size of a playing card in his hand. He placed it next to my wine.

I slumped in my chair.

"Don't you ever tire of your tricks? I certainly do. Try thinking of others for a change."

"Whaddya think of her?"

I focused on the photo. Pretty girl. Blond. Ocean-green eyes. Bikini. Sexy curves.

"Hot," I said, and bit my tongue with a look at Anselma. She bounced her head in agreement, no offence taken.

Steven said, "Would you date her?"

I considered the question with a bite of steak.

"I might, but I'm engaged. Michelle's just as hot."

Anselma prodded me, "But you would date her, wouldn't you," more statement than question.

"He'd do her too," Steven said.

Anselma flipped her hand at him.

"All men are pigs."

Steven jutted his jaw at me. "What if I told you she's fifteen? Would you do her then?"

I stiffened and took a closer look at the girl in the picture.

"Fifteen? Fifteen going on twenty-five…"

Anselma said, "Girls do mature quickly. But she's still only fifteen."

"Who is she?"

"My niece," Steven said. "My wife's side of the family. A future supermodel." He leaned forward in his chair, blue eyes sharpened steel penetrating my befuddled gaze.

"What's the point?" I said.

Anselma leaned forward in her chair as well, her sultry voice dulling the daggers in Uncle Steven's glare.

"You know she's fifteen," she said, "but that doesn't mean you're not still attracted to her; you simply have to think one way and act another."

The daggers in Steven's eyes flared into laser beams.

"No more flying around shooting videos like a war correspondent. You have enough videos. You like catching the shitheads in action, and know how you feel about them, but you must dominate your emotions and act in a manner best to your self-interest."

"I haven't shot a video in quite a while…"

Prefer to bash their brains…

"We can beat the motherfuckers," Anselma said. "All of them, not just the state's prosecutors aligned against you. But you must enjoy the process, like a competition, and act in a manner that won't give us all away as killers."

"Metaphorically speaking," Steven was quick to add. He reposed in his chair, drank some wine, and seemed to swerve the subject: "You're an expert in the water, Colt, and an expert fisherman. What's a surfer's biggest fear, aside from the fear he must channel when faced with a giant wave?"

The question required some thought.

"I wouldn't call it a fear, exactly. More like a remote possibility that's always in the back of every water rat's mind, if he has any sense… A shark attack."

"And what ocean creature has no fear of sharks due to its superior agility and intelligence?"

That was an easy one.

"Dolphins or porpoise. Orcas too, and—"

Steven waived off my expanded answer.

"Orcas are part of the dolphin family. They never attack humans and have no fear of sharks, and you've little-to-no chance of running into them outside of extremely cold water… You're surrounded by sharks, Colt. Be a dolphin."

I slouched over my food, what remained of my steak and lobster, and brought a pensive hand to my forehead, my fingers massaging the frown creasing my brow.

Dolphins are a surfer's best friend, and hunters and killers as well…

I looked up at Anselma.

"Who are you?"

"A brilliant self-made attorney," Steven said. "The American dream incarnate."

Anselma accepted the complement without a hint of bashful unease.

"No other country on the face of the earth could have afforded my grandmother and her family such opportunity to succeed. And I know how to demonstrate my appreciation." She cut Steven a quick glance. "I'll accept your case. Frankly, Colton, your public defender looks as though he's on the take, and he represents all I despise within the justice system and diseased *wokeness*."

"As does Dr. Bolton," Steven said. "Dr. Bolton *IME*."

"What is that…*IME?*" I'd meant to look it up after reading Bolton's business card to Steven over the phone.

"Ignorant Morons Eternal," Steven said.

Anselma huffed. "Yes. But don't underestimate her kind, Colton. No doubt they're ignorant, but they're not stupid."

Steven polished off his ahi.

"She's ignorant and stupid. Kick her ass."

"You know her?" I asked Anselma.

"International Multicultural Education," she enunciated. "—IME. I know who she is."

"The only good thing about those kinds of Critical Race Theory degrees," Steven said, "—Multicultural Education, Diversity Studies, Environmental Justice Studies, Intersectional Social Justice—is that the graduates are horribly trained. They haven't learned how to think. Anselma tears them new assholes when she gets them on the stand."

"When I have the opportunity," Anselma confirmed. "It can be difficult though when the judge is on the take—a product of the same anti-American and anti-critical-thinking mindset. But your case won't come to trial, Colton…if you allow me to represent you…"

"I'd be honored," I said, and retreated into myself. Anselma represented a tremendous asset…yet…

"What about the others out to devour me, those not directly involved in my legal troubles?"

"Like who?" Steven said.

"Goddamn zombie doxers, for one."

Anselma arched her eyebrows at me.

"You've been doxed?"

"Me and some friends who own the hardware store next door to my business I was forced to close."

"Are the doxers responsible for shutting down your business?"

Steven knew the answer to that question: "No. The lockdowns did that."

"We have to be able to identify those who doxed you and show damages to go after them," Anselma said.

"They gave my friend's mother a stroke. They're rioters and terrorists, basically. And like the rioters and terrorists in Portland, L.A., Seattle...all they do is cause damage, and get away with it."

Anselma quickened her pace, "Are you sure the stroke wasn't caused by a preexisting condition? And do you know who the doxers are?"

"They caused her stroke and—"

"You may be right, Colton," she intervened, "but that can be difficult to prove in court. And who are they? Why did they go after you?"

"For removing BLM graffiti. According to them, we're all privileged white racists—"

Steven snorted. "That's original. The hubris of the infallible woke cancel culture."

I recalled the bum I'd nearly shot in the alleyway—*they all look the same...*

"And they all look the same, with their masks and clothing—black clothing, mostly. I don't know who they are. But they demonstrated outside my friends' hardware store last Saturday night. I should be able to get a license plate number from a vehicle if I follow them next time..."

Hunt them down and kill them.

"You need to show damages," Anselma reminded me. "Unfortunately, that means you have to wait until they actually accost you or destroy your property to be able to take legal action..."

I sagged in my chair and grumbled inwardly.

Best to get them first…

"They gave me this," I said, and pointed to the scar on my neck.

"That didn't happen this last Saturday," Steven observed. "Did they assault you?"

"Yes. Yes they did. I was rescuing my friend's mother from them outside her home."

"So what are the damages?" Steven said. "A few stitches?"

"And Edna's stroke."

"And you have friendly witnesses to the assault," Anselma inferred. "A video as well?"

"Not of the assault. No."

"And you can't identify your assailants," she stated flatly.

"No. They all…"

"Look the same," Steven said. "I'm afraid Anselma will need more specifics to go after the sonsabitches."

I regarded Anselma once more, sipping her wine.

"Who are you exactly? I mean, is a case like my defense against the state up your alley?"

"Everything's up Anselma's alley," Steven said. "Whatever, wherever, and whenever the hell she chooses."

Anselma took a knife and fork to her steak. Elegant and proper, and with the feeling of cutting a throat.

"I'll have the assistant DA buried in paperwork by Wednesday."

"And still have time for her ADF work," Steven added.

"ADF?"

"Battling the conspiracy," Steven advised, shrewd finger tapping his temple. "Alliance Defending Freedom…. All men are pigs, right Anselma?"

Uncle Steven had touched a nerve. Anselma pointed her knife at me. "Why aren't females transgendering and competing in men's and boy's sports?"

I was taken aback again and swallowed a last bite of lobster with effort. Our conversation had taken an odd turn.

Anselma answered her own question: "Because it's biologically untenable for them to have a chance at winning against maturing and matured, well-trained males. And the principal reason males supposedly transgender...or decide they're female...and then compete against girls and women is because they're gutless and incapable of winning blue ribbons and gold medals against male competition."

Steven said, "We're pigs, or pig-sharks...pig-dogs...pig-wolves... Pigs...the ones who aren't dolphins." He poured us more wine. "And the girls and women forced to compete against pigs in sports need legal assistance to ensure a level playing field, that they are competing against other girls and women—biological girls and women."

"They're *bullies*," Anselma emphasized, "—the males competing in girls' and women's sports, along with the entire woke cancel-culture creed and cults propagating nothing but lies...as if trans-women can get away with murder simply by declaring that the male DNA found at the crime scene cannot possibly identify them because they self-identify as female."

"The biology lie," Steven rejoined, "—*to define gender by chromosomes, DNA, and reproductive organs is inconsistent with science*—is a whopper, as big a whopper as the 1619 Project... and Critical Race Theory. Can't wait till you get the murder case,

Anselma, the knockout death blow from a trans-woman in the cage against a biological woman. You'll gain fame along with your fortune."

Anselma shook her head minutely.

"The breakout case probably won't go down that way. But women are abused, as usual, by men and every woman who goes along with this LBGTQ alphabet horse manure... And fame is a pain in the ass. I'll settle for a fortune." She lifted her chin to me. "But your case won't cost you personally, Colton. And I wager we'll have it wrapped up by the holidays..."

CHAPTER 22

MICHELLE

Tonight was a good night to go zombie hunting. Another demonstration in downtown L.A. would provide an opportunity to put into practice a new strategy, part of a grand masterplan I'd devised to strike the enemy before they struck me.

Anselma's admonition might have been lawfully sound, but no way in hell was I gonna sit on my hands and wait around for the zombie enemy to attack before taking action. Galvanized zombies, the entire woke cancel culture and their BLM-Antifa and political-corporatist-media allies were deadly, bloodthirsty and deadly. They had to be stopped before they devoured me and a great majority of the country.

I strived to know the enemy better and better but already knew them well. You gonna wait around until your house is torched by the killers and arsonists you know are preparing to burn you and your family alive before taking action? No way in hell. Kill first... like Brando said in *On the Waterfront*:

Wanna know my philosophy on life?.... Kill the cocksuckers before they kill you…

No sittin' around waiting for evidence or legal proof for me. Wait long enough and you, your family, pets and stuffed animals are dead.

Thanks to Anselma and Steven, my preoccupation with the state's trumped-up charges had been alleviated. Now I could focus my energy where it belonged: going on offense. Much like my Jack and Zodiac strategy, this new strategy required that I stakeout and stalk the enemy, yet unlike Jack and Zodiac I would not strike with alacrity an immediacy. I refused to sit on my hands in anticipation of a galvanized zombie attack, but nor would I kill without consideration of a grand masterplan that would not make martyrs of the enemy but still destroy and slaughter them.

My grand masterplan was an ultimate cure, my *raison d'être*, and had not simply sprung from nowhere but was a result of months of experience, gathering information, and writing— making lists and keeping notes. Investigative work remained before I could set my masterplan into motion, a piece of that work a strategy to hunt zombies—stake them out and stalk them—so I might learn their individual habits and continue to know the enemy better and better.

In a sense, I'd be surfing, swimming, hunting, and behaving like a dolphin rather than Jack and Zodiac, and tonight would be a good night to go zombie hunting…if not for Michelle—my other raison d'être.

Michelle had given me the news yesterday. Tremendous news. International travel restrictions had finally been eased and she'd booked the first flight possible back to the States and Los Angeles…due to arrive this evening.

We began stripping right away, starting with our pandemic masks outside the terminal. I asked her, "How was your flight?" but other than that our conversation revolved around "I love you" and "I missed you." It took us a half hour to get out of the parking lot, not due to traffic but our inability to keep our hands and lips off each other.

Like her black skirt, Michelle's legs were all silk. We held hands on the drive home but mine wandered to her knees and thighs while hers teased my chest, groin, and the back of my neck. I'd told her of my new attorney, Anselma, over the phone, and we touched on the subject once more without traipsing over every detail of my case. Those damn zombie doxers came up as well, but I brushed off the topic with assurances that they had disappeared from our neighborhood. I'd protect Michelle with my life but saw no reason to inject fear into our reunion with an admission of my fears…and my acquisition of a firearm.

We were all business upon entering our apartment and headed straight for the bedroom. The next day, Sunday, was spent in bed, for the most part, the sheets and air slick with the scent of sweat and sex. Jetlag overtook Michelle and she slept more than I did. I admired her while she slept—her long lashes and the gentil slope to her nose, nubile figure and the curve of her hips and back, her dark hair parted over a slender shoulder—and traced a finger over a scratch she'd marked on my shoulder, unable to follow its length over my back.

I was sore, but the penis has a mind all its own, a mind impervious to a bit of irritation. We made love…and fucked and sucked…in between naps, a bite or two to eat, and beer and water breaks. Conveniently enough, Michelle's jetlagged sleep schedule allowed us to bathe together before I began my Zoom English lessons at 4:30 Monday morning.

Michelle had work to do as well. She reminded me in Spanish while brushing her hair before the bathroom mirror.

"Tomorrow I go to the office to pick up computer equipment. We're scheduling appointments from home now due to the pandemic."

Michelle had a work permit and scheduled appointments in Spanish and English for a medical technology firm based in downtown L.A. and with an office here in the valley. She puckered her lips at her reflection and swung her hips beneath her white slip.

"You were good on Zoom this morning," she said. "And you speak Spanish and have certification to teach English as a Second Language. Let's put out some ads, get you some publicity so you can teach English to Hispanics here in the States and L.A."

Michelle knew that teaching English as a Second Language (ESL) was not a career choice of mine, but we could expand my ESL work to augment our finances and save money in preparation for any future opportunity to reopen another incarnation of Fisherman's Shore Bait and Tackle. Michelle was inspiring, and the idea seemed a logical option, perhaps the only logical (and somewhat ambitious) employment option available to me.

Michelle did recall a mnemonic of my masterplan when, while multitasking between her iPhone and my laptop at the dining table, she mentioned the term "Latinx."

"What the hell is that," she remarked, "some sort of insult to Latinos?"

"Where'd you find it?"

"In a news feed on my phone. And it comes up every now and then on Facebook—the use of *Latinx* instead of Latinos."

I was reclined on the couch and practicing Spanish by reading the translation of a book I'd read in English—*The Sun Also Rises*. I set the book aside and closed my eyes.

"It's a woke technique to control your language," I replied. "Gender neutrality bullshit."

"Gender neutrality? Sin concordancia, no podemos entendernos en español."

"That's the point," I said.

Michelle was referring to an elementary romance-language fundamental: without gender agreement between articles, nouns, and adjectives, the frequent result is an ugly incoherent language without rhyme, reason, rhythm, beauty or poetry. Introduce gender neutrality into the syntax and the effect is destruction of the language all together.

Gotta get the hijos de la chingada first, before they destroy everything, language included...

Michelle said, "The point is to stifle communication and destroy the language?"

My mind slowed. I had to get up early. It was time for bed.

"Basically... Or...huh... More like control language in general...all language. Control language and you control the future, as well as the past." I opened my eyes with a "right Princess?" and blanched at the empty loveseat opposite me.

Princess was gone. I startled myself upright. "Where's Princess?"

CHAPTER 23

THE CURE

I removed Princess from the closet in the spare bedroom before noon Tuesday morning and spoke to her for the first time since Michelle's arrival: "Sorry Princess. Let's just be thankful she didn't toss you in the trash."

That was it. No exchange of ideas, no pleasantries, no explanations…no conversation at all. And we remained silent on our drive to Princess' new home.

"I'm here now," Michelle had admonished last night. "We can leave your roadkill confidant in the closet for the times you might still need her…"

In good conscience, I couldn't do that—leave Princess in the closet like a hostage. She was much more than a "roadkill confidant" to me and I couldn't find it within myself to leave her locked up when there was somewhere for her to go where she should be appreciated.

I'd called first but Charlie didn't pick up—a good sign. Meant he was home. Charlie often left his phone off while working, but that didn't mean he couldn't be interrupted. Whenever I showed up after reaching his voicemail, he welcomed me. Not a demonstrable welcome but resolute…

We'd grown accustomed to each other's company.

Other than myself, I'd never seen another guest at Charlie's place and received a surprise upon arrival. The door opened just as I knocked, and I was greeted with a "Ho-ha ha… Here's the man himself—Charlie's favorite antipode."

I flinched and stammered, "D-didn't expect to find you here."

Ned appeared to have grown an inch, the door's threshold lifting him to about my height. Along with his imperial Roman nose, Ned had blowsy, ponderous cheeks and a malleable mouth, attributes of his I hadn't seen in person since the pandemic outbreak.

"We both look healthy and handsome without our masks on," he said, the corners of his mouth turned up. "Ho-ha ha…I suppose you're excited to have Michelle back with you."

Ned's clairvoyance set my teeth on edge. "How did you—?"

"A couple of days ago I read that international travel restrictions have been eased." He appraised my figure, "I see you've kept yourself in good shape for her," and patted his belly. "Ho-ha ha… fortunately I do not require your endurance after thirty years of marriage."

Ned's ebullience and active nature belied his age, his beetled brows, creased forehead, and balding pate sprinkled with gray the giveaways that he was pushing sixty. He bowed me into the apartment. "Charlie's been expecting you."

Charlie had probably noted my voicemail.

I stepped into the apartment and spotted Charlie, seated at his desk in the far corner of the living room, eyes on his computer screen.

Ned said, "Keep up the good work. I see you've brought along an extra head for the job. Lovely creature, and three heads are better than two."

"That's Princess," I said, focused on Charlie, emersed in something or other on his computer, woolly afro covering his ears and blending to his beard. "She's pleased to meet you."

Princess was on my back, in my backpack, her head above the rim.

"Ho-ha ha. Pleased to meet you as well, Princess. Like so many, looks like you've been through a trauma. Bloodied but unbowed, eh? With trauma comes experience and, hopefully, wisdom. You should be a fine addition to the team."

An eerie chill whispered up my spine, like finding a long-lost keepsake on my nightstand—where did *that* come from? Who left it here? Did I always have it? I swiveled my head around to Ned and searched his face, his features alight in exalted rapture, dark eyes retaining that sagacious glint from the evening he'd spoiled my plans to go on a killing spree...

"Are you part of the *team* as well, Ned?"

"Four heads might be better than three...but that also runs the risk of having too many cooks in the kitchen." Ned raised a beetled brow, lips pressed together in an expression of intimate confidence. "At times you feel isolated, but you do indeed have a majority with you. There are fans hungering for inspiration." He blinked and smirked...and patted his belly once more. "And speaking of kitchens and inspiration, it's time for lunch. Ho-ha ha...don't want to keep my own fans waiting." He stepped out the door and lifted a hand to me as if to Salaam. "Au revoir, anti-pode de confiance. Till we meet again…"

I stared vacantly out the door, through the space Ned had left, baffled at this new habit of his—an uncanny ability to interject himself into my life at unexpected moments and affect my actions and thought process like a force of nature.

I shut the door and muttered, "Antipode de confiance." Trusted antipode.

Ned knew of my masterplan and had conferred upon me a ti-tle—trusted antipode—a diametric opposition—that conformed to one of Charlie's socio-political variables.

Charlie said, "The tyranny of the minority is infinitely more odious and intolerable and more to be feared than the tyranny of the major-ity," as though reading it off his computer screen. "They will rule and ruin, although in the minority." He glanced over his shoulder at me. "And lie, cheat, steal, intimidate and kill to achieve their ends…"

"You quoting someone, Charlie, or did you come up with that yourself?"

"Paraphrase, paraphrase, paraphrase. McKinley…yes, yes, yes… President McKinley…while still a member of congress." He returned his attention to his computer screen. "Lenin's and Mao's minorities overran Russia and China."

I crossed the living room and looked over Charlie's shoulder, his computer screen filled with what looked like shopping lists—food, cars, television sets, all manner of goods to be purchased.

"Is Ned an alien, Charlie, or one of our coconspirators? Both?"

Charlie read off a list: "Red, green, Ariane, Empire, Ambrosia, Golden Delicious, McIntosh…"

"An alien on our side could prove a huge advantage."

"Concorde, White, Bartlett, Red Bartlett, Green Anjou, Red Anjou…"

I turned from Charlie's customary ramblings, gave his master-piece up on the wall across the room a lingering look, and headed for my station at the dining table. Charlie kept a corner of the table clear from books and clutter for me, my yellow legal pad with its notes and lists occupying its own little space. I pulled the chain to the overhead light, dropped my backpack to the floor, and sat Princess on the chair next to mine, directly across from Charlie's back.

"I've brought you a new friend, Charlie."

"Organic, non-organic… All species within a ten-mile radi-us of this apartment. Can't find that in China…no, no, no…or Europe for that matter…"

I thumbed my iPhone and took my seat next to Princess. The notes and missives I kept on my phone were accumulated while away from Charlie's apartment, entered when an insight struck me at a moment's notice. I transposed the useful ones onto the legal pad, then reviewed my work from the top—a list of causes I'd be fighting for rather than against…

Think one way, act another…

I was now in favor of BLM-Antifa riots to reach political ends, and would refer to them as social-justice peaceful protests; in favor of indiscriminate lockdowns and pandemic regs as applied to all but social-justice warriors and political-corporate elites and cabals; in fa-vor of the academic elite's Critical Race Theory and the resulting in-quisition against whiteness and America itself; in favor of stifling free speech and controlling language; in favor of destroying monuments and all remnants of America's heroic heritage; in favor of the institutions, corporations, and political hacks who ignored Chinese atrocities and genocide to make a buck and Chinese yuan…and then virtue signaled with donations to woke organizations supporting "justice" and "equity"; in favor of woke cancel culture and labeling all opposition "racist fascists"; in favor of declaring national emergencies as a method to destroy the Bill of Rights.

No cops, no walls, no USA at all would become my mantra…

A tricky business, knowing your enemy and keeping them close; dangerous too, perhaps more dangerous than confronting or hunting and killing galvanized zombies. If I were discovered as an infiltrator my life, and the lives of those I recruited, would be forever ruined if not ended.

Not all my recruits—Manny, Jaime, Antonia…Michelle—would be infiltrators; I imagined various roles to be played within my masterplan, a masterplan I'd been piecing together with Charlie. Eventually, my masterplan would require extensive recruitment and I'd have to be leery of the enemy infiltrating my own ranks. At the moment, however, my masterplan remained in its nascent stages, and stage one was infiltration of the enemy. Jaimie would make a good infiltrator. Young, strong and bright… and he had firsthand experience with the enemy while guarding Nuestro American Hardware. Yet I'd take it upon myself to begin the infiltration process, mindful that I'd been doxed and might need a disguise…and also mindful of Jack and Zodiac, how they were able to blend into society and avoid capture.

"Antipodes will collide, right Charlie? Infiltrate, double-cross, collide."

"Quickly, quickly, quickly," he answered. "The advantage is a heritage of liberty, but the memory can be diluted and lost."

Charlie rose from his seat, retrieved a marker and eraser off his desk, and strolled the wall of whiteboards and collages opposite his masterpiece. He paused before the whiteboard of graphs and erased and redrew a few lines.

"Next will be an ethnic bio-virus…just a matter of when…"

"Ethnic bio…virus?"

"Targeting DNA. That's why China mines DNA from around the world… Just a matter of when…when, when, when…"

Charlie was like a doomsday machine, routinely adjusting his time schedules for disaster to hit. We were on the same page when it came to acting quickly, but his invariant quantities, nomological networks, and calculations and recalculations of timelines and socio-political outcomes were strictly his purview. As an antipode, I had a different function—action. Yet I needed to get my mind right, get myself clear on motives and goals, like an actor preparing for a role, and flipped to a page in my legal pad where I'd been stumped: defund the police.

Charlie read my mind and picked up right where we'd left off during my last visit.

"Federalize, nationalize," he said. "The government, bureaucrats, and elites will choose winners and losers… Nationalize and federalize everything…everything, everything, everything—the economy, education, elections, police…especially the police. Remove local control of governance and law enforcement and the people will be isolated, unable to have individual needs and rights addressed, rights that are no longer natural and unalienable but the province of government; and what the government and their oligarchs bestow they can and will take away. The people are then forced to either unite in love for Big Brother or rebel..."

Charlie drifted to the whiteboard near his desk and added an equation to the bottom of it.

"So I'm not for defunding the police, exactly, but defunding local police in favor of a federalized police force—Mussolini Blackshirts, government-corporate blackshirts who enforce woke demands as a method to destroy the Constitution. Outwardly, this conforms to my desires, yet our predicted outcome is that it will force the people to choose liberty over tyranny. The woke strategy for a takeover of the country will blow up in their faces..."

Charlie released the eraser, pivoted and raised his arms overhead, marker sustained in his left hand, assuming the pose of a conductor.

"She knows!" he exclaimed, opaque right eye rolling around in his head, lucid amber left focused on Princess. Charlie pointed his marker at Princess, "You've always known, haven't you Princess?" His smile contorted into a grimace of pained elation through his beard, as in reaction to the arrival of a valued guest he was unprepared to receive.

I dropped my gaze to Princess—the bonnet angling over her inverted crown of blood, the stuffing oozing through the scar where her left ear should be, her twisted and bloodied snout, the blood splatter on her jumpsuit, and the single stich left behind by her right eye. Princess didn't have an afflicted right eye like Charlie but no right eye at all.

"Great news," Charlie said. He stood over Princess, his visage slackened and head cocked to her...listening.

"Yes, yes, yes," he replied. "Of course you're welcome here. Stay as long as you like. You're inspiring…and can remain Colton's confidant."

Charlie blinked up from Princess and focused his eyes on me—both eyes, his afflicted right eye streaked in swirls of amber.

Something cold passed through my chest, a shudder that shivered my shoulders and prickled my scalp. Charlie's stricken eye had come to life, his reedy tenor pitch heightened and dulcet, yet his lips did not move to the voice needling my ears:

"This way we won't leave a blood trail."

Princess. I stared back down at her. Princess' stitched mouth stretched into a broad flying-W smile…and her head listed onto my bicep.

"Or the blood trails won't lead to us," I said. "And I'll have to begin one at a time, right Princess? Ingratiate myself and have them bring me into their confidence one at a time before we strike."

Princess agreed: "One at a time, one at a time, one at a time… Yes, yes, yes…one at a time. Quickly, quickly, quickly…one at a time… and liberty will spring forth like a geyser in revolutionary spirit…"

I glanced up at Charlie and his glowing gaze. Age seemed to have fallen from him like ashes, his rejuvenated eyes—both eyes—limber and embracing. I flashed him an alligator smile…

Charlie had been transformed, and I was cured.

THE END

ACKNOWLEDGEMENTS

My sources for *Surfing with Sharks* were personal experience, interviews and interactions with associates, friends, and others in Los Angeles and Portland, innumerable media outlets, voracious reading, and imagination. *Surfing with Sharks* took me eighteen months to write and have edited and by November 2021 was ready to publish. I knew from experience that self-publishing takes time and the intervening months offered me an opportunity to think about this acknowledgements page. The support of my wife and family (including my mother, whose edits and critiques are boundless) was indispensable, yet it occurred to me that perhaps my greatest debt of gratitude is owed to fellow writers who have both inspired and incensed me, often all at once. Aside from the inspiration I have enjoyed from fictional works by the likes of Twain, Dostoevsky, J.D. Sallinger, Ayn Rand, and Joseph Heller, shortsighted and misguided non-fiction has incensed as well as inspired me, works like *The 1619 Project* (which should be listed as fiction), Zinn's *A People's History of the United States*, and most anything by Saul Alinsky, Herbert Marcuse, or Karl Marx himself. As is often the case with an acknowledgements page, I'm bound to overlook some people, yet I do value and appreciate the thoughts and writings of Mark Levin, Douglas Murray, Candice Owens, Gaad Saad, Andy Ngo, Thomas Sowell, Victor David

Hanson, Steven Mosher, and Michael Pillsbury…not to mention Montesquieu, James Madison, and Aristotle…

Thank you.

And thank you dear reader. Please feel free to leave a review of this book—good, bad, indifferent—at Amazon, Barnes and Nobel, or the media outlet of your choice.

Seve Verdad is the author of the novel *Finding Devo—a novel adventure*. He earned three graduate degrees from Oregon State University after studying abroad as well as in California and Oregon. He was born and raised in southern California and lives there now with his wife, never too far from the beach.

Visit Seve at seveverdad.org,
and contact him at seve.verdad@seveverdad.org